Y0-BEM-120

MORNING SONG:

MOURNING SONG

Marje Blood

IMAGE IMPRINTS

EUGENE, OREGON

IMAGE IMPRINTS
PO Box 2764
Eugene OR 97402

ISBN: 09615233-4-4   HC (Limited Edition 100)
ISBN: 09615233-5-2   PB

Library of Congress Catalog Number: 87-81670

IN APPRECIATION

For the expressions of confidence from colleagues,
For the sharing of information by respected professionals,
For reassurances from close friends and family members
who never seemed to doubt I could bring this book—
and its companion volume—into being:
My thanks to all of you.

1837

Narcissa lay without opening her eyes, warm in the featherbed, listening for Marcus' movements about the cabin. Then, sensing silence, she came awake with a start.

Lying on the pallet, looking up into the room, she seemed to be at the bottom of a block of pure cold, the space between floor and sloping roof filled with light reflecting from the snow covering the world outside. It seeped in between the logs where the mud had fallen out, and around the edges of the blanket hung over the windowpane.

Twin to the cold was the isolation. Drowsing, she pictured herself in the bone-chilling room, roofed and walled by the cabin centered in loneliness; the nearest help at Fort Walla Walla, a long day north across a sea of drifted plains; the closest mission at Lapwai, five times as far away past frozen hills and rivers; her family east to the Atlantic, a continent of snow separating them from her. The only sign of human life within sound of her calling was the cedar longhouse of Umtippe and his savages. And nothing between them and her except a shallow river.

—three days she had been alone here, and the Cayuse

knowing Marcus was gone. She'd tried to talk him out of riding to the Fort in this weather. She didn't need Mrs. Pambrun yet, she insisted. They could get along without her if they had to, Marcus being a doctor.

But there was no changing his mind once it was made up. "The baby's due any day now. I've already waited too long. Once the weather warms and the snow melts the creeks could flood. I might not be able to get there at all."

"Then let me go with you."

He just looked at her, perched there on the low stool like a humpty-dumpty. "You'll be all right until Richard gets back."

Her eyes moved to the window. He read the glance easily enough. "You don't have to be afraid of them, 'Cissa. Umtippe won't bother us as long as Stikus is here."

She thought of Umtippe's hatchet face with eyes like a rattlesnake's; thought of him sitting his wild horse with his head thrown back so his long hair fell free except for the brush of bangs across his forehead, his mouth turned down at one corner in that terrible smile, as if he knew some evil secret he could use against them. She doubted Stikus could help much if Umtippe got angry.

"It's lucky for us it was Stikus got that bellyache from rotten fish when we first came," Marcus said. "If it had been Umtippe he'd probably have been mean enough to die just so the tribe could demand my head for it."

He was trying to joke; trying to make her feel better about staying alone. She didn't think there was anything funny about Umtippe. "Someday he's going to, Marcus. Every time you go over there you take your life in your hands."

"It's what I came here to do," he reminded her. " Figure I'll die when the Lord decides it's time; until then my conscience rests better knowing I've done all I can for these people."

2

She didn't answer. He stood there looking at her, saying finally, "I'll have to start now. The sooner I get going, the sooner I'll be back."

She shouldn't have cried like that. But seeing him struggling into the old sheep-lined jacket to start out through the snow, him alone in Indian country and her alone in the cabin—

"I can't leave you crying, 'Cissa, and I've got to bring Mrs. Pambrun. We'll need a woman to help after the baby gets here. You know it. As busy as I am—"

She nodded, but the tears swamped her face, falling on her skirt where it belled out over her swollen abdomen.

"You'll have Trapper to keep you company while I'm gone."

The little airedale frisked about, hearing his name. "You take good care of her now." Marcus patted the shaggy head and the pup crowded against her skirts. He gave her an awkward kiss that almost missed her mouth. Then, walking fast, he went out where the big gray waited head down as if apprehensive of disturbing the untracked expanses of snow.

She watched him out of sight, answering aloud his last wave before he disappeared into some trees. "Hurry, Marcus—" And Trapper barked, starting after him. She put down a hand, feeling blindly for his ears; the rough tongue licked at her fingers. He'd licked her hand that way the first time she'd held him when Dr. McLaughlin had given him to her for a present.

Trapper stayed close to her as she barred the door. She sat back down on the stool then and cried, her head against the rocks of the fireplace, until the little dog whined to go outside. She peered out before opening the door wide enough for him to squeeze through, and stood looking out through an inch-wide crack, hoping he wouldn't take a notion to chase his own tracks in the snow as he sometimes did.

But Trapper, as if sensing the seriousness of their position, performed his necessary act and returned at once, not lying down until she had the door closed and the iron rod dropped into the catches.

As least she'd got her unhappiness out of her system, she thought, washing her face and pinning up her hair before settling down to get through the day. She'd been building up to a good cry for a long time.

Had it only been six months since she'd stood by the river in the dark saying goodby to Dr. McLaughlin? So much had happened since that leave-taking at Fort Vancouver. If she had known what lay ahead of her, those first months, she likely would have stayed longer at the Fort. Dr. McLaughlin had done his best to persuade her and Eliza to stay the winter there, but she had wanted to be with Marcus in a home of her own.

He'd promised to have one waiting when she got there, and he'd provided it, such as it was. But the log lean-to with a canvas hung over one side for a doorway had been all he could manage before she arrived. It was finished now. She wouldn't let herself think about being alone at night.

The Indians would come snooping; they'd seen Marcus leave, and they'd be like curious children. They used to crowd into the lean-to at all hours before Marcus got the wall finished. She'd look up from making bread to find three or four of them inside the opening, watching hungry-eyed.

With Trapper to warn her and the strong rod on the door, she was safe enough. It was the idea of the Cayuse prowling outside while she slept that made her nervous.

She sewed all that first day, finishing the diaper hems, and cutting the scraps into belly bands. She browsed through her books: Plato and Bacon and Blake. She used the last sheets of writing paper getting letters ready for the spring express.

But when the shadows crept up from the river at dusk, pushing the silence before it, she felt herself filling with shadows and growing silent too; holding her breath and listening.

Anger came to her rescue, building slowly against the growing tension. Why had she allowed Marcus Whitman to leave her here alone? He could have waited for Richard to get back from his hunting trip. He could have paid one of the Indians to go to the Fort.

But anger gave way to fear when Trapper, dozing in front of the fire, lifted his head, his ears pointing a warning, a low growl grinding in his throat. Her heart seemed to stop—waiting, waiting—as she listened. It could be the wind rising—

Trapper got to his feet, his tail sharpened toward the east. Even if they are out there, she reminded herself, they can't get in. Her eyes veered to the barred door. She held herself stiff against a betraying movement. Maybe they'd go away if there was no sound—

No, that was wrong. They lived like animals, fought like animals; maybe they could be frightened away by noise, the way animals ran before a sudden shout.

She'd be dead from fear before morning if she stayed like this, barely breathing, waiting for something unseen, unheard, to attack. She reached for a book to read aloud.

It was the hymnal left there after Sunday services. All right, then! Singing was better than reading anyway. The pages fell open and she sang the first words she saw, her voice wobbly,

At length ther dawns the glorious day
By prophets long foretold—

She sang hymn after hymn, her nervousness pushing her until she was shouting the words; sang until her voice broke in the middle of a phrase and her breath was gone and silence rushed in like a thunderclap.

Trapper blinked in the stillness, circled twice in his tracks, and dropped to the floor with his head on his paws. Painfully she rose from the stool. There was a different feel about the darkness now.

Finally, wearily, she found the courage to go to bed.

Next morning when she went outside for water and wood she found moccasin tracks in the snow, and the haunch of venison Marcus had left hanging by the door was gone.

Anger took possession of her; she felt her heart would burst with its wild beating. She glared at the camp across the river, hating them all. They knew she was alone. They wouldn't risk coming like that in the night if Marcus had been here, to steal from the porch.

She crusted some bread on a stick over the fire and made tea. Mama always made tea and toast when they weren't feeling well, served on the rosebud china, the bread hot and dripping with sweet butter—

She hadn't even tasted butter since they left Fort Vancouver. The charred bread stuck in her throat and she gagged, sick and frightened.

Mama, I want you here when my baby comes; not some fat indian woman who barely understands English, with a tribe of young ones crowding the cabin to overflowing. All the indians smell, even the Pambruns, and closed up together like we'll be here, we won't be able to breathe—

She wiped her eyes and rested her face against the window glass, searching the expanse of snow to the north for something moving. It would help if she could tell someone how she really felt about the indians, but who would that be? She couldn't tell Marcus. He felt pity for them. She felt—betrayed.

She tried to recapture the compelling reasons that had

urged her to give up her way of life to come out here. They eluded her. Where were the childlike natives she had come to save? The indians here were dirty savages who haunted her days like dragons. Not once had she looked into the eyes of an indian and found an answering understanding. It was like trying to see into the soul of a crocodile. There was no way, no way at all that she had found, to bridge the gap between herself and the Cayuse.

And she was committed to spending the rest of her life trying to rouse an answering spark in them. *The rest of her life—*

Anger shook her again. If God really wanted her to help these creatures, why couldn't He help her see them with compassion instead of revulsion?

If she'd had no answer to her plea for understanding of the Cayuse, neither had she had further trouble from them. Marcus would be home by evening. She had this last day to get through. She stirred the coals ablaze, shivering, and tried to think of chores to make the day go faster. Even with her clumsiness the rooms were pin-neat in no time, and evening seemed as far away as when she awoke.

In the afternoon she ventured to the river for water, keeping a lookout toward the camp as she slipped and slid her way back to the house. It was a cold blue day, padded with snow that sparkled under the pale sun.

By contrast the cabin was dark; musty. She went to the door again. The hill wasn't far; from the top she would be able to see Marcus coming two hours away.

Umtippe's frozen camp showed no activity; the dogs were quiet. No doubt they were huddled around their smoking fires, prisoners of the weather, as she was. It wasn't likely they'd bother her in broad daylight, knowing Marcus' anger would descend on the tribe like the heavens falling if they dared harm her.

Trapper, eager to run after days of idleness, enticed her across the meadow and up the hill. Near the top she sat on a fallen tree to catch her breath. Her face tingled. A handful of snow crashed against her shoulder, jarred from the heavy-laden boughs of a young fir. Snow spread like a cloth on the flat land below, rolling to the edges of the world.

From here the indian camp was deceptively neat among the naked trees, sketched in charcoal lines against the snow. It was hard to believe that distance could blot out the stench of the camp, where families lived in cubicles no bigger than pantrys, the air thick with smoke and body smells and dog odor; the children covered with scabs and crusty scalp dirt, and most of them with eyes running with matter.

The snow drew the landscape together, uniting the camp in the background and the cabin like a doll house into a scene by Currier and Ives. And it hadn't any more movement than a painting. No matter how she searched to the north, nothing moved anywhere. By the time cold forced her back down the hill the evening shadows were reaching out around the cabin, ringing it in loneliness.

The walk and the fire worked together to induce a fatigue she had not felt in weeks. She yawned while she waited for side meat to cook. After she'd eaten she sat in the rocker, thinking to read. If Marcus was coming he should be here soon . . . .

She was jerked from sound sleep by a pounding on the door, and Marcus calling, " 'Cissa? Are you all right in there?"

Her weight was intolerable; struggling to get up from the chair her feet caught in her skirts and she fell with a thud that jarred her through. And all the time Marcus was pounding as if he'd break the door in, before she could get there to lift the bar.

Then there was hardly time to talk, with the three children to be fed, and beds to spread while they ate fried meal with molasses. The little boys' eyes were bright and black as they watched Trapper wriggling his joy that Marcus was home. Maria, the girl, sat nibbling at her food, and followed her mother to the curtained-off corner after they'd eaten.

Once the children were settled Marcus and Mrs. Pambrun ate by the fire. She pretended to eat too, but slowly, hoping the indian woman would go to bed soon. She was happy to have her here; no doubt she'd talk herself hoarse tomorrow. But tonight she wanted to talk with Marcus without having to be polite for company.

"You didn't have any trouble from across the river?"

"They stole the venison—" She gasped as pain struck a savage blow to her lower back. She stayed in a strange, bowed position until the pain had passed through her; then, slowly, she let out her breath.

Marcus worried over her. "You all right now?"

"I must have hurt my back when I fell."

"You'd better get into bed and rest."

She didn't intend to do any such thing. "I've spent the last three days resting. I want to visit now."

He went back to his chair reluctantly. Mrs. Pambrun smiled and rocked in the firelight, all bronze in a dress of rust merino that matched her skin. Only her white leggings, beaded in red and blue, rescued her from monotony.

It *would* be a blessing, having a woman in the house to talk with about the baby. Marcus could understand better than most men, she supposed, what was happening, and why, and when it would be; but no man could really know *how* it would be.

She reached to set her cup on the table and was struck by a second pain. She looked up at Marcus as he lifted her

9

to her feet and led her to their bedroom.

"Is it the baby?"

He nodded. "You rest now while you can. Mrs. Pambrun will help me get ready."

The cruel pains played cat and mouse with her then in the cold room—streaking out to cut through her pitilessly; releasing her to languor; biting again as she accepted the truce; snatching her back at the last moment, reminding her she was without control of herself; demanding complete surrender to this sacrifice of all dignity—all identity.

—no wonder women talked of this process in whispers; no wonder they warned brides of its terrors. This was what fathers and ministers threatened, out of their guilt, when they thundered of damnation visited to women who took motherhood lightly, without the safeguards of marriage. Marriage was the concession men made to induce women to allow infliction of such merciless torment in the name of love—

She bit down hard on cries of pain; she would not allow Marcus the satisfaction.

Toward morning the pains were overlapping, one hardly giving way before another began its slow grinding in the deep of her back. Her moans could not be held back now, seeping out first in a barely discernable keening, rising to a crescendo as the pain mounted, mounted, riding her like a demon.

Marcus' frantic face hovered over her, circled by a nimbus of lamplight, imploring, offering his hands in a pathetic effort to endure what he had done to her. She clamped her fingers around his, forcing his participation in the destruction his body had worked on hers. Let him feel the pain through her hands! Let him see what was happening! Let him live with it, too! All he knew of birth was pleasure in the night, his body promising that happiness would sing forever in her. Now let him deny the truth if he dared, while the pain clawed and rocked her, tearing her apart.

She ached with the need to go outside, but he held her down. She felt the sheets warming—knew a moment's exquisite release—and cried as the wetness cooled under her.

"Now look what you made me do—"

Marcus called for Mrs. Pambrun. She was caught again and again between crushing pains, and at their worst felt strong hands dragging her up from the pallet. *"Aux pieds!"* a strong voice grated; she opened her eyes and Marcus' face had become an indian's, chanting sternly, *"Aux pieds! Aux pieds!"*

She fought the grasping hands as another pain buffeted her; in a brief second of relief was pulled to her feet. And she could not stand—could not—

"Marcus—

He loomed a giant, seen through her suffering; he sounded like God calling from heaven. "What are you doing, woman?"

The woman squatted, a frightening stranger, pointing between her own legs; grunting—straining—gesturing to the pallet, crying in that vulture voice, *"Hyas chee tenas. Kloshe kopa tenas—"*

"That's not our way!"

She heard thin crying from a distance. The indians, acting up again? She would ask Doctor . . . . But he was bending over her, holding a spoon, and his voice boomed a dreary echo, "Dri-n-k th-i-s-s-s."

She knew a time of calm, then, the pain withdrawn to a distance that made it tolerable; was jerked again from her dreaming by a monster wrenching her apart inside, and she screamed, and the child Maria bent over her, big dark eyes watchful as she writhed and screamed.

— this was not for a child to see. She caught at Marcus' hands; tried to tell him to send the girl away. From the shadows the hoarse voice grated, "Maria woman. Stay."

Twelve years—

And the agony was at her again, mauling her; and she forgot Maria—forgot Marcus—

An angry mewing brought her awake. Marcus was beside her, holding a bundle of blankets. "Here she is—" His voice thinned; recovered itself. "You hold her—keep her warm—while I clean up here." The slight weight of the bundle settled lightly, warmly into her arms. He lifted the blanket corner for her to see the red face.

And this was the product of their mutual joy? This the result of that—that tearing apart, that enduring agony; the ending of that journey begun—

"What day is it?"

"March eighteen. You got a fine birthday present this year, 'Cissa."

The first days after the baby's birth were chaotic. She woke the first morning to the sound of outraged crying from the bundle of damp blankets beside her. Turning carefully, keeping the quilts high against the freezing air, she unwrapped the baby to find her naked with a sodden diaper wadded between her tiny legs.

Her voice calling Marcus caused the doll face to contort, and a thin scream cut the air.

"Why's she crying like that?" he said, thrusting his head through the door opening.

"I'd scream too if I was left naked and wet all night. Where are her clothes?" She held the blanket aside to show the squirming infant.

"Mrs. Pambrun took care of her last night, but she's down sick this morning."

"Sick?"

"They all came down with la grippe except Maria. She's

12

up, but she's moving slow."

There was no use fussing at him about it. "Bring me her clothes box. I'll dress her."

"I'm not sure you ought. Soon as I get breakfast over I'll do it."

She hadn't strength to argue. "Just get me the clothes and prop me on the pillows."

Her exasperation grew as she struggled with the crying baby in the cold room. After all the trouble they went to to bring Mrs. Pambrun, she had to come down sick and the whole family with her. Now Marcus would have all of them to take care of as well as her and Alice.

She was exhausted by the time she had finished the baby and eaten breakfast. But Marcus insisted she try to nurse Alice before she went to sleep. The tug of the baby's mouth set her writhing inside; it was like being eaten alive. She had to force herself to hold the baby to her breast. She knew she could never endure two years of it.

Finally she slept, to be awakened by a disturbance outside. Blinking she raised her eyes to the small window and saw dark faces pressed to the glass; indian faces.

"Marcus!"

He came running. "Make them go away!"

"They just want to see the baby. Stikus and one of his chiefs is waiting to pay their respects."

She was too tired to entertain indians, chiefs or not. But he insisted. "Let them come in for a minute and they'll all go away sooner."

She knew he was right. They would stay until their curiosity was satisfied.

Marcus brought the two chiefs—oily, wrapped in musty blankets. Stikus wore a battered military hat gleaned from some accidental encounter at the Fort. His eyes were friendly as he looked down at her. Not like

Umtippe's. She held the baby for him to see.

"*Tenas Cayuse,*" Stikus smiled. "*Tenas Cayuse.*"

"That means little Cayuse baby."

Stikus pointed to the crowded window and asked a question of her with his sharp eyes.

"They want to see the baby too," Marcus said.

All of them in here? She couldn't stand the jostling and smells and noises. Not this soon.

"We'll hold her up to the window so they can see," Marcus said, understanding her silence.

The chiefs stood proudly, one each side of Marcus, while he held the *tenas boston klootchman* for the Cayuse to view through the murky window.

Later she was to look back on that first day as peaceful. The little boys recovered first, scuffling underfoot, running in and out, tracking snow, forever forgetting to shut the door. Marcus, back at his outside work, tried to keep them occupied, but his offerings were too much like chores. Indian boys did not work.

If only Mrs. Pambrun would get well— Here she was, trying to take care of the baby and manage the house from her bed with only Maria to help, and the little boys into everything—

The hardest chore was keeping clothes washed and dried for the baby. The first week they froze dry outside, but the weather changed to rain, forcing them to dry diapers in front of the fire.

Maria didn't understand about diapers. Indian children ran naked below the waist once they could walk, but surely the tiny babies used diapers—

She asked the girl.

"The *te-cashe*—carry board—is filled with moss, with grass."

"No diapers?"

"No washing, too."

"But don't the babies get cold?"

"In winter board is filled with feathers."

Struggling with the wet diapers in the crowded cabin she thought it might not be such a bad plan after all.

The boys drove her out of her mind with their romping. She tried reading to them, but they didn't seem to follow the stories, and their runny noses made her ill.

Lying in the darkening room late one afternoon, watching the streaming window glass, she thought she would send the lot of them back to the Fort next day, rain or not.

She heard Marcus coming and sat up, brushing at her hair. Maybe they could have some time together alone while the two boys were napping.

But he was talking with someone— If he came bringing more indians into the house she'd scream them all outside. It wasn't Richard; he'd set out hunting again yesterday.

It never crossed her mind it would be William Gray, but there he was, tracking more mud across the floor, pulling off his hat and dropping it on top of the baby's clothes.

"Marcus run me right in here to see the new girl," he said.

She spoke, but her heart was heavy as a brick. What was wrong at Lapwai this time? Whenever William showed up it meant trouble.

Marcus held Alice for him to see. "She's a beauty," he said, pride tempting him to brag a little.

"She's kind of red, ain't she?"

"New babies are," Marcus said, his voice stiff, handing Alice down to her and leading William back to the other room.

Why couldn't William have said something nice about Alice? Even if he had to fib a little? She should have known better than to expect it, though. William didn't know any language but complaints.

—why did he have to come *now?* Wasn't it bad enough that she had to lay here in bed with the house like a hog pen and the baby's clothes turning yellow from being half washed, without having to put up with William?

She could hear him at it the minute the chairs scraped up to the table: "Soup needs more salt, don't it?" and "Got the bread kind of brown on the bottom, didn't you?"

She set her bowl on the floor and scrunched down, pushing her face into the pillow. She couldn't stand another single thing; not William or the Pambruns or the mud or this terrible cabin or this awful place—

She *wouldn't* cry and let William hear! But the pillow was thick, and no one heard her whispers, "I wish I was home. Oh, Papa, I wish I was home!"

The next morning she got out of bed, ignoring Marcus' protests. Mrs. Pambrun was working in the main room. The sun had come out, too, signalling change in the weather. Gradually, then, they brought some order to the house.

There was no easing William's presence, though. Worst of all, he was moving back permanently. He had decided to build his house here at Waiilatpu. They should have expected it; he'd mentioned it before, and it was certain him and Henry didn't get along.

"I'm going to the Fort tomorrow for supplies for the house," he announced one night at supper. "Anything you need, you better make a list."

Mrs. Pambrun looked up from her plate. "I go," she said.

She hoped her own eagerness didn't show. "Are you sure you feel like making the trip?"

Mrs. Pamburn nodded. "Good," she insisted. "Good." She grabbed the boys, wiping their hands on her skirts.

16

"We go home?" they shouted, their eyes catching the light from the fire and throwing it about like sunbeams. "We go home to Papa?"

"We go." She shooed them out of the way and began clearing the table. She had worked swiftly, once recovered, as if to make up for the inconvenience caused by her illness. Watching her at the dishpan silencing the unruly children with a look, Narcissa felt regret that things had worked out so badly while Mrs. Pambrun was here. One thing sure, she'd leave things in good shape.

The indian woman looked up suddenly; their eyes met. "Maria stay?" she asked.

The thought hadn't crossed Narcissa's mind. But why not? Maria sat sewing by the fire. She had a look about her of waiting for something to bring her to life; in the meantime she did not waste her emotions.

"Would you like to stay with us, Maria?"

A shadow smile crossed the girl's face, light as a feather, and retreated. "Yes," she said, her voice soft.

"She can learn talk out of book," Mrs. Pambrun said. "She help with *bebe*—"

"We'd like that fine, Mrs. Pambrun," Marcus said. "We'll take care of her like she was our own."

Spring accomplished miracles overnight in the trees bordering the rivers, washing the fields with a faint green; scattering blossoms with wild extravagance along the brushy places. The cattle began dropping their calves. The pasture was populated half again with the awkward, noisy new-born.

And summer followed before she expected it; the seductive warmth of spring changing overnight to oppressive heat.

This afternoon Maria sat on the blanket with the baby while Narcissa watered her orchard. The rye grass swayed around her, dotted with blue and yellow flowers like a piece of calico. Waiilatpu meant 'place of the rye grass.'

She filled her bucket at the creek and carried it back to the feathery twigs of trees, nursed from seeds she'd carried with her from Vancouver. "Save the seeds from the apples you eat here," Dr. McLaughlin told her. "Plant them at your new home. Some of them will live. The seeds for the first apple trees here at Vancouver came from England in my pocket." He smiled then. "And every time you look at your apple trees you'll remember your friends here."

In five years they would bear fruit. She looked around at the small stretch of rail fence beside the trail; at the beginnings of the mill pond; at the plowed fields, sprouting now. Some day they would have a mission here at Waiilatpu that would offer as many comforts as Fort Vancouver.

She'd pictured the house often enough in her thoughts, built there by the cottonwood, with the Blue mountains to the south for a background. It would be white, with a gallery, and a white fence around the flowers. The orchard would be green, then; and the north fields fenced for more cattle. Marcus had already ordered sheep from the Island mission. They could graze in the foothills of the Blues. And there would be—

She broke off her thoughts, thinking she heard the baby cry, but there was no further sound, and she went back to her work. Marcus worried when she carried water for the trees. "Let Maria or Richard do that," he'd say. "They're young."

He wouldn't believe she enjoyed it. He promised he'd have the canal finished another year. He was down by the mill shed now, stripped to the waist, deepening the ditch from the river to the low place he'd planned for the mill pond. The mill stones would be here by fall.

Indians leaned against the fence, watching. They wouldn't dream of helping, but they'd be at the door with their hands out the minute he started grinding meal. They'd have the whole camp to feed again when cold weather started.

The indians roamed the mission grounds at will. She tried to keep them out of the house, but Alice Clarissa drew them like flies around a sugar bowl. They shook their heads in wonder over her white skin and yellow hair. But they had to be watched every second. She'd caught one boy tucking her green glass ink bottle into his waistband.

Automatically she checked the clothes drying on the fence. The Cayuse had picked up one thing from Marcus' sermons—the idea of sharing. Alice's missing diapers had begun to turn up as scarves for Umtippe's young men.

Surely by winter the new house would be finished. It wouldn't be the big house they planned for later, but it would have an indian room the Cayuse could sprawl in. She was tired of having sick indians in her kitchen. The house smelled for days after.

If William hadn't taken it into his head to start his own station they'd have the house half finished by now. The foundation dobes were finished, and a big pile of brick. But William had got his feelings riled about something and went looking for a new site, saying he was tired taking second place.

Marcus had tried to argue him out of the idea. "Don't be a fool, William. We're hard put to raise enough supplies for the two missions we have now; we can't support another station yet."

"The Lord will provide," William said.

"How are you going to pay for what you need?"

"As soon as I pick my site I intend to petition the Mission Board for orders."

"You have to have some qualifications, William. What have you got to offer besides a strong back?"

William's mouth trembled like a girl's. "So now you're saying a carpenter ain't qualified to head the Lord's work among the indians?"

He'd never overlook a reference like *that* one, Narcissa thought indignantly.

"I'm tired being looked down on because I didn't have a well-off family to buy me an education," William went on.

Marcus' irritation showed strong when he answered. "You're a bigger fool than I thought, Gray. My father died when I was a boy. Henry never even knew who his father was until he was past school age."

She shook her head at Marcus. There was no need bringing up Henry's parentage. But William wasn't listening anyhow.

"You're just saying that because you're afraid I'll show you up."

"You'll be lucky to accomplish half as much as Doctor has in the time he's been here," Narcissa said quickly.

"You think so, Missus? Well I'll tell you, if it'd been me here I'd have had a school going by now. Instead of trying to get them plowing and planting, I'd be teaching the Word."

"You can't have a school without students, and the Cayuse can't stay in one place until they learn how to grow food so they don't spend all summer hunting."

"Henry Spalding's had his school going at Lapwai ever since he got there. Of course, Mrs. Spalding ain't got her fancy house yet, and they haven't raised fences all over the countryside. But they're teaching the indians."

"The Nez Perce are different from the Cayuse—"

"Let it be, 'Cissa." Marcus took her arm. "William's got his mind set on moving. Guess we ain't going to change it by any reasonable argument."

That same day William rode off to go exploring, leaving Marcus to work eighteen hours a day with only Richard to help.

Where was Richard? The dobe pile was deserted. Marcus had told him at dinner time to work at the bricks this afternoon. From the looks he hadn't been near them.

She walked along the creek to where Marcus was attacking the ditch. He straightened, wiping his face as she came up. The indians took no notice of her.

"You shouldn't be watering those trees with the baby so little." He repeated his protests automatically.

"You're a fine one to talk. Let Richard dig for awhile and you come rest."

"I don't want to take him off the bricks."

"He hasn't been near that brick pile all afternoon. We're going to have to do something about him, Marcus."

"Seems like he won't do his share any longer, doesn't it?" His eyes were worried. "He wants to spend his time with the young fellows from the Cayuse camp." He wiped at his neck again. "Can't say I really blame him on a day like this."

"No wonder he doesn't pay any attention to you. He knows you'll make excuses for him—"

"Well, it's hard work being a boy, 'Cissa. When you hit fourteen or so you got something inside you just busting to be a man, and you look like the same little kid you were at thirteen, so it's hard knowing where you are sometimes."

She wasn't in a mood for any of his preaching. "I know Richard belongs on that dobe pile this afternoon. And if you don't speak to him, I'm going to!"

"Don't interfere with Richard, 'Cissa. I'll take care of it."

When he used that tone of voice it meant the subject

was closed. "At least come have some tea. You know you'll work here till dark."

"I can't afford to stop work in the middle of the afternoon."

"You can't afford to be sick, either." He couldn't argue about that, with his side bothering him again.

He straightened, stretched, picked up the bucket and shouldered the shovel. "I might as well go rest and get it over with," he said, "so you'll let me get back to work."

It was seldom she could persuade him to leave his chores as long as there was light. And as summer progressed the results began to show. Most of the indians had started their yearly travels, following the wild food crops as they matured. But a few had stayed behind this year, held by Marcus' story that they could make their own food grow by dropping seeds on the earth. They believed, seeing the corn stalks shooting up; the potatoes flourishing. They begged to plant for themselves.

He explained it was too late this summer, but promised to share his crops if they would help him this year; and to furnish them supplies next spring to plant crops of their own.

They helped—if the sun wasn't too hot. And at the end of each day they demanded buttons. Pambrun had told them the indians would work for buttons, but Marcus considered it bribery. He refused to pay them.

"Well why not, Marcus? If it's the only way we can get them to work, why not pay them in buttons?"

"Because I can't preach one thing and practise another."

Often, as summer slipped toward fall, he'd say, "We've got to get the school organized, 'Cissa. The indians will be coming back before we know it."

She would look at the fields of pumpkins to be gathered, potatoes to be dug, corn to be harvested, and

22

shake her head. "There isn't time now. When the crops are in—"

"Henry's had his school going almost a year," he answered her one day. "All we've done is manage Sunday sermons, and I have a feeling the Lord finds them pretty skimpy."

"All the indians come."

"There ain't a tenth of the Cayuse left in camp this time of year."

"Our services last two hours, at least."

"Two hours of singing," he said. "Except for a prayer, and a few words from me."

"What's wrong with singing?" The singing was her idea. No indians would come unless they offered something to catch their attention. Marcus didn't preach with fire and spirit, the way Henry did.

"They don't understand a word I say, and you know it as well as I do."

"Most of them know some English—"

"A word here and there is all. We can't just teach them to memorize Bible verses. That's the way the Jesuits do it: teach a savage his catechism and baptize him quick to add another soul to the score. I won't have any part of that."

"Just because Henry boasts all the time about reaching his indians you don't have to belittle what we're doing. If Henry had to raise his own food he wouldn't have time to learn the language, either. Eliza wouldn't get many primers copied if she had to harvest corn."

"Don't you belittle what they're doing," he said "Henry is reaching his natives with the Word of God, and I'm not sure we are. That's about the size of the matter, 'Cissa, and raving around won't change it."

"I'm not raving around," she said, her mouth tight. But she wanted to! Henry could run his mission any way he liked; but they had the same privilege. She was furious that Marcus felt he had to run down his own work in comparison to Henry's.

Nevertheless his accusations nagged at her. One morning she decided. "We're going to start school today, Maria." Just like that.

The girl's hands went still on the churn dasher. Her eyes took on a brilliance as she thought about it. "I will learn to talk books?"

"*Read*, Maria. I'll teach you to read."

A smile touched the girl's mouth and stayed there as she worked the dasher up and down, up and down.

They held school each afternoon then while Alice napped. Maria mastered the simple reader quickly, and learned to print on the slate, starting the first day with her name. Her eyes would light when she triumphed over a difficult work, or added a row of figures correctly, as if a similar light had gone on in her mind. Maria's soft questions excited Narcissa's own interest in teaching again.

Marcus discovered the school one afternoon when he brought an indian to the house to bandage his cut arm. That night he looked up from his reports for the Board. "Too bad you only got one student in your school, 'Cissa. But the Cayuse will be coming back any time now. There'll be more."

She frowned. "I couldn't crowd more than a dozen in here."

"You've got all outdoors."

"As long as the weather holds. But what about later?"

"If we try to wait for the right time and place we'll never have a school," he told her.

"I haven't enough books or slates."

"You can teach them to write their names and to count if they take turns. Let them try. At least we'll be making a start."

24

He was unexpectedly tense. Make a start where? At teaching the indians? Or at overtaking Henry?

The Cayuse began trailing down out of the Blues during the sunburned days of late August, shirts and calicos still bright from summer trading. Dust raised by their horses rose along the trail well into September.

Marcus took word of the school to the camp. After the first few days, when curiosity drew old and young, the number fell to less than twenty and they settled down to school under the cottonwood each afternoon.

The indian children learned with amazing ease, running through the alphabet and the first numbers in days. Narcissa copied pages from the primers and they practiced reading from these. Reaching back to her teaching experience in Steuban County Narcissa began each session with a song, and was delighted to discover the Cayuse children had an ear for tone and rhythm. They liked singing. She'd organize a choir for Sunday services— She could teach them English and hymns at the same time; and grooming, too, by insisting they be clean and have their hair combed when they sang.

Marcus could not resist bragging when writing to Henry. A return letter from Lapwai noted Eliza had plans for starting a choir, too. She was already translating some of the simpler hymns into Nez Perce—

As the crops came to harvest Narcissa went out in the mornings to help. Marcus made his usual arguments which she ignored. There was no one else—

The rows of corn stretched seemingly without end, their rustling a reminder that it was time to pull the ears. Marcus had hoped to recruit the returning indians to help. They came one morning: a band of men on horseback herding a troop of women ahead of them.

It was apparent the men planned to watch from the

shade while their women worked. "What about the men?" Marcus asked Umtippe. "Let them work too."

The chief shook his head vigorously. "No. No. No."

"You'll need food. Cold weather's coming."

"We find food; plenty salmon, plenty camas."

"Enough to last all winter?"

Umtippe did not bother to answer.

Marcus put the women to stripping the ears, finally, while the men raced their horses along the edges of the field or lounged under the trees.

"I don't like this working women while the men have fun," he insisted, his mouth set. "It's against what we're trying to teach here."

Narcissa wiped her hair back from her sweaty face. Her hands were cut from the dry stalks; she itched all over. He'd better not do something foolish like refuse to let the women help because the men were too lazy! He'd better not!

That evening each woman received her basket of corn without a word and they trudged back across the field to the camp. The corn was roasted for a feast. Singing and chanting sounded across the river all night.

The indians never returned to the corn field except after dark. When Marcus protested to Umtippe about stolen corn the chief, with great arrogance, denied any knowledge of the matter.

"Umtippe, there's cobs all over the ground here. Where did they come from if they aren't out of my fields?"

"You give. Give women."

"That was weeks ago. These cobs are still fresh."

"You give, Umtippe insisted, his tone admitting the lie, his manner challenging Marcus to prove it.

So in the end there was Richard and Marcus and herself to do the dusty work. Once, staggering from heat and fatigue, she complained, "We've got to get some help, Marcus. The three of us will never get this finished—"

He'd turned on her. "We *will* get it finished, and by ourselves. There isn't anyone else."

"Then I'll dismiss school until we have the corn in."

"I'll work all day."

"No you won't," he said. "The sun is too hot. You need to take care of Alice, anyway. She's beginning to look like one of the Cayuse babies."

"Maria's doing the best she can," she flared. "She's only a child herself."

As he bent to pick up his corn knife a sound between a sigh and a groan escaped him. She wanted to cry. She shouldn't snap at him. He was trying to do the work of three— "At least let Richard help you."

"He can help in the mornings like he does now. In the afternoons he'll stay in school."

Oh, his stubbornness! "All Richard does is keep the girls upset with his tricks."

He rubbed at his shoulder; conceded from necessity. "Richard," he called, "let's get back to work now."

Richard sat unmoving as a stone.

"You'll have to help afternoons now until we get the corn put away," Marcus told him, attacking the stalks with vicious strokes.

Richard's mouth moved; he half turned away; bent finally to the row and began his own wrathful assault on the corn.

Narcissa gathered an apron full of ears to carry to the house for supper. She walked slowly, hoping the baby was down for a nap. She hadn't had time to get lessons ready. It was a waste of time to pass the first readers around again; the girls had memorized them.

If she could only persuade the Board to send her books and slates. Did they expect her to make her own readers because Eliza did? If Eliza had to work in the fields chopping corn she wouldn't have time to make books either.

She decided to read with the smaller children. "Not *kly*, HoolHool. *Cry*. Try it again now. The baby will cry."

HoolHool's braids fell along her cheeks; her bony shoulders hunched as she brought her face close to the page. "*Te bebe will k—l-l-y—*" She sat back then, head high, waiting for *Techa's* praise.

Narcissa hadn't the heart to correct her again. "Thank you." She shooed the little girl back with the others.

"*Techa?*" The pixie face was overshadowed by the bright black eyes. She thought how much HoolHool resembled the mouse for which she was named.

"*Temora sing, Techa?*"

"Yes, HoolHool. We sing every day."

"*Sing clean-clean?*"

She drew a deep breath. Of course. Tomorrow was Sunday. And she hadn't any cooking done; she hadn't planned services. Nothing was ready—

"*Techa—?*"

"Yes, HoolHool," she sighed. "We sing tomorrow." The shadows of the cottonwoods on the far bank of the river were reaching across the water. "Let's sing our goodby song now."

As the children sang she heard hoofbeats far off and behind her. If the indians would spend half as much time working as they did racing they could accomplish miracles—

The children ran when she dismissed them. She sent Maria to find squash from the garden for supper. "I'll bring Alice."

As she carried baby and books toward the house the sounds of the horses were louder. She looked toward the foothills; stopped short. It wasn't indians coming. There were at least six men.

—and here she was in her field dress; and Marcus looked like a ruffian, working half naked, streaked with sweat. She began to run to the field shouting, "It's company, Marcus! And they aren't indians!"

He squinted to the northwest. "Looks like you better get out the big kettles."

"I'll lay out clean clothes for you," she called, running for the house again. "Wash in the creek—"

"As soon as I tell Richard what to do here."

She had twenty minutes, maybe, to get out of her dirty dress and get her hair combed. And to get Alice out of the dirty white stockings she'd been crawling in since morning.

Maria came with the squash. "Put them in the kitchen, Maria, and put on your new dress. Company is coming."

A smile tugged at Maria's mouth. "It is papa."

"Your father—?"

"Yes."

"Hurry, then. We want to be ready."

It was half an hour or better before Marcus came, walking with Pambrun, still bare and streaked with field dust. Their first real company and he looked like one of the Cayuse.

"Now don't get mad, 'Cissa," he said quickly. "Pambrun caught me down at the field and I couldn't get away till we got his men started pulling corn. I'll put my shirt on right now."

Pambrun's eyes danced in his ugly face as he bowed over her hand. "Waiilatpu makes you more beautiful than ever, Madame."

"Aren't your men tired after the trip, Mr. Pambrun?"

"Those? *Non.* We send them something to eat, they will work all night." He looked around carelessly. "And now. Where is my Maria?"

"Right beside you."

He stared; his eyebrows shot up like arrows. "This young lady is my Maria? *Non! Non!* I cannot believe

29

this!" He bowed over her hand as he had over Narcissa's. Maria's eyes shone.

Suddenly the little man swooped her into his arms in a powerful hug, and for a moment her reserve vanished. She flung her arms around his neck and pushed her face against his shoulder.

"She is good girl?" he demanded, his voice brusk.

Marcus came back from the wash bench buttoning his shirt. "She's a wonder, Pambrun. I hope you're not thinking to take her home with you."

"Oh, *oui. Oui.* I think of it. But I will not take her. Maria is learning to be lady. That is what I want for her: to be beautiful lady."

There was pleasure in cooking a company dinner. And just in sitting at the table long enough to enjoy it, holding the baby and feeding her bites while the men talked. It gave a woman a feeling of pride to have a man eat the way Mr. Pambrun did. "Ah, Madame. It is *superbe*— I have not tasted such food for—" And he would cut off his sentence with another enormous bite.

When he had finished he wiped his mouth with his hand.

"Maria—" He cocked an eyebrow at the table.

"I'll help, Maria," Narcissa said, handing Alice to Marcus.

The men moved stools back to lean against the wall. "Now we must talk," Pambrun said.

"You got something on your mind?"

Pambrun nodded. *"Mon ami,* you need help here. These Cayuse no good for work. These Cayuse are lazy, no good, *cochon—"*

I don't know what you called them but I doubt I can argue with you from the way it sounded." Alice struggled to stand up in his lap. "Looks like me and Richard is going to have to take care of things ourselves."

"Non! Non! Non!" Pambrun reached over and lifted Alice to his knee, bouncing her very fast in spite of her

30

squeals. "I go to Vancouver from here. If you like, I ask Dr. McLaughlin to send you kanakas to help with harvest."

"I can't be forever calling on McLaughlin for help. Sooner or later I got to stand on my own feet."

Pambrun nodded, chucking the delighted Alice under her chin. "It must be later, my friend. And there will be no later if you do not get your crops safely in."

"Kanakas couldn't get here in time even if I wanted to ask for them."

"How long it will take you and Richard to harvest that corn? Even with Madame's help—" he shot a shrewd glance in her direction, "—too long. Tonight I send man to say Pambrun is on his way; get supplies ready. Same time I tell him to send Dr. Whitman kanakas *vite.*"

"I hate being under obligation to McLaughlin."

The little man went still, holding Alice's outstretched hands, looking over her blond head with brooding eyes. "Every man in this country is under obligation to every other man; it is the way we survive. If you insist to live alone, you will die alone."

Narcissa looked up from gathering the plates. Pambrun's words were a warning; and he was talking about something more important than borrowing workers from Vancouver.

"Why don't you, Marcus?"

"Maybe we better—"

Pambrun laughed. "Good. Good. And now, Madame, I give you your beautiful child for some needed attention." He lifted Alice high above his head and into her arms, revealing a large wet spot on his knee.

She flushed. "I'm sorry. I'll bring a towel."

"*Non, non. 'Pas de quoi.*" He waved her away. "She is *bebe—*"

The sticky days of late summer gave way to fall; the

nights cooled to frost between hot noons. The kanakas—
four of them—went to the mountains to cut trees for
boards after the harvest was finished. Marcus spent most
of his time shaping dobe blocks from the sloppy clay,
paying no attention to the Cayuse who lounged like
brown slugs, watching. When they laughed at him for
doing women's work, he laughed back at them.

There was only one thing in their favor. They loved to
play with Alice. Narcissa never grew used to seeing near-
naked men on their knees teasing the laughing baby with
a feather. Time and again she would go to change Alice
and find some strange carved animal they'd left for her.
She was for throwing these gifts into the fire but Marcus
would not allow it.

"She'll grow up in this country, 'Cissa. Better let her get
used to the dirt from the start."

With a supply of new-shaped bricks baking in the sun,
Marcus started laying a wall. And when the wall was
shoulder high, Narcissa began to dream again of the finished house. They would send to Vancouver for the furnishings. Marcus would make the chairs in his spare time.

"Do you think I could trust Dr. McLaughlin to send
something suitable for curtains, Marcus?"

"Don't get in a hurry, now. It's a long time yet to
curtains."

She laid aside the dress she was hemming for Alice.
"How long?"

"Hard to tell. Depends on the weather."

"You can work on it this winter."

"If everything goes right."

"Why don't you keep Richard at work on the house,
Marcus? It wouldn't hurt him to make dobes along with
you."

He closed his book and removed his spectacles. "Someone had to take supplies to Walla Walla in time to catch

the HBC train to the West Forts. If William really brings recruits back here next spring they'll be needing supplies by the time they get to Fort Boise."

"William Gray will have a hard time finding anyone who'll come west with him, I'll guess."

"Better quit running William down, 'Cissa. So far he's done just what he said he was going to do. He might be put in charge of all the missions after he's talked to the Board."

"David Greene knows better than to put William in charge out here," she said, resisting the idea. "That man is a trouble maker."

"I was just having a little fun with you." He leaned back, stretching his feet to the fire. "I'm glad to have Richard to run my errands for me. I'd have lost two weeks if I'd had to go to Lapwai myself."

"They could have come for their own corn after we raised it for them, or sent some of their indians."

"Richard enjoyed the trip." He tipped his stool forward and stood up. "How about another piece of that pumpkin pie?"

She noticed that Richard was put to work again at the bricks next morning, but disappeared as soon as Marcus was called to another job.

"I'd like to know what's the matter with that boy." She hadn't realized she was speaking aloud, but Maria, folding clothes, said softly, "Richard is Nez Perce."

"Richard is like our own son, Maria."

Maria did not look up. "Richard is Nez Perce," she repeated.

She could not put the words out of her mind. She told Marcus what Maria had said.

"Maybe she's right, 'Cissa. Maybe we can't take an indian boy and turn him into a white boy just by changing his clothes."

"What about Maria?"

"She's half white already. Richard's another matter."

"But he's been with us so long."

He put an arm around her shoulders. "Quit worrying about Richard. He's going through a stage."

Richard began eating at the Cayuse camp. Every day he seemed more a stranger, his face closed to them; his mind closed to them.

Seeing him one noon sleeping against the half-finished wall, Narcissa felt an impulse to try to talk with him. She buttered some fresh bread and went to the new house.

He opened his eyes when she said his name, and for a second she saw into them before the flat, closed look came over his features. There was little of Richard as she knew him in the way he pushed himself up against the wall. He was all indian—unsmiling, taking the plate but not eating; looking straight ahead without meeting her eyes.

"Richard, are you ill?"

"No. Not ill."

And talking that way—like one of Umtippe's young bucks—It was as if she were watching Richard being transformed to a savage before her eyes. She knelt beside him.

"Richard, please listen to me."

He looked at her without expression.

"Why won't you talk with us any more?" she managed, nervous under his steady gaze.

His eyelids flickered; his tone stung with malicious humor. "What you want I talk?"

"Richard, what's changed you? Why won't you—" her eyes fell on the bricks beside her, "—why won't you work?"

He was on his feet instantly, kicking at the bricks. "This not work for man," he charged, outraged. "This

34

work for women—for slaves—"

"And please don't talk trade English, Richard. You sound like one of the boys from the camp over there."

"That wrong, too?" Not bothering to keep contempt out of his voice. "For Nez Perce to talk like Cayuse?" Deliberately mocking her—

She stood up slowly. "But you've been taught our ways."

He sliced at the air with his flattened hand. "You tell me to think like you. But I *feel* Nez Perce! I *want* Nez Perce! You say Nez Perce way wrong. Umtippe say your way wrong." He pounded at his leg with his clenched fists. "You made me *no-thing!* Not indian. Not white. I am *no-thing!*

"Richard—" She reached out to him instinctively. He jerked away as if her fingers were of fire. "No! he shouted. "No!" and ran suddenly, around the wall and across the mission yard, toward the Cayuse camp. They did not see him again.

As if Richard's defection had opened their lives to the chill of winter, they woke next morning to the heavy drumming of rain on the low roof. "I'd better go for the kanakas," Marcus said. "No use them staying now that winter has set in."

By the next day the kanaka boys were on their way back to Vancouver. Narcissa's mood was heavy, watching them ride off through the blowing rain.

"I wish they didn't have to go," she said, and went to stand in front of the fire to drive away a coldness that had little to do with damp weather.

"We haven't room to keep them here even if we could afford them," he reminded her; and that was true. But even so—

"We're all alone out here now," she said.

Maria came from the bedroom carrying the baby. "Well," Marcus smiled, taking Alice, "we got two mighty fine girls here to keep us company." He tossed Alice up and caught her high in the air. "And we'll have plenty of sick Cayuse cluttering up the house before very long, I'll wager."

The cluttering started sooner than even Marcus expected. Sunday evening, near bed time, they were startled by three young indians who thrust the door open without knocking and stomped into the room, trailing muddy tracks from door to fire.

"Umtippe say come," the tallest one said, thrusting a finger under Marcus' nose. "You, Doctah!"

"What's wrong with Umtippe?"

"He *sick sick.*" The spokesman rubbed his stomach; thumped it twice with his bunched fingers. *"Muck-amuck—"* He circled his head with his outstretched hands, frowning. *"Sick kopa latet."*

Narcissa felt the swift uprush of fear that swept her whenever Marcus was called to the Cayuse camp. "He's only been drinking spirits again, Marcus. Wait until morning."

"I'd better go, just in case the old devil's really got something wrong with him."

She was so astonished at hearing Marcus call Umtippe names she said no more.

The bad weather held for weeks. They went to sleep to the droning of the rain; roused in the night to hear the wind tearing at the house; woke each morning to a steady beating.

"What are we going to do?" she would ask, looking out the window at the pile of bricks dissolving to a muddy mess. "If it keeps raining there won't be anything left of our house."

"You might as well stop stewing, 'Cissa. It will quit

raining one of these days and freeze tighter than a drum."

"But the bricks will be ruined."

"Then we'll have to make more next spring."

Before the rains stopped word came from Lapwai that Eliza was nearing her time.

"I have to go," Marcus said, "but there's no sense of you and the girls travelling in this weather."

"We're going. I won't stay here alone."

They left for Lapwai in dark, blowing rain. Snow was mixed in the drops falling against their faces. Marcus sheltered the baby in front of him; Narcissa and Maria paced their horses behind his. They arrived at Walla Walla late that night, drenched, shivering, exhausted.

After the first night they camped in the open, or under dripping trees. It was a miserable trip. Narcissa was sorry she hadn't left Alice at the Fort with Maria.

Eliza's baby was born two days after they arrived at Lapwai; a fragile child whose thin kitten-cry sounded as often as it was still. Narcissa had ten days of impossible confusion trying to care for two babies and a sick woman in a rude shelter with winter rain pouring every minute and the men coming and going.

The Sunday before they left for home Henry baptized the two babies and held indian services. She had to admit the Nez Perce seemed more interested in religion than the Cayuse. Most of them appeared to understand the meaning of Henry's preaching. And he conducted part of his sermon in their own language.

Eliza talked more than she needed to about her school; bragging, almost. But she offered two copies of the primer they'd printed by hand.

Narcissa's reluctance to admit Eliza was ahead with the Lapwai school was tempered by her own need for the books. She could use a dozen if she could get them.

Because of the heavy snow they made the return trip to Walla Walla by canoe. Their horses would be returned later. Wrapped against the cold they traveled in comparative comfort, their dugout guided down the Sweetwater and into the Columbia by their Nez Perce boatmen. It was the long day's ride from the Fort to Waiilatpu that tired them.

Marcus made a new fire while she got the children to bed. They sat for a time then, absorbing warmth and pleasure at being home. "It will be good to have some peace and quiet," he said, yawning.

And before he'd closed his mouth the door burst open and a dozen young Cayuse crowded into the room, jostling, shouting. One grabbed for the kettle on the hook, begging, "Tea? Tea?" in a rusty singsong.

Exhausted more than she was frightened, her first impulse was to cry. "There isn't any made," she choked.

The dripping youths turned to Marcus, keeping up the chant, "Tea? Tea?"

"You better make some, 'Cissa. And put some molasses in. Maybe that will quiet them down."

They drank the mixture from the circulating indian cup, squatting on the floor. When it was gone the spokesman faced Marcus abruptly. "You come, Doctah."

"What?"

"Much sick. Sick. Sick. *Cayuse hiya sick sick.*"

"Lots of Cayuse sick?"

Narcissa was furious at their greed. "Why didn't you tell us when you first came?"

Marcus shook his head in warning. "I'll be there at once. You tell Umtippe."

"Come *alta.*" The boy grabbed his shoulder. Marcus shook off the hands and stepped back, his face tight. "Not without my bag."

38

How dare they touch him? Those boys!

"Be careful," Narcissa called as he trailed the band to the creek. He raised a hand without looking back.

It was daylight before he returned. He stood by the fire rubbing his hands at the flames while she made breakfast. "They have measles over there," he said. "Bad."

"Will Alice get them?"

"Alice can tolerate measles. But do you realize what's going to happen to them?" He jerked his head in the direction of the camp. "About day after tomorrow they're going to start their death chants, and they'll go on for a long time. There's half of them down now, at least."

"Are any of Umtippe's family sick?" She asked it fearfully; if death struck the chief's family, it meant—

"Three of his children," Marcus said. "And his wife."

"They might die, Marcus—"

"Maybe they'll all die. What can I do for indian measles? They won't stay in bed. The minute the fever comes up they jump in the river. It don't take long for them to catch pneumonia in this weather."

"Can't you do anything."

His eyes were somber. "Pray."

The death chants began lifting from the camp the next night, fading at times during the following days, to swell again as more Cayuse died. Marcus was at the camp as often as he was home now.

She argued against his going. Umtippe rode out from the camp each day like a demon, returning as the firelight began to wink under the naked trees. He hadn't openly threatened Marcus with his traditional right to claim the doctor's life if his family died, but he would. He would.

"They don't do anything you say, Marcus. You're just setting yourself up to be blamed when they don't get well."

"Your girls try to follow my instructions," he said. "But

their fathers tell them to listen to Kalakala. Girls can't do much against their fathers."

And wives can't do much against their husbands! she thought.

Marcus was dragged relentlessly from one day to the next by the demands of the indians. Coming back from camp at dawn he'd fall asleep at the table, often as not, waiting for her to get some hot food for him. They never seemed to come after him except in the middle of the night. Seeing him like that—gaunt, exhausted—she fought another terror: that he would become ill himself. It was a chance he took each time he went into the filthy longhouses, breathing the same foul air the dying breathed in and out.

And what if he did come down sick? What if Alice and Maria did?

He was careful, he assured her when her fears burst out in angry questions. And then one morning he came carring a child wrapped in a dirty blanket. She met him at the door. "You can't bring it here, Marcus."

He pushed past her. "Her mother died this morning. There's none of her family left to care for her."

"But we can't run the risk—"

She watched, numb, as he laid the child on a pallet, blind to any need but her own desperate desire to protect her children. That Marcus would expose the girls for the sake of an indian! He was called to help them, yes; but to choose between an indian and his own—

"*Techa*—?" HoolHool's pointed face emerged from the blanket, eyes hot in the blotched face. "We sing?"

Tears started in her throat; her anger dissolved to a crushing sense of shame. "Soon—" She knelt to smooth the matted hair. "Go to sleep now."

She looked up; met Marcus' sober eyes. "I didn't know it was HoolHool—"

"What about the others?"

"You're doing all you can."

He bit at his knuckles. "It's not enough! How can I answer these people when they say, 'You! God man! You say your God love Cayuse. Why He make Cayuse sick?"

"We aren't making them sick! They're killing themselves because they won't listen to you!"

"If there was some way to keep them from trying to cool the fever by jumping in the river. When I try to stop them, they remind me I've told them the way to find God is to be pushed into the river—be baptized—and they say they will look for God in the river and ask Him to make them well."

"Who says this to you, Marcus?"

"Kalakala."

"He's trying to turn them against you. He's jealous."

He nodded. "Probably. I guess I'd be jealous too if a witch doctor moved in and tried to tell me how to take care of my patients."

"We need a hospital." She had a picture in her mind of her school girls huddled ill in their blankets, pulled up by savage hands and thrown into the icy water, crying for help.

"We'll have one some day, 'Cissa. But it won't help these."

"We'll have to bring them here." It was easy enough to insist she wouldn't have sick indians in her home. She couldn't deny her girls care when they were helpless.

He brought only those who had been left orphaned. But there were usually some sick children sleeping near the fire that winter, tumbling with fever or shivering with chills.

Each time Marcus left to go to the camp Narcissa waited, sick with fear, for his return. Mr. Pambrun sent word that one of the Walla Walla chiefs had died—a cousin of Umtippe's. The same day Umtippe's younger brother rode to Walla Walla and killed the *te-wat* who'd nursed him.

She suffered nightmares then that one of Umtippe's family would die, and he would come for Marcus. But by some miracle they all recovered. She could not believe their good fortune. "You said his wife was dying, Marcus. Why did she get well and not the others? Why didn't his children die?"

"Umtippe's mean but he's smart. I told him at the beginning that measles was a white mans disease and if he wanted me to save his family he'd have to let me do it with white mans medicine. When his family got better some of the others decided I might be more powerful than old Kalakala." His eyes were thoughtful. "Maybe this epidemic was sent for a reason," he said, "to give me a chance to show the indians that our ways work."

The walls of the new house were washed away by the flooding creek one night. Narcissa accepted its disappearance with fatalism she had never felt before. She should have known it was too much, expecting a decent house out here miles from nowhere. She looked around the cabin, her face grim. The size and shape of her dreams were to be outlined by these rough walls—tiny, rude, final.

1838

Winter wore itself out finally. Narcissa looked out the door one day to see signs of spring on the land: the brush along the creeks feathered in green; the tender grass showing beneath last year's stalks.

The grayness inside her was beginning to lift, too. One day she sent word to the camp that school was beginning again. But not all her girls returned; seven had died.

Strange indians were seen in the valley. Some of Umtippe's hunting parties reappeared after being marooned in the mountains by snow. Small chiefs brought their camps and set them up near Umtippe's summer lodges. The whole camp had moved south from the winter's devastation, so it was hard to guess the numbers of the newcomers. Enough to be worrisome, she knew.

"Where are they coming from?" Marcus demanded, watching a family trailing past the house, the man riding ahead, the woman supervising the sleds made of lodge skins and poles. They looked sideways as they passed the mission but they did not smile or wave.

The indians came one morning unannounced, unexpected. They woke to find the west field crowded with Cayuse on spotted ponies. As they watched, a troup formed and galloped toward the house through the greening stubble of last year's corn field.

Narcissa's fears leaped to life at sight of Umtippe and his son leading the band. "Don't go out there, Marcus!" she begged, but he was already through the door, buttoning his shirt as he ran.

She watched from the porch, astonished to see Marcus mount an indian pony and ride off with Umtippe to the north, and back to the south; veering to the west and across to the east. The baby cried then and she ran to pick her up. When she returned the indians were racing back to the camp and Marcus was running toward the house.

"They want to plant crops!" he yelled. "They said I promised last spring to help them plant. These new ones are relatives; they want to plant too!"

He kicked the dirt from his boots and pulled her into the house. "I have to send to Vancouver for plow points, and I'll have to go up to the Fort to—"

She handed him the baby. "Not before breakfast, I hope."

He barely touched his food, on fire with his plans. "Let's ride around the fields and measure them," he suggested out of the blue. "Come on. Pretty needs some exercise."

"I can't go off riding, Marcus. I've got work to do. And so have you."

He leaned on his elbows, his blue eyes searching hers. "It's the first warm day of spring, 'Cissa. Pretend you're back in Steuben County and you're going riding with one of your beaus."

She laughed, embarrased, and pleased too. "Don't be foolish. I'm a married woman with a family to care for."

"The work will wait. Come on."

"There's the baby—"

"Maria can take care of Alice for a while. Let's go."

They rode along the river's edge beside the brush. The

briar bushes were lacy green, heavy with buds that would bloom wildly when the weather warmed. They made a wide circle around the camp, but not wide enough to escape notice. The dogs with their yapping brought the Cayuse women from the lodges to watch as they made their way across the flats. Narcissa was nervous under their eyes. They knew Maria and Alice were alone at the cabin—

Marcus guessed her worry. "They won't hurt the baby, 'Cissa," he said gently.

But uneasiness shifted beneath her pleasure. The brightness of the day dimmed; the scent of spring was lost behind a cold wind that seemed to blow up from nowhere. She was relieved when they turned back toward the mission.

Back from Walla Walla, Marcus gathered forked sticks from the willows along the creek for plow handles, whittling them into shape for drying them. He fitted three with points he had among his tools.

"We'll have to get a shop set up here," he told her. "We can't be sending off to Vancouver every time we need a piece of iron."

"What happened to the shop materials we brought with us?"

"They're at Lapwai. Now William's left I think I'll ask Henry to send them down here. We're going to have a farm community here in a few years that'll make those Pennsylvania places look like kitchen gardens."

"Henry won't like it."

"He ain't got much room for farming up there. We can take care of his equipment for him and have the tools here where we can get more use of them."

She rescued Alice from some greasy gears and started back to the house. Henry would scream like a goose being plucked alive if Marcus tried to take those tools from him.

But Marcus' ambition sparked her own. She started the school girls on fine sewing, ripping her embroidered petticoats apart and cutting them into choir capes for them to hem. She had some doubts about the elaborate trim.

"Do you think they'll look too much like Catholic robes, Marcus?"

He barely glanced at them. "They're fine."

Inevitably, with the approach of summer, her thoughts turned to the house. Marcus had no time now, but it worried her that the sunshine was going to waste with no one making bricks. There was no use trying to work the indians; they were stretching their willingness to the limit in plowing their fields.

Richard's words came to her mind several times. "That work for woman—" The Cayuse women—? She put the idea aside reluctantly. Marcus wouldn't like it.

There wasn't any reason why *she* couldn't work at making bricks, and Maria too. She went to the lean-to where Maria was making bread. "Why couldn't we make bricks, Maria?"

Maria nodded and went on kneading the dough.

Alice pulled at her skirt. "Me too," she begged. "Me too."

She hugged the chubby baby against her knees. "Yes, Alice. You too."

They never quite got the project under way. Marcus paced off the foundation lines one evening after supper; a much larger plan than the house they'd lost to the floods. That was as far as they got with it until fall. But it was a start.

"Might as well do it right," Marcus said. "it won't wash away this far from the creek; and no telling how many rooms we'll need when the others start coming."

"Marcus, we've hardly seen a soul all winter and you're measuring off a mansion big enough for a hotel."

He stopped on a corner, careful to keep his left foot in position. "William's bringing a bunch this fall."

"Oh, *William!*"

His eyes followed Alice as she ran toward the fence where Maria was folding clothes. "Well, it ain't unthinkable Alice might have some brothers and sisters for us to find places for, is it?"

She went after the baby. He should know there might be doubt of that, a doctor and all. Things hadn't been right with her since Alice was born. Her time of month couldn't be counted on at all, going weeks past, then lasting for days, the flow so heavy it frightened her; so heavy she'd be hard put to keep cloths clean.

Sometimes she would feel sickness gathering inside her like a pool, and at night, lying down, would feel herself flooding with a slow-spreading nausea that could only be contained by lying still as death until sleep came.

It was a strange thing that she could never bring herself to talk of this to Marcus. A woman ought to be able to talk of such things with her husband.

The months of isolation were ended by the arrival of four kanakas, come up river with the trader LaVarech making his spring run to Forts Hall and Boise. Marcus had seen them across the flats and come running to warn her, excited as if someone had lit a hot fire inside him. "They're bringing my plow points, I reckon."

They arrived in late afternoon, pack mules piled with bulky cartons trailing behind them. The kanakas grinned like jack-o-lanterns seeing her and the girls waiting at the fence. They recognized two of them—Adam and Ebenezer—from the year before.

LaVarech was a thick, fair, inarticulate man in aged buckskins. He slipped up to the table in the silent manner of the trail men, handing Marcus a packet bearing the seal of Dr. McLaughlin.

Mail— A big bundle, this time. Narcissa's heart beat a heavy rhythm. There'd be mail from home, finally. All the letters that had been following them all this time—

She watched and waited while Marcus fumbled at the waxed strings; reached and took it from him, only to find the knots too strong for her own shaking fingers. LaVarech lifted it from her without speaking; she caught a glimpse of understanding in his eyes as he untied the bundle. Everyone out here knew this terrible longing for word from home—

She waited impatiently while Marcus shuffled through the stack; went through them the second time. "There's something, surely—"

"Yes," he said, "but not what you're looking for. These others are from the Board."

She was looking for anything! Anything from anybody! She turned it to see the signature: *John McLaughlin, Governor, Hudson Bay Company, Oregon Territory.* She tossed it on the table and went to the window, looking out on a world blurred by her tears, pressing her tongue hard against the roof of her mouth to keep from sobbing aloud.

"Madame—?"

She half-turned at the gruff word. "More mail is due on the RELIANT this fall."

She nodded. She should be used to this particular pain by now, but she was not; would never be. She could not believe her father could hold her leaving against her to this extent.

"He's coming to visit us," Marcus said abruptly. "Some time next month."

She whirled. "Dr. McLaughlin?"

"I thought you'd be glad to see him. It's certain we owe him some hospitality.

"But *here?*"

"This is where we live, ain't it?"

Narcissa's dread of the impending visit almost damped out her disappointment about the mail. How could she entertain the Governor in this cabin? How *could* she? She couldn't picture *him* shaving at the kitchen table; or washing up in a bucket outside the door. And if he brought Mrs. McLaughlin—
They would have to sleep in Maria's little corner. Marcus could contrive a cupboard out of a box, and she'd put their own bowl and pitcher in for them. But there weren't any coverings on the windows. She'd have to cut into another petticoat. That would only leave her one good one, but they were too full to wear under calico anyway.

There was no use complaining to Marcus. He'd just say if it was good enough for them all the time, McLaughlin could stand it overnight. His mind was full of plows for his indians. She fretted about the curtains in her own mind and didn't talk out loud about her misgivings.

LaVarech was barely out of sight before a new set of guests rode in unannounced. Narcissa was trying to persuade Alice to take a nap while the girls read when she was startled by a knock. Before she could move a familiar voice called, "Mo-ther? Mo-ther?"

She went still. Her girls were caught in poses of expectancy, like a covey of small birds listening to an alien sound. Her heart began to beat in thumps that jarred her like blows.

—it's Richard. It's Richard, after all this time—

But it was not Richard. Another tall, slender, dark-skinned boy in a red shirt stood there, his hair tied back neatly, his teeth white.

"John!" She embraced him before he could pull away; released him quickly for fear of embarrassing him. His smile widened. He let her pull him inside while the girls giggled softly.

"Let me look at you. You've grown a foot at least. But you're so thin, John." There were circles under his eyes, now that she saw him in the light. "Have you been ill?"

"No more." He beamed at her.

She dismissed the girls. "Put away the sewing, Lakit. Maria, you check in the needles."

"Father Spalding has come," John offered shyly.

"Mrs. Spalding, too? And the baby?"

John shook his head. "Father."

Not even Henry's bragging could dull her enjoyment of having news from outside. She was still talking when they went to bed. "Henry's looking good, Marcus. He doesn't seem so bony any more."

"Well, Henry's feeling prosperous and self-satisfied. He's got his indians at Lapwai moving toward the church at a trot."

She felt a swift distaste; Marcus being envious wasn't becoming. "Don't make fun."

He lay with his arms behind his head watching her brush her hair. "I'm just curious. He has his school going full time. And according to him the Nez Perce are just begging to be baptized. What's he doing that we're not? We haven't even got one Cayuse asking to be baptized; we'd probably get stuck in the belly with a lance if we tried to baptize one. We're lucky if we can keep our school open an hour a day."

"How many miles of fence has Henry got in?" she countered. "How many acres has he got plowed and planted?"

"Not many. But he's got a printing press coming from the Islands on the ship this summer. He's going to print his own books. He's kindly offered to make ours, too, when it gets going."

"Well, you've ordered sheep from the Islands," she

said, stung by his evidence that Henry and Eliza were pulling ahead of them. "We'll have our indians supporting themselves in five years time. Being able to read and write won't keep the Nez Perce alive if they don't know how to feed themselves."

"Henry insists we came out here to save the indians, and anything else should come second."

Her hairbrush caught in a snarl; she jerked angrily and the pain made her more impatient with Henry's smugness. "Is Henry always right?"

Marcus took her hand. "Henry's a preacher and a teacher; maybe he can talk his indians into understanding. But I'm a doctor. I have to *show* them the good life. I can't take time out to learn the language; I'm doing good to pick up a few words to tell them how to cure a bellyache."

"The indians are coming to us, too," she insisted. "They're planting right now. They call on you when they're sick. Doesn't that mean as much as what Henry's doing?"

He patted her wrist. "I keep telling myself it does. But I can't help wondering how the Board will look at it when they read the reports."

What *would* the Board say about the difference between the two missions?

"We have to get the house started, Marcus. That's all!"

"And prove that we're spending our time building and planting instead of preaching and teaching?"

"But if we can get moved into the big house we can use this one for a school. And maybe, if we had a place for him to live, David Malin would come. We need a preacher here. And it should satisfy the Board so we could go ahead with our plans."

He smiled. "Satisfy everyone? Don't you know that's the surest way of pleasing no one?"

She wanted an answer, not more questions! "When can we start the house?" she asked, looking straight at him to keep him from looking away.

And his eyes changed. "It will have to wait awhile, 'Cissa. It—" He turned over suddenly and lay back. "We'd better get to sleep now."

She blew out the candle and lay beside him, vaguely dissatisfied. He was keeping something from her—

She found out next morning. Henry, saying his good-bye's, said, "Why don't you bring the baby and come to Lapwai with Marcus next month? Maybe you could learn something useful from seeing the school in operation. Eliza would welcome your company."

She whirled to face Marcus. He had known last night he was going to Lapwai. He had been afraid to tell her.

"Henry's ready to start his house," he said. "I told him I'd come help him as soon as the planting's finished."

"What about *our* house?"

His fingers closed hard on her shoulder. "We'll talk about it later, Narcissa."

She threw off his hand. "I don't want to talk about it later! Why don't Henry and Eliza build their own house, the way we have to? No wonder they have so much time to set up a school and hold revivals; we do half their work for them!"

"Henry helped me build the house we're living in. The agreement was that I'd help when he was ready to build his."

"He can wait until we finish ours!"

Henry mounted his horse. "Let me know when to expect you," he said to Marcus, and rode past her with a nod. John waved as they crossed the creek. She was too upset to wave back.

"I'll be there inside three weeks," Marcus called.

She hoped he wouldn't come into the house with her,

but he followed her to the lean-to. "All right now," he said, "let's get it over with."

"Why didn't you tell me last night instead of waiting until we were with Henry?"

There was a heavy silence. Finally he said, "Because I didn't feel like an argument last night."

Her anger waved. There was such a weight of weariness in his voice—

But he wasn't being fair! She was tired, too. She was tired waiting for a home. "You know I can't entertain the McLaughlins here," she cried, seizing on the first irritation that came to mind.

A cry from the porch, a knocking at the door, saved her from one of his sobering, logical answers. "Doctah, Doctah! These two break my plow—"

A heavy sigh escaped him. "I'll fix it, Chaka. Come to the mill house."

She never had the least hope he'd change his mind. But her disappointment was too deep to push aside. They lived under a wary armistice, not talking about the Lapwai trip. A few days later, a messenger came from Walla Walla to say Dr. McLaughlin would not have time to visit at Waiilatpu this trip.

"He wants us to meet him at Walla Walla next month," Marcus said. "It will work out better that way all around."

She didn't answer. If it was a relief to know she would be spared the problems of playing hostess to the Governor; it still didn't settle the trouble between them. Marcus was planning to leave his own house barely started to go build one for the Spaldings. She didn't care about his agreements and promises! It wasn't fair!

She got him ready for the trip but this time she did not ask to go with him. Marcus used the Walla Walla trip as a peace offering, as if that would make up for what he was doing.

"You be ready," he said, packing his saddle bags. "I'll come back in plenty of time to go to the Fort."

The tired lines around his eyes showed even when he smiled. She almost wished she could be happy about the trip to Walla Walla. But she'd used up all her emotion fighting his going to Lapwai. She'd be ready; she'd go. Only she couldn't find any enthusiasm for the idea.

Maria had enough for both of them. She talked constantly about the journey. Used to her silence, fighting her own unhappiness, Narcissa thought she could not endure the chatter. But she could not refuse to listen; it would be like brushing aside a hummingbird. With so little to anticipate in this isolated place, their first trip away had been spoiled by Marcus' obstinence. She fought a secret jealousy that Maria could look forward to it with pleasure.

But she found it hard to hold to her resentment in the face of warm weather that teased her with promises of summer just around the corner. The kitchen garden sprouted green feathers where onions and radishes and carrots would thrive later. Every time the girls stepped outdoors they came back with fists full of the blue flowers that grew in the rye grass. She arranged these in a small dresden swan she'd managed to carry unbroken through the mountains.

But the sight of the vase and the blue lace flowers against the rough walls revived her grievance and she had to fight her resentment anew. It wasn't fair of Marcus to keep her living in this cabin while he went off to build a better one for Eliza. She had a right to a home where a vase of flowers didn't make the rest of the room look disgraceful.

Still, almost in spite of herself she began to look forward to the trip to the Fort. By the time Marcus returned she had put down her disappointment and was actively planning for the outing. No telling what visitors would be at the Pambrun's. There'd be coming and going and people to talk with—

Marcus spent two days catching up with chores that could not wait. He turned the calf in with Bess to take care of the milking and got them all to bed early the night before they were to leave, planning to start at daybreak.

He called her at four o'clock. "You make breakfast while I get the horses ready."

She was uneasy as she fried the cold mush slices. It was impossible to ignore the smell of a storm, and the lowering clouds hiding the new day.

She met Marcus at the door when he came back from the horse shed. "How does it look?"

"It's going to be a good one."

"Shall we go?"

His eyes were murky as the sky. "I don't know. It won't hurt me none, and maybe not you, but the girls don't have rain ponchos." He bent to peer out the window. "It might not let loose before evening. Maybe we can be there before it hits."

He was leaving it up to her. She too peered out into the darkness. But what was there to see? Nothing but shadows rolling and churning across the heavens.

"Maria will be heartbroken if we don't go."

"You say."

Maria came from the bedroom carrying Alice. "The baby is ready," she said, her eyes excited.

Narcissa made her decision. "Eat breakfast, then. We'll have to hurry."

They rode out across the flats under villainous green clouds that rolled and tumbled as if the sky were in torment. The sun was rising, or trying to, but its rays couldn't break through that ominous barrier. The best it could do was outline the storm bundles as if trying to warn them of the size of their adversaries.

The horses were nervous as butterflies. Marcus was having trouble with the gray mare. Thank goodness Alice knew enough to sit still when she was riding with her father. Narcissa could feel Pretty's uneasiness, too; the sorrel's body twitched as if wires were jerking beneath the lovely skin. Maria, bundled into an old coat of Marcus', was working hard to keep her pony in the line.

A drumroll of thunder cut loose above them, at the same moment a tongue of flame darted across the sky. Narcissa anticipated Pretty's instinctive jump to one side, and held her under control with difficulty. The big gray was sidestepping, too. Narcissa managed to pull Pretty to a stop and sat there, shaking. They should never have started out in this weather. Already they were under attack by the storm.

"Marcus—"

The wind snatched his name from her and whirled it away. She was afraid to put Pretty to a run; the little mare, already wild with fright, might lose her head completely.

Marcus looked like a bundle of dry goods hunched over to shelter Alice, his rubber hat merging with his poncho. His horse plunged ahead as if breaking a path for the ones behind. She could never make him hear.

Without warning the rain sluiced down on them; great sheets of icy water beating at them without mercy. Marcus stopped the mare and sidled around until he faced the buildings. She opened her mouth to shout that they must turn back, and tasted the storm, strong and earthy on her tongue.

He sat while she and Maria turned their horses, then all together they rode back the way they had come, heads bent against the rain. The gloom followed them inside the house. Even after Marcus got the fire blazing they stood in their separate silences. It was hardest for Maria. Narcissa had never seen her cry; she thought now with sudden insight that it would be a shattering experience to witness Maria's tears.

"Well," Marcus said, putting the kettle on the hook, "this weather won't last forever. We'll leave when the rain lets up."

"You can't wait if you want to catch Dr. McLaughlin."

His eyes were troubled. There wouldn't be time later to see the Governor. It was today or not until fall.

Alice began to cry. Maria took her to the bedroom to change her.

"You have to go today," Narcissa said quickly.

He nodded.

"Can you take Maria?"

"That'll leave you here alone with the baby."

"I don't care. You have to take her."

Maria did not understand when they told her. She looked at Narcissa. "We try to go again?"

"You and the doctor are going, Maria. We can't take Alice through this storm."

Maria sat down on a stool. "Then I will stay here too," she said, and did not move until Marcus was on his way again.

Soon enough they had more company of their own. Thomas McKay had trailed his string of mules into the mission yard late yesterday evening, a full week ahead of time, loaded with supplies from Vancouver. And gifts. Dr. McLaughlin knew the things a woman would be longing for after a winter in a place like Waiilatpu: dried apples and raisins, some thread, sewing materials, letter paper.

And Captain McKay had brought the chickens as part

payment for his daughter's keep this winter. Narcissa walked carefully with the eggs she'd just taken from the nest Marcus had rigged in a corner of the mill shed.

She would have expected Margaret McKay to be small, like Maria, and shy. Instead she was tall—as well developed as a woman at fourteen. She had her father's bone structure, and his fluid carriage; she had the same narrow high-cheekboned face. But where Captain McKay moved with animal grace, silently, she walked almost with disdain. It didn't seem right for a girl that young to hold herself apart like that.

She had left the two girls chopping fruit for a cake. They were still at it, one each side of the table, when she returned. Like they hadn't spoke a word while she was gone—

There was a small mountain of fruit between them. "We only need three cups for the cake," she said, and they looked at her, startled, as if afraid they might be told to put the bits back into a block.

"It's all right." She measured what she needed into a crock. "You girls take what's left now and make candy." Maybe that would make them act like girls instead of— wooden indians. "Get the small crock and stir a cup of honey into the fruit. Then spread it on a damp cloth about that thick—" she measured with her fingers"—and we'll put it up on the roof to bake in the sun. It ought to be ready by the time the company gets here."

Narcissa put the cake in the oven, thinking ahead to the rest of the meal. She wanted it ready when Mr. Lee and his party got here, and she wanted it nice. She'd have new potatos and peas, and wilted lettuce, and green onions. They'd have to make do with side meat, though. Marcus hadn't time to hunt. She'd been embarrassed not to have anything better than fry stew to offer Thomas McKay.

58

She'd been surprised at the way he'd talked. He'd been so quiet on the trail two years ago. They'd been totally unprepared when he asked to leave his two older children with them for the winter.

"It isn't really a school yet—" Marcus made excuses. "We haven't much for supplies. We improvise. We're still waiting for books and slates from home. Until then—"

Captain McKay completed the sentence. "—until then, it's the only school available. There's no teacher at the Fort now." His voice was soft; his eyes were shadowed. "I do not wish my children to grow up as savages."

Dr. McLaughlin had had the same expression in his eyes when he'd asked her to teach his daughter Eloisa when she stayed at Fort Vancouver while Marcus came ahead to get the cabin started. She was uncomfortable, thinking of the men in the Territory, white or raised as white, whose children shared indian blood in equal part with theirs; who worried that these children would revert to the mothers' way of life.

They'd have to find room for the McKay children—Margaret could share Maria's corner. Maybe they could fix a bed for John among the potato sacks in the lean-to.

But Marcus settled the matter another way. "We'll keep the children, Captain, if it's what you want. But I'm wondering if we can't do better for John. How is he at his studies?"

"More serious than most. Dr. McLaughlin feels he should be sent east for his education, and my mother agrees." He glanced over to where Maria and Margaret were showing the boys how to make cat's cradles with waxed string. "She spoils them shamelessly."

"Why don't you send John east to school, then?"

"I could only let him go so far with someone I trust."

"Would you be interested in entering him in my old

school for medical training?"

McKay's face went still. "I would be most grateful if it could be arranged," he said carefully. "But it is a long way to your country, Doctor Whitman."

"Jason Lee's going east. He'll stop by here next week. It would be a fine opportunity for John to make the trip."

"I had not thought to send him so soon—" He was hurting already at the thought of parting with the boy.

"At least think it over," Marcus said. "Lee's planning to stop at Walla Walla on his way back from Lapwai. You could catch him there."

"And arrangements at the school?"

"Fairfield will consider it an honor to have Dr. McLaughlin's grandson as a student. I'll send a letter with Lee."

Narcissa's anticipation of Jason Lee's visit died down when she saw Henry Spalding with him. He'd had Mr. Lee for a week or more; why did he have to take over their visit, too? It was obvious something was bothering Henry. He could hardly wait to get to the house to start talking. His face was red, almost as if he'd been drinking spirits, and his voice as shrill as a nervous woman's.

He fidgeted while the others lingered over the food. She was furious. At least he could let the rest of them enjoy their meal. But before they'd finished the apple cake he pushed aside his plate and stood up, his head brushing the ceiling, his bony face all shadows. "Is there some place we can meet privately, Marcus?"

"I have to milk Bess. Come on out with me."

The cream was rising on the milk before they returned. It was like Henry to demand the men shut themselves up together and leave her sitting alone.

She strained the milk and walked down to the creek to rinse the pail. Usually she didn't go out into the dark by herself. But she wouldn't stay where she wasn't wanted, and she would not allow Henry Spalding to force her to her bed before she was ready to go.

The shadows bunched under the bushes; the fields stretched empty in the moonlight. The Cayuse camp was quiet. She walked slowly, letting the night air cool her arms. She had thought to serve more cake and tea, but it was getting so late now she wouldn't bother.

They all looked up as she went back into the house. Henry's eyes held a curious exasperation, as if she had, by her entrance, forced their minds from matters of grave importance.

"You'd better read this, 'Cissa." Marcus handed her a paper. "Move over here by the light."

She read the first lines; re-read them unbelievingly. Her eyes met Marcus', then turned to intercept Henry's hot glare. She glanced at Jason Lee who sat looking into the fire as if avoiding a scene of embarrassing privacy.

—Henry was asking for *thirty* ordained ministers, when they hadn't been able to get one, up to now; for *thirty* farmers, *thirty* school teachers, *ten* more doctors, and mechanics, and their wives. . . .

They had no place to put these people. It was idiocy to ask for them! She read more of the letter—

> . . . *you can do no less than send them with*
> *proper outfit. . . There must necessarily*
> *be. . .thousands of immortal souls take their*
> *leave of this world and pass beyond the border*
> *of hope, leaving the blood of their souls on*
> *the skirts of somebody. . . .*

That Henry would write to the Board that way! He was unbalanced! She turned the paper fearfully. On the back, a solid list of items demanded. In Marcus' writing—

> *2000 gun flints; 100 dozen scalping knives*
> *for trade; irons; bolting; 500 yards of*

striped or checked cotton; school supplies;
books; saws; axes; planes. And furniture.
And kitchen supplies . . . .

She faced them then. "Have you lost your minds?"

"We've just come to our right minds, Sister." Henry's face was lit like a ghost from the candle.

Jason Lee slipped outside and no one tried to stop him.

"We've gotten nowhere with our begging letters," Henry went on. "It's time the Board realizes we have to have materials to work with if we're to accomplish anything at all."

"The Board hasn't funds to finance an order of this size."

"People will come forward with money if they know of the need." Henry's voice was rising like a leaf on a spiral of heated air, tossing and shifting.

"We can't grow without supplies, 'Cissa," Marcus said; and Henry broke in to add, "We have to meet the opposition at their own game."

She leaned on her hands, brought her face close to Henry's. "How could we possibly compete with Mr. Lee's mission, with a solid wall of mountains between our territories? Aren't there enough indians to go around?"

"'Cissa, Lee brought word from Vancouver that the Catholics are getting ready to set up missions. They're bringing a Vicar General from Montreal this year."

"We lose face with the indians when we're treated like poor relations by our Board while Lee gets anything he asks for," Henry cried. "We can be as big as the Methodists in two years time if we demand our rights."

"And where are we to put these people if they come?"

Marcus gathered the papers into a stack. "We'll talk about it later," he said. "Mr. Lee is coming."

She and Marcus lay awake long after Henry's snoring began to rumble through the house.

"You think it's wrong, don't you, 'Cissa?"

"David Greene will believe you're raving mad if you send that letter."

"We ain't asking for half what Lee's sending for."

"He's been here five years."

"We can't wait five years. We've got to be ready when the settlers start coming."

"Nobody was waiting here with a ready-made settlement when we arrived."

"McLaughlin helped us plenty. But the missionaries is one thing and settlers is something else. Once Americans begin coming in here, HBC is going to be out of businesss. McLaughlin knows it. Lee's carrying a letter signed by the Americans in the valley asking the President to establish jurisdiction over the Willamette Territory. You think McLaughlin's going to help them set up claim to this country?"

"That will be years in the future."

"It's beginning now. McLaughlin's already got orders not to sell tools or cattle to the Americans, nor to indians either, for that matter."

"You don't know that for sure—"

"McLaughlin told Lee when he stopped there on his way up river. He wants to discourage us from sending reports that the settlers can do well here."

She shivered, pulling the blankets around her shoulders. The letter was a terrible mistake! But she'd never convince Marcus. He thought the time was ripe for his dream to start coming true.

Henry and Marcus were in a fever of planning after Jason Lee left. The Methodist acres already flourishing on the banks of the Willamette was a spur they could not bear. Henry stayed over a day, and the two made plans that could not develop for years, as far as she could see.

But if Jason Lee hadn't done anything else with his big talk, he'd succeeded in putting down Henry's jealousy of Waiilatpu. Henry laughed with Marcus over Lee's warnings that they'd do better to abandon one mission and unite forces.

"That's mighty good advice from his point of view," Henry said.

"I reckon neither McLaughlin nor Lee is going to be too happy when William gets here with more missionaries," Marcus agreed. "This is one time I'm going to be happy to see Gray."

The next day Marcus was summoned to the Cayuse camp. The indians were coming down with ague. He gave them what medicines he had and sent to Vancouver for more. They gave him no rest for more than a week.

One night, rousing from sleep and grumbling as he answered a knock, he ran back to the bedroom shouting, "It's mail! Get up, 'Cissa! It's mail!"

This time there was letters from everyone they'd left behind. Touching the paper was like touching hands with parents and friends and relatives. Her eyes blurred, seeing her father's heavy scrawl on one envelope. He hadn't disowned her after all—

Marcus worked from first light to midnight now, cultivating fields and setting fence, in spite of frequent midnight calls from shivering indians who would be burning with fever before he could get them bedded down in the kitchen. Narcissa worried over his lack of sleep but to tell the truth, he showed no signs of fatigue. Events were moving them forward at a pace that would certainly show progress at the end of the year. The indians seemed to be responding at last; the school was showing results. Narcissa gradually regained her sense of well-being in spite of the letter.

In early fall Marcus came leading a stranger to the house: a slender man—indian or part—but lighter skinned than the Cayuse. And his eyes were free of the suspicion that burned in the eyes of Umtippe's people. He wore dark trousers and a blue and white striped shirt. His only concessions to his indian ancestry were moccasins and his long hair bound with a red handkerchief.

"'Cissa, this is Compo. I told you about him guiding Doc Parker and me the summer we came West." Marcus fairly beamed at finding someone from that summer.

Narcissa held out her hand, and thought later that Compo took it as naturally as Marcus would have. And that's what they were trying to do, after all: to make the indians into people who could enter the civilized world and know how to act.

"Compo wants to stay," Marcus told her. "He's got his family with him."

"Where will they live?"

"He's setting up his lodge by the mill shed. If the kanaka boys get enough lumber before bad weather, we'll try to finish a room in the shop for the Compos."

"Umtippe will be jealous if we let them live on mission grounds."

"I'll think of some way to pacify Umtippe. Compo's a Christian. We need him."

Within the month Narcissa was grateful for Compo's presence. Marcus was called to the Methodist mission at the *dalles* to deliver Mrs. Shepherd's baby in mid-August.

"You'll be all right," he assured her as he left. "Things are quiet at the camp."

"How long will you be gone?"

"Not more than a week, probably." He smiled. "Come Sunday you can lead the indians in song for hours and I won't be here to interrupt with a sermon."

That same night she was wakened by the indians

knocking. They would expect her to come in place of Marcus and she could never go alone to Umtippe's camp at midnight. But it was a woman waiting at the door, carrying a blanket-wrapped figure. Her eyes begged for help she could not put into words.

Narcissa's efforts to talk with the woman roused the girls. "Wrap something around you and run bring Compo. Hurry."

She had come a long way against her husband's wishes, the woman told them. She wanted the doctor to help her child. Faced with his absence and nowhere else to go, she allowed Narcissa to examine the little girl.

The child was unconscious, her cheeks red along the bones under the tight skin. Narcissa knelt as she had seen Marcus do; felt the slight pulse and listened to the heartbeat. Compo knelt beside her at the pallet.

"She is dying," he said, his voice grave, "but I do not know why."

"Ask the mother how long she has been ill."

The woman held up five thick fingers.

Narcissa did not know what to do. She bathed the little girl with salt water to bring down the fever and went back to bed, leaving the mother squatting beside the pallet.

The child was dead next morning. She felt her helplessness like a weight. Compo led the woman, carrying the child, from the room. Soon the death cry sounded. The girls rushed to the kitchen in their nightgowns, fright and understanding on their faces. Alice broke into wails of terror. Narcissa herded them into her bed and waited with them for Compo to return.

"The mother wishes the child to rest near the mission," he told her. She would have to arrange some kind of service for this afternoon, then.

No one wanted breakfast. Each of them felt the child's dying, as if it pointed up the vulnerability of the mission.

66

The cabin was no longer a refuge; death could enter in spite of the bar on the door.

It was cool and green under the trees at the bottom of the hill. She stood beside Hind's grave, remembering the gentle man and his kindness to her on the trail. He had cared for her as if she were a child, times when she felt she could not go on another day; not another step—

"Missus—?"

Compo was standing with the shovel, waiting, "Here, Compo. I think Hinds would like having the child next to him."

The shovel bit into the grassy sod. "Wait until the children are down from the hill. We'll hold services later this afternoon."

"The man sleeps here alone?"

"Some of the indians are buried where the rocks are piled."

"The Cayuse do not use burial platforms?"

"Doctor persuaded some to use the burial ground. He believes disease spreads from bodies left unburied. I was surprised Umtippe allowed it. He's against us in everything we do."

"Umtippe is a clever man, Mrs. Whitman. He will accept any white customs that are to his advantage. It is too bad he is also a cruel man; he could be a big help in bringing his people to the mission."

"Why does he hate us so, Compo?"

"Umtippe is afraid his people will lose their land and their ways; afraid they will be cheated out of the things promised to replace what they must surrender."

"But his people suffer because of his ignorance."

"I think it is because Umtippe is not ignorant that he is afraid. He sees beyond this moment, but he is cruel and fears others are cruel, also."

"Mother Whitman!" Narcissa looked up to see the girls

running down the hill path, skirts flying behind. "Company is coming. We saw them in the meadows."

She stopped them beside her, smoothing their braids. "Quiet, now. Which way are they coming?"

Maria pointed north and east.

It couldn't be Marcus yet. She walked up the path to see for herself, and recognized the people from Lapwai. For once Henry Spalding had come at the right time.

When they went to the hill that afternoon they found the Cayuse already there. They listened in impressive silence as Henry preached the service; when he knelt some of them fell to their knees in the blowing grass.

She and the girls and Compo joined Henry in the Lord's Prayer, their voices thin on the busy summer air. But voices began following the words from scattered places in the crowd, and she realized with pride her girls were repeating the words she had taught them.

Henry insisted on staying until Marcus returned. She didn't mind this time. His mellow mood was holding. He'd been stirred by the number of indians at the service.

"I felt a quickening there," he told Marcus later. "I believe the time is near when they'll come to God freely." He paced the floor in his enthusiasm, holding aside the tails of his coat, speaking with unaccustomed approval of their project.

It surprised her to hear Henry speaking this way. Was it possible that she and Marcus were moving faster at Waiilatpu than they realized?

"I've felt something this spring," Marcus said, "just under the surface. Maybe you ought to stay awhile, Henry. Show them the way. I doubt I can."

She bit back a protest. She wished Marcus wouldn't always underrate what he did. As if it was Henry's right to claim the credit for saving their indians after she and Marcus had worked to lead them to this moment!

68

She hoped he'd refuse, but Henry nodded, brooding on saving the Cayuse. So he was at Waiilatpu when William Gray and his new wife came with word his party was arriving within the week. He created an uproar as usual, stopping by the lumber mill and gathering the kanakas to ride down with him and his lady, the troup of them clattering in past the shop and bringing the Compos on the run.

None of them had had any idea of his marriage. Henry didn't hesitate to ask bluntly, "Where's your recruits, William? And who's this young lady?"

Narcissa kissed Mary Agusta warmly, then held her away to look at her. "You're a pretty thing," she smiled. And she was: golden and delicate in the soft green sprigged muslin, her face shaded by a summer bonnet with a green ribbon poufed under one ear. Her hazel eyes were shaded by deep lashes; her brown hair framed her face neatly beneath the bonnet brim.

Where in the world had William found a girl like this? She had to admit there was a difference about him. He hadn't complained once while they waited for her to make breakfast. He even looked better; almost handsome now with his clear eyes and tanned face. Some of the softness had disappeared during the trip.

But his old self emerged soon enough. When Marcus asked, "Now, William, we're all curious about our new workers," he leaned back in his chair.

"I'll tell you, Doctor, they're honest and dedicated, but they won't be easy to live with."

Narcissa caught Marcus' quick wink as he helped her serve the food. It was the pot calling the kettle black if ever she heard one. She glanced at Mary Agusta and wondered how it would be for a girl to live with a man like William. Was he at odds with her, too, or did he need her as a source of peace when his contentiousness made his relationships with others too sharp to live with?

"There's seven, you say?" Henry prompted. "Who's the odd one?"

"Cornelius Rogers. He's a good enough boy, I suppose, but he's got a spark of fun about him that might get out of hand if unguided."

"A streak of humor never hurt anyone, William."

William's eyes seemed to hold some secret about Cornelius Rogers better left unsaid. "He spends a lot of time fiddling and singing."

"We can put his fiddle playing to good use," Narcissa said. "The indians love music."

"I want to hear about the preachers," Henry said.

William pursed his lips. "They're an odd lot. Walker don't say much. It's like he's afraid of his own voice." he sniffed. "He's different when he's dealing with his wife, though. Had the poor woman in tears most of the way with his criticizing. Not that she don't deserve some of it, with her faunching around and sticking her nose into others' business—"

"William—" Mary Agusta murmured.

"They might as well be prepared." he leaned across the table. "I'll tell you, Sister Whitman, he'll spatter your kitchen good with tobacco juice if you let him."

She stiffened. Mr. Walker nor anyone else was not going to chew tobacco in her house! She decided to pay no attention to William's warning. She knew William. He'd get trouble stirring ahead of time if he could manage it.

Narcissa was tempted to ride out with the others to meet the newcomers, except it would take what time she'd have to get ready for them. So she tried to visit with Mary Agusta, questioning her about the women. But apart from mentioning that Myra Eells was several years older than her husband, Cushing, and that Sarah Smith was inclined to be sickly, she didn't add much to what William

70

had told them. Somehow the impression came to her that Mary Agusta didn't care for Mary Walker.

She seemed embarrassed around Margaret and Maria, and drew back from Alice as from a muddy puppy. A strange girl— pretty, yes, but without much warmth. As if all her prettiness was on the outside.

She was glad when the Grays decided to make a trip to Walla Walla. It would be easier for her to get ready for the others without a strange woman in the house. There was so much to be done: along with William's recruits, there'd be Eliza and the baby. Henry had sent for them the day William arrived.

Narcissa drove herself to be ready for them. Marcus was forever after her to let Mrs. Compo and the girls do the heavy work. But there were things she couldn't pass on to others when she was to be entertaining women she'd never seen; women fresh from houses with polished floors and billowy curtains and fine chairs and tables that gleamed from years of polishing.

She should have listened to him. She was ill again before they got there. To lie down sent pain and nausea spreading through her. Marcus, finding her still awake in the early morning hours, would rub her legs to ease their aching until she fell asleep.

Later she was to look back on these days as peaceful and private. For the summer that had begun so pleasantly was shattered by the gathering of the missionaries. No one seemed able to find a place in the group that suited him. It was as if a wind of discontent blew against a tapestry, rearranging the figures almost hourly.

Once they were past exchanging news of relatives and family, hearing about new fashions and books and events in the east; once the pleasure of the things women discuss when they first come together had faded, the irritants surfaced.

Within days she felt as if she'd been attacked by a swarm of wasps. These women expected the kind of hospitality they had known in the States. Out here entertaining was a different matter, with everyone helping, and an acceptance of inconvenience a matter of course. The newcomers expected service as if they were renting rooms in an inn.

She escaped from the house whenever possible. She followed Marcus to the milk shed every evening. And he let her express her complaints, listening patiently.

"Sarah Smith gave me her laundry this morning as big as you please, with instructions on how to starch the Reverend's collars."

"They'll learn to pitch in, 'Cissa. Give them time."

"So far all they've learned is how to sleep late on a corn husk tick."

"Seems like Mrs. Walker's always helping."

"Mary's a worker," she admitted. "And it isn't so much that they don't help anyway. It's their attitude. Myra Eells looks around with her mouth turned down like she thought she'd find cockroaches. How's she ever going to live with indians if she's so squeamish?"

"I'll trade you the men for the women," he said. "At least the ladies don't voice their opinions so loud."

"Are they still arguing about Mr. Walker using fermented juice for Communion?"

"That's settled. But I'm dreading the battle when William finds he ain't going to the Flathead station."

"Wouldn't it be easier to let him have the site than fight with him about it?"

"Nobody will go with him. They're all so tired of his loud mouth they refuse to settle anywhere with him. Every one of them has said flat out they won't live with the Grays even if they have to go back to the States. I'll tell you I don't look forward to tomorrow."

72

The arguing went on all day of that First Annual Meeting of the Church. The men met outside. Narcissa was grateful for that. The women had enough contention among themselves without taking over the men's quarrels. It was sundown before they reached an agreement. The Walkers and Eells would establish a mission among the Spokanes, with William and Mary Agusta going to Lapwai, and the Smiths staying on at Waiilatpu. Cornelius Rogers would divide his time among them as he was needed.

Narcissa would have chosen the Walkers to stay with them if she'd had her say.

They voted to spend as much time as possible during the next year learning the indian languages; to build a flour mill and blacksmith shop at Waiilatpu; appointed committees; and asked Marcus to go to Vancouver for supplies. They would hold Communion at the indian services on Sunday with Henry explaining in the Nez Perce tongue, which many of the Cayuse understood. The newcomers would be accepted into the Church. Thank goodness they'd gone ahead with the organization and election of officers before these others got here—

The weather turned cold overnight and they were crowded in the cabin all day. The women complained of having nothing to do, but they would not turn a hand unless asked, and then wasted more than they were worth. Narcissa smarted, watching Sarah Smith making sweets as if every day was a holiday; like all she had to do to get more sugar was stroll to the market. Finally she told her straight out that supplies couldn't be used so extravagantly. After that none of them would enter the lean-to. For several meals Sarah Smith pointedly refused all but the barest portions of food. Naricssa almost hated the woman. It was easy enough for Sarah to be self-

73

righteous; it wasn't *her* winter's supplies that were being eaten in a month. And Mary Walker was whining now that Elkanah had gone looking for a site with Henry. Being in the family way didn't give her the right to spend the next three months in bed whimpering for her mother.

They managed to close down her school with their sniveling. Narcissa had thought this would be one place they could help but they turned up their noses and edged away from the girls in their dirty calicos. For a second she saw her girls as Sarah Smith and Myra Eells were seeing them: with lice in their braids and grime under their fingernails; and Naeta with a patch of ringworm on her head bigger than a spanish dollar. But they were gradually getting better about these things, and when they smiled shyly they had the whitest teeth in the world. What help Narcissa had came from Margaret and Maria. She wouldn't have blamed them if they had rebelled against being ordered around like maid servants. But they did what they could, and when the orders came too persistently, quietly disappeared.

She was half sick with a cold the day Marcus left for Vancouver. Alice was fussy with a sore throat. He wouldn't wait for her to get the baby to sleep, but insisted on packing his saddlebags himself. No sooner would Alice's eyes droop than he would stomp into the bedroom and she'd cry for him to hold her.

When Narcissa whispered to him to please be quiet he turned on her sharply. "I been planning this trip for days. Where are my clean clothes?"

She fought not to cry; she wouldn't let those women see her with red eyes. Marcus wouldn't have spoken to her that way, except for them causing so much trouble for him.

She kept on rocking after Alice had given up. When

Marcus tiptoed to the door and asked cautiously what he could take with him for food she laid Alice on the bed and went to the lean-to, head bent to keep her unhappiness from the prying eyes of the visitors. She was sorry to see him leave, but mainly because the responsibility would be hers now for keeping the peace.

That night at supper, with ironing still in its basket, Narcissa laid the plates on the table boards. She'd never set guests down to a bare table in her life before; tonight she didn't care.

She offered a short grace in spite of Mr. Smith's objections to women praying in public—anything to save them sitting through one of his lengthy supplications. In the silence following she heard Myra Eells whisper, "It's a disgrace to ask people to sit at a dirty table without even a cloth to cover it."

Narcissa stood up abruptly, and never mind that she was crying. "This table has never been bare until today. No one has ever complained of the food served at this table until you came!"

They stared at her without a word.

"But no guests have ever before intruded without offering to help. You might have brought me another pair of hands, since I'm to be a slave to all of you."

Later Mary Walker came to the doorway of her room. "Are you all right, Mrs. Whitman?"

She nodded.

After a long silence Mary said, "Nobody means to be cruel—" and ducked back to the outer room.

The bitter weather did not let up. Tensions increased as the cold held. Feelings were rubbed raw by the friction of conflicting beliefs; unintended discourtesies ballooned. Narcissa felt herself on the point of bursting; thought that only her skin kept her from flying apart. They passed their colds from one to another as if they were playing *Button-Button*. Mr. Smith's hacking cough kept them awake night after night.

Marcus worked on the new house as soon as he returned from Vancouver. Narcissa would bundle herself into a heavy jacket and go with him just to get out of the crowded cabin. She would stand in the roofless rooms, teeth chattering, and imagine the house finished and furnished; the curtains hung; the shutters green against the whitewashed brick.

Asa Smith helped when his cough permitted, but grudgingly. Sarah was at him every minute to get her a place finished where she could be by herself.

"If the weather holds we'll have the corner room roofed by December," Marcus announced at supper one night. Mary Walker's baby would be born in December. Once the Smiths moved, they could partition the little room to give her some privacy. Elkanah was forever after his wife for exposing herself unnecessarily. Now Mary spent most of the day in bed, crying, refusing to come out to the fire when the men were in the house. Narcissa thought she would scream if the dry sobbing didn't stop. She tried to talk to Mary; the girl only sobbed she wanted a room of her own. Sometimes she invited Mary to use her own room, remembering the feeling of being penned in by watching eyes.

The birth of the baby didn't improve the situation. Mary could not nurse the husky boy. He cried day and night, and Mary's cries joined his when they held him to her breast to try to stimulate the milk flow.

"Marcus, you have to do something!"

"I'm doing all I can, 'Cissa. Is she using the pump? And the cold packs?"

"It's freezing in that room. She'll have her lungs congested too if we keep putting packs on her—"

"Then move her to our room. I don't know anything else to do."

Narcissa gritted her teeth to keep from shouting that he was a doctor—why didn't he know something else to do?

She made Mary comfortable in her own bed, but the thin wail of the hungry baby followed her all morning. In desperation she put him to her own breast. Mary watched from dark circled eyes and said nothing. Narcissa felt the sharp tugging at herself with distaste, but at least the baby was quiet for a time.

There was some peace then, but with two children drawing nourishment from her she felt as if she were being eaten alive. And Mary Walker wept now because she wanted to nurse her baby herself.

Marcus finally ordered her to stop nursing both children. "I'll find a bottle for the Walker baby. Alice can use a cup."

"Where will we get milk? Bess is ready to dry up."

"We'll keep her milking till Posy comes fresh." He rummaged in a box and found a medicine bottle and a red nipple. "Start right now."

Alice made no more fuss about giving up the breast than throwing away a stick, but the cow's milk was too strong for baby Cyrus. Narcissa bit her tongue against his constant crying; finally ran to where Marcus was working. "I can't stand this, Marcus!" She held her hands over her ears as if the crying would follow her outside. "I can't stand it!"

He held her against him, soothing her. "I'll do something," he promised.

He brought Compo's wife to the house. "She'll nurse the Walker baby," he said. Narcissa watched, fascinated and repelled, as the woman unbuttoned her dress and lifted out one of the large bronze breasts dripping milk from the dark nipple. She leaned over Mary's bed like some monstrous cow; the small lips reached as she lifted the baby to her; fastened, tugged— From the first feeding Cyrus Walker began to thrive.

1839

Narcissa's brief peace was broken when Marcus received Henry's call from Lapwai. Marcus followed her into the lean-to to break the news. "Henry needs help, 'Cissa. His indians are ready now to come into the Church."

She covered her face with her hands, leaning against the rough wall. "Why can't the others go?"

"If we're to catch up with the Methodists we have to take full advantage of every chance. The others don't realize."

"You're going to leave me alone here with these people to go help Henry catch up with the Methodists?"

"Yes," he said, his voice earnest, seeing nothing wrong with the idea.

She climbed the hill every afternoon he was gone, in spite of the cold. The day he returned she had Alice with her, bundled into heavy wraps against a persistent sore throat. Seeing him in the meadow she started down the hill. "There's papa coming—"

When he saw them he came at a gallop. Narcissa started to run, letting Alice follow through the dead grass as best she could. Breathless, she leaned against him and rested for the first time in two weeks. He gave her time, holding her, before he asked, "What is it, 'Cissa?"

"Don't ever leave me behind again—"

And he promised, with anger underlying his words. "You don't ever have to stay here without me again. That's my promise."

He held Alice on the horse and walked beside Narcissa. As they neared the buildings she said, "I can't stand to go back inside."

"It's our home—"

She stopped, letting the wind push her without resistence. "Not anymore. They've taken it away from us."

He turned her to see her face. "All right. Let them have it. The three of us will go away."

"Where would we go?"

"We've been invited to spend some time with Joseph's people. And that's just what we're going to do."

"At Lapwai?"

"No. No. Chief Timothy is camped on the Clearwater now. The spring flowers will be coming up soon, and there are evergreens all around to break the wind.

She let the thought of that peaceful setting grow in her like sleep creeping up on her, softly—softly—

"And you know the best part of it? No one can complain. Timothy's going to teach me the language."

She made only one condition: that they take Margaret and Maria, too.

They left next morning in a soft mist, before the birds were awake, moving north and east through the prairie grass. Marcus led the way holding Alice in front of him; the girls followed on their black and white ponies; she was last.

The gray sky suited her mood precisely. She nursed her resentment at those interlopers back at the mission who still slept while she and Marcus and the children were forced from their home to try to find some peace in an indian camp. She had no desire to talk, not even with Marcus. What was there to talk about except the trespassers who had taken over their home?

But when the clouds broke in the early afternoon her depression lifted. The girls raced their ponies ahead and she rode up beside Marcus, taking her turn at holding Alice.

"It's time you put it all out of your mind," he told her, and went on quickly, "I hope Timothy has a watch out for us; I'm not sure I know my way around in these hills without a guide."

Th chief himself was waiting for them at the junction of the Clearwater and the Snake. He was taller than she remembered, standing with his young warriors; dignified in his fringed elkskin robe with bands of blue beading at cuffs and neck and armholes. Once the greetings were made he led them into the hills along a waterway bordered with willow and birch, and down to the valley where his people had set up spring camp.

She felt peace around her when she woke in the dim lodge scented from the pine boughs under their blankets; heard it in the splash of water pouring over the rounded stones of the creek bed, and in the bright bird whistles. From their lodge they could see the narrow canyon fenced with willow poles where the ponies ran, dark manes blowing—the older horses splashed with contrasting color, the yearlings just beginning to frost in patches of white.

But peaceful or not, her surroundings could not ease the bitterness she'd carried with her from Waiilatpu. Constant criticism could mark a person with cuts that festered until there was no room left for gentleness. It took what energy she had just to get through a day at a time.

Marcus had done everything he could to help her enjoy

herself here. He'd put the girls in charge of Alice so she could sleep late. But sleep was a habit she'd outgrown in Oregon country; she'd wake in the dark with Marcus breathing evenly beside her, the irritations stinging like scorpions in her mind.

The hurt she could never forgive was that she and Marcus had spent the years surrounded by savages, taking what little there was and building the best they could, only to have these latecomers destroy their pride in their accomplishments in a matter of days.

Did they think she and Marcus didn't recognize their efforts as pathetic, compared to what they *wanted* to do? It was a terrible thing to tear down a person's sense of his own worth. There was some truth in their complaints, no doubt. But surely the effort in time and will power showed too.

—The truth was, she wanted to be admired for her efforts, even by unlikeable people—

She tried not to spoil the outing for the others. Marcus spent half of each day learning the Nez Perce language from Timothy and his *te-wat*; the rest he talked with the men or fished or hunted. She was startled more than once to hear his laughter. She couldn't think how long it had been since Marcus had laughed that way.

Alice ran free with the indian children, dabbling in the pools at the creek's edge, tossing dried twigs into the current and watching them out of sight, watching ponies. Her blond curls stood out like goldenrod beside the crows-wing heads of the indian youngsters; and where their shirts faded into the trees from a distance, Alice's red knit pullover burned like a summer rose bush.

Strangely, Maria and Margaret made no places for themselves among the Nez Perce. They walked alone, or sat together watching the indian girls. Somehow, here, the white blood showed plain compared to the indian.

Maria's fragile face was alien beside the rounded features of these people; Margaret's dignity showed more as white determination than indian pride.

It was a thought new to her: she'd always thought of them as indian. But the difference was plain to see. How much of it was because they'd lived at the mission? How much of it could be traced to their white fathers?

Curiosity gradually pushed her unhappiness to the background. With more than a hundred people she never saw dirt in the camp. Game and fish were cleaned on the gravel near the stream and the offal thrown to the dogs. The meat was parceled out and cooked promptly, with none left in the sun to draw the swarms of flies that buzzed hungrily over the food in Umtippe's camp. Observing now, Narcissa thought it might be true, as the traders said, that the Nez Perce were as nearly civilized as indians could be. And when they started back to Waiilatpu she left Timothy's camp with reluctance.

The first evening home Asa Smith brought up the subject of making wine for Sunday services from spring berries, knowing Marcus was dead against it. Straightening the house next day she came across a letter from Mary Agusta to Myra Eells, full of bitter accusations against herself based, as near as she could tell, on an outright lie.

"I didn't mention Mary Agusta's baby to anyone," she stormed. "I forgot it, to tell the truth."

"Wouldn't have made any difference," Marcus said, angry himself. "William's been bragging among the men about her being in the family way ever since they got here. He's told all the details, too, like a snot-nosed kid just sneaked away to a woman for the first time."

She quieted down then, uncomfortable that he could talk that way. He wasn't a man to waste his thoughts on such things. Or was he, and she didn't know? She'd heard women whisper among themselves sometimes. If she thought Marcus ever mentioned her that way— She glanced at him and flushed when he looked up suddenly and met her eyes.

Walker and Eells returned from their scouting trip and the allegiances changed. Walker and Smith went to Lapwai, leaving Cushing Eells and their wives behind. Within the week word came calling Marcus and Cushing to a meeting of the Board.

"I'm going with you, Marcus," she insisted. "You promised."

At Lapwai the air tingled with tension. Narcissa found herself smarting often from Mary Agusta's jibes. The quiet little bride, burning from imagined hurts, had become as vindictive as her husband. For once Narcissa lined up with Eliza, who went about her routine seemingly unaware of the group. And she had to admit Eliza had done wonders with her school. But if she felt admiration for the work at Lapwai, Marcus did not. "Anyone can beat these creatures to obedience," he said, his voice sharp.

"What in the world are you talking about?"

"Henry's using whips on these poor people. They do what he asks because they're afraid."

"Henry wouldn't—"

"Don"t tell me," he said. "I saw it myself! He ordered ten strokes laid on a poor devil because he went hunting instead of working in the garden. And last week he gave an indian woman *seventy* lashes because she ran away from the brute Conlon—the one that works the smithy."

"Henry whipped a woman?"

"He ordered it done, and that's the same thing."

An appalling picture came to mind, Henry in a frenzy, striking, striking at the woman while she endured the painful punishment silently—

"I can't believe it, Marcus. Not a woman."

"William saw it. And the indians."

She could not bring herself to be around the Spaldings any more than was necessary after that. She spent her time with the babies. Little Eliza was delicate, with long dark hair and black eyes, painfully thin in contrast to Alice's sturdy legs and round arms. When Narcissa lifted the little girl to her lap, she would look up uncertainly, her eyes all questions, before settling back against her. Didn't Henry or Eliza ever hold the child?

Henry made it a point to go on about Eliza's health and the extra work. Narcissa didn't bother to answer. Eliza had always been thin; she was white, and her eyes were shadowed, but she'd always looked that way. As for helping, it was surely enough, keeping the babies out from underfoot.

She was reading to the little girls one rainy morning when Marcus burst in, spraying them with drops from his jacket. She got up quickly. "What happened?"

"They've voted to start a new station on the Palouse River."

"For William?"

His eyes met her and she saw disbelief there. "For us," he said.

But that wasn't possible. They had Waiilatpu—

"They're giving Waiilatpu to Smith," he went on. "They've decided since Smith don't want to live with us, we'll have to move."

The anger Narcissa had tried to suppress blazed now like a forest fire. "Let Asa and Sarah Smith go to the Palouse or wherever," she shouted. "Waiilatpu's our home."

His hand gripped her arm. "Be quiet now," he ordered. "We'll go wherever we're sent."

She was sick— Sick— How could they justify taking Waiilatpu from them just when things were beginning to work out?

"They say as the only doctor I'm needed in a central location," Marcus said. "But the truth is, Smith and Gray have squawked so loud they'll do anything to shut them up."

"Is it settled for sure?"

"They're taking the vote now. We've been lined up all day: Rogers and Walker and me against the others."

"Why aren't you up there?"

"I'm sick of fighting, 'Cissa. I told them to settle it to please themselves." He stiffened. "Here comes Rogers now."

They waited in silence. They didn't have to hear Rogers say the words—they read the verdict in his manner.

She turned abruptly from the pain in Marcus' eyes. He hadn't really believed they would do it. And, "I'll never forgive Henry Spalding for this," he whispered.

Spring had come to Waiilatpu while they were gone, as if to taunt them with the treasure they were losing. Narcissa went about her work untouched by the renaissance. She had taken refuge in indifference, determined not to be reached by any further humiliations.

She watched unmoved as the Eells and Walkers packed their supplies and prepared to follow the Spokane chief Ellis who had come to guide them to their new site. She said goodbye, but distractedly. When Mary Walker hesitated beside her she was indifferent to her overtures. They had had their day of hurting her; none of them would have another opportunity.

Strangely, the Smiths made no mention of her and Marcus leaving. It was as if, having forced their expulsion, the older couple had no desire to enforce it.

—but I can't forget it! she thought time after time when, in spite of her efforts to divorce herself from the mission, a rush of hurt pride and fierce hunger for her home tore at her like a hurricane.

Marcus left to explore for a new site. She watched him ride away with the same detachment she'd felt on seeing the Eells and Walkers leave. Sometimes, searching the sky high-piled with white clouds, she felt the earth spinning madly; felt the moment might come when she would be flung off into space, bumping about among the soft bundles.

Maria and Margaret watched her silently and kept Alice with them, as if she might forget the baby if they didn't care for her. Narcissa kept the school going, but automatically, setting her students to work each day; feeling relief when they left in the afternoon.

Marcus returned from his trip despondent. "I can't find any place, 'Cissa." He leaned with his arms crossed on the window sill, looking out over his fields—*his* fields—and his head fell until his forehead touched his wrists. "Or maybe I ain't really looking. I don't want any other place.
"I want Waiilatpu."

She felt nothing with which to comfort him. She was dried up inside; of if she wasn't, she didn't dare unlock the gate that held back her feelings. Once released, her anger, her sense of betrayal, might set the world on fire.

Marcus went back to work as if pursued by furies. Alone with her he raged at Smith's ignorance of the philosophy by which Waiilatpu had prospered. "He don't believe in teaching the indians farming. He says flat out the only way to help them find salvation is to keep them chasing around the mountains away from the vice and corruption of the settlers."

Night after night Narcissa lay staring into the dark. Where would they go when they were forced to leave? To the Spaldings? Without a site they would be condemned to spending the winter in someone else's home, at the mercy of one of those wives who despised her.

Then one morning they woke to find the Smiths packing their gear to spend the summer among the indians. She hardly breathed as they hurried through breakfast and packed their horses. A cautious hope grew in her as they rode away. Just like that, with barely a goodbye—

"When are they coming back?" she asked, her mouth dry.

Marcus squinted after them. "He didn't say."

As if released from a spell, Narcissa returned to running her home, and Marcus began plowing his land. He issued plows to the Cayuse who claimed their plots, working beside them as long as there was light. If the fields were planted when the Smiths returned there was nothing they could do about it.

Word came from Vancouver that the Reverend Hall and his wife had arrived from Owyhee with the printing press. Narcissa looked around the house, freshly whitewashed, windows gleaming in the sun, and felt pleasure at the thought of visitors. Before Marcus left to meet the Halls at Walla Walla he sent word to Henry to come to Waiilatpu.

She ran with the girls to greet them as they splashed their horses across the irrigation ditch. Once they'd made out the dots of movement through the grass the hours had crawled slower than the caravan creeping towards the mission. Now that Narcissa dared feel again, she was on fire to see another woman; to talk with someone. Part of her bitterness had been from knowing she was still alone. A woman in this forsaken spot needed someone.

It was different with men: they grew up with roughness; could cope with the solitude; were strong enough to meet the demands of a primitive country. They had the problems of food and shelter to hold their attention. They could overlook minor difficulties. It was the accumulation of matters too trivial to bother a man with that broke a woman down, heart and body—

So she was waiting for them: Marcus, and the man and woman, and behind, two kanaka boys carrying between their horses what appeared to be a chair on poles.

Mrs. Hall was a big woman, riding indian style, ample hips overflowing the saddle, clutching the reins with both hands. Mr. Hall looked no bigger than a gnat. He hopped to the ground and ran to help his wife as she heaved herself around and slid down the side of the horse like some bulky cargo being lowered over a ship's side, while the kanaka boys came racing with the chair.

She beamed up at Narcissa from the pile of gray checked gingham skirts bundled around her in the chair. "Land sakes, girl; I haven't been on a creature like that for years. Mr. Hall told me it wasn't ladylike to come riding astraddle, but it's the way I learned, and it's the only way I can stay on an animal."

"It doesn't matter, Mrs. Hall." Narcissa knelt to kiss her cheek. "Just so you got here."

Mrs. Hall's smile revealed two gold teeth. "And you got a baby! Let me jist hold her awhile. I ain't seen a little yalla haired baby for so long I almost forgot what they look like. Come on and see Auntie," she coaxed Alice, who crawled into her lap obediently. When Narcissa tried later to take Alice Mrs. Hall shooed her away. "She's just as hungry for a grandma as I am for a little one. Leave her be; leave her be. I'll set her down when I'm tard."

Margaret and Maria were fascinated by the gleaming teeth. She called them her 'girlies' and included them in her bountiful good will. They loved her unconditionally.

It was obvious Mr. Hall thought of his wife as frail and of himself as her protector. He was forever fussing over her. "She's ailing," he explained often. "It's her legs. She don't walk more than a few steps at a time. They sent us with the press hoping the change of climate would help."

"Mrs. Hall reminds me of Mama," she told Marcus.

For the first time in months his eyes were teasing. "Cissa, if your mother heard you say that she'd faint away. It's like saying an old felt carpet slipper reminds you of a leather button shoe."

She laughed with him. "I don't care. There's something about her that reminds me of mama."

He slipped his arms around her; put his face against hers. "It's because they're the same ages as our parents," he said. "they make us feel young again." His hands touched her breasts through her gown; she felt a strangeness, almost apprehension— and then the swift answering awareness she'd felt the first time he'd touched her that way.

—she didn't want to grow old! She didn't want him to grow old! She covered his mouth with her fingers. He was making them sound old, even so—

His lips moved against her hand, freeing a hot, painful aching in her—wanting him—wanting him—

She felt his arms bending her to him in the dark, and no one listening to stop their coming together as there had been all this winter.

Narcissa woke in the mornings now eager to be up. It was a pleasure to work in the open air, stirring the boiling clothes while Mrs. Hall, sitting on the wood block, thumped the dasher up and down in the wash barrel as if she were beating the devil out of the work shirts along with the dirt.

She did not mind working in the garden while Mrs. Hall sat on a blanket in the shade helping the girls piece quilt blocks and singing hymns in a voice as plain and comfortable as her face.

The first day Mrs. Hall had shuffled over to her saying, "I got you a present here, Dr. McLaughlin down to Vancouver said to give you when you were planting your garden."

"What is it?"

"Flower seeds. He wouldn't say what kind; said the surprise would last longer if you had to wait a while to see what came up."

"I'd like to see Dr. McLaughlin. He sends so many things."

"And I'd like to see them flowers when they're blooming. I tell you, Cissy, I used to get that hungry to see a trumpet vine or a morning glory when we was at The Islands! I got so tard of them big bright red flowers I could of screamed. They don't seem natural. They grow too fast. I swear I used to wake up sometimes a dreaming they was trying to eat me."

"They'll be blooming when you come back in the fall."

She'd known of course the Halls were going to Lapwai to visit with Henry and Eliza. Now, seeing Mrs. Hall's chair waiting beside the porch, she realized she would be alone again. She held onto the older woman, saying goodbye. "You can't go," she cried against the heavy shoulder.

"Why mercy, child! Of course I can go. I got to look after Mr. Hall."

"But you're coming back?"

"Indeed I am coming back. I'm coming to see those flowers a blooming." She patted Narcissa's head and loosed her hands. "I'll be back before you know it, sassy as a squirrel."

. . . But she had come back. Thank God Mrs. Hall had been where she could come when they needed her so desperately. Thank God for that—

Time had just been standing still those weeks after she left; the flowers blooming in the garden, the vegetables bright. Harmony seemed to have softened the earth, the sky, the world, so that even the indians were under a spell.

"I feel so good I'm afraid," she told Marcus one evening.

He took her hand, under the spell himself. "Look at that big yellow moon up there laughing at us. Don't it look to you like he's saying everything is going to be all right?"

"I'm afraid, all the same."

"I got a feeling we'll get to stay here 'Cissa. Henry says Smith is talking of living up there at Kamiah."

—but she hadn't even been thinking of that. Truly, she'd all but forgotten the sentence hanging over their heads; and even now, reminded of it, the whole matter seemed far away. It wasn't leaving Waiilatpu that troubled her—

Sunday had been a beautiful day. She'd dressed Alice in the white tucked dress, just as if they were going to the big Church back home. "Hold still, baby; we'll be late." And Marcus had preached a short sermon.

> Now from the fig tree learn her parable; when
> her branch is now become tender, and putteth
> forth its leaves, ye know that summer is nigh;
> even so ye also, when ye see all these things,
> know yet that He is nigh, even at the doors.

Her eyes wandered to the window through which she could see the apple trees, and the cottonwoods farther back, and she thought that if summer meant the presence of God, then Waiilatpu was blessed with His presence indeed—

After family worship Marcus took Alice with him for indian services, the two of them walking hand in hand across the meadow to where the indians were assembled. She had dinner ready when they came back, the table set with the green and white china on a linen cloth. She'd baked pea beans the day before, and made a fresh rhubarb pie. The little china swan sat in the middle of the table, a handful of pinks like lace against the cloth.

After the table was cleared Margaret and Maria went for a walk. They'd asked to take Alice, but the baby wanted to stay with Marcus. Maybe, she thought now, her heart beating thick and heavy, nothing would have happened if—

—but something had happened! That terrible, terrible thing had happened and—

She jerked her thoughts back from that, and blinked, and looked around her. She was sitting on the bench in the sun, alone, and Marcus was— Where was Marcus?

She got up to look for him, and then she remembered where he would be, and sat back slowly, and tried to breathe deep to drive away that sick feeling that came over her—

She felt a movement at her feet; Trapper, sitting patiently, his black eyes dull, his ears drooping. He knows, she thought, and bent to place an arm around the shaggy neck.

At dusk the death cries began again in the Cayuse village, clouds of sound filling the summer night. Marcus came to take her inside for supper, but she wasn't hungry—would never be hungry again. She sat on alone as the night deepened.

He came a second time and knelt beside her. "I can't leave you sitting out here by yourself, 'Cissa."

She didn't answer; couldn't answer.

"At least come eat a bite. You haven't touched food for two days now. You'll make yourself sick—" his voice broke "—and that won't help Alice none—"

She shook her head.

"Maria's in there crying her eyes out. Can't you at least say something to her?"

She jerked her hands up to cover her ears. "No!" she said. "No!"

"What good does it do to sit out here in the dark? Come back and sit with—with the baby—"

She turned her head away, and he held her hands and begged her. "Please, 'Cissa. You been sitting with her all the time—"

All at once she sagged against him. "She looks different, Marcus. She's changing—" She clung to him. "I have to wait out here for Mrs. Hall."

He rocked her gently. "I'll wait with you," he promised.

Hours later he had said, "I hear them coming now. Shall we go inside?" But she shook her head, and he left her finally to light a lantern to guide the party from Lapwai to the house . . . .

And now she heard the shuffling steps she'd been listening for; at last—at last—the soft arms wrapped her close and Mrs. Hall was saying, "I'm here now, like I said. You go ahead and cry if you want to. It'll make it easier for you."

But she didn't cry. She never did cry.

All through the funeral she had been dazed, as if nature, taking pity on her, had drugged her in advance. She felt nothing—heard nothing—except at the beginning of the services when, for a moment, her numbness was penetrated by Henry's voice reading the scriptures:

Is it well with thee? Is it well with thy husband?
Is it well with the child?

And she looked for Alice, and couldn't find her; and in looking for her saw the casket covered with a black shawl. She started to run; was held back by someone; and after awhile they were walking back across the plains with the

94

others . . .

—but she hadn't cried—

Marcus cried. She saw him, later, out beside the mill shed, his shoulders bent and moving with his crying. She wanted to go to him but she was empty.

Late in the afternoon she went by herself back to the grove at the foot of the hill. The wind blew her skirts and wisped her hair and she thought, Why didn't we put her on top of the hill? But when she saw the grave, mounded and clumsily covered with chunks of rye sod and flowers, she thought that the wooden marker that headed Hind's grave sheltered Alice, too.

After supper that first night Mrs. Hall followed Narcissa outside to the bench where she had waited out the first ravages of grief, lowering herself painfully to sit beside her. "Now tell me how it happened, Cissy," she said, her voice tired and old.

As if she had been waiting for someone to ask her, Narcissa began almost as if she were telling a story. "Marcus was reading and I was writing letters and Alice was playing in and out. I must have missed her, because I asked Marcus if he was watching her and he said she was playing. The girls came back from their walk then and went to get some onions from the garden. Marcus told them to see what Alice was doing—"

"Take your time now. We got the whole night for this."

"When they didn't come back I went to look for her myself. Alice wasn't with the girls. They'd looked for her, but instead of coming to tell us they couldn't find her, they went on to the garden first. I don't know why— Maria's been taking care of her ever since she was born. I can't think why she didn't call us—"

"That little girl keeps crying and asking herself the same question."

"And then Compo came and asked Marcus what the

little cups were doing floating in the river, and Marcus flared out at him to come help look for Alice, and we ran along the river through the brush, all of us calling her—"

She drew a hard breath. Mrs. Hall patted her knee, slowly, but she didn't speak. "And then, as we were coming back, one of the indians dived into the water where we'd seen the cups, and I stood there and watched him swimming underwater, and when he came up . . ."

She turned and took Mrs. Hall by the arms and talked as fast as she could. "When he stood up he was holding her, and the water was running from her hair and her face, and her dress was streaming, but her shoes weren't even muddy." Mrs. Hall made a little sound of grief, and she rushed ahead with her words to smother it. "I tried to take her, but Marcus lifted her and pulled her dress down; and Mrs. Hall— I swear she breathed— I swear it—"

Mrs. Hall said heavily, "You better not go on with it. It's too hard on you."

She couldn't stop halfway; must go the painful length of the story so nothing of this would be unfinished.

"We tried everything we knew to save her, but it wasn't any use." She leaned her forehead against Mrs. Hall's arm. "What am I going to do now?"

"Pray," the older woman said without moving. "Jist pray. Thy will be done— I've kept going time and again on those words—"

1840

Narcissa scooped a bucket of brackish water from the creek and straightened, reluctant to leave the shade of the willows. Summer had brought one more revolution of the relentless seasons whose primary purpose seemed to be to crush what life remained in her to an uncaring zero.

This day felt like yesterday and the day before: thick with blind, breathless heat. Already, before nine o'clock, her dress hung limp, wet spots spreading under her arms and between her thighs. She'd given up wearing her petticoats days ago.

It hadn't rained since March. The water in the canal was a scummy layer of mud. Marcus had been after her to let the flowers die. "I'll keep the vegetables watered," he told her, "but I haven't time for flowers now."

An inherent need would not allow her to abandon the marigolds and zinnias; the bright mass of oranges and yellows made the only color as far as they could see.

"You haven't any business out in that sun," Marcus protested. "First thing you know you'll be down again."

But she persisted, struggling to fill the buckets with the syrupy water; and the flowers maintained a dusty, rag-tag bravado in their tangled bed. She was driven to keep them alive if only to remind herself that color and life would return to Waiilatpu when the rains came.

Silence as oppressive as the heat hung over the mission this year. The indians had deserted winter camp early, after a winter of deep snow, and no game, and measles and whooping cough. They'd moved out, half-starved, looking straight ahead when Marcus begged them to plant before leaving for the mountains. What few planted refused to venture into the fields to work under the broiling sun.

Marcus had only Compo to help him, beside Asa Munger, who was as good as no one. She'd have to stop by the Munger's room when she'd finished with the flowers.

They'd come rattling up to the mission late last fall, skin showing through their rags; a chubby girl with soft brown hair, already rounding under her dingy skirts with a baby on the way, and a boy still growing out of his coat sleeves; unfinished, both of them, as if nature was still experimenting with their final forms. Asa's whole being was afire, bent on preaching to the indians, and what did a boy of nineteen have to say that could be of value to anyone, savage or white? He hadn't lived long enough.

Marcus' concern shifted between sympathy and anger. "That little girl belongs back with her mother. She's got no business out here with a baby on the way and no roof over her head."

She felt a mirthless laughter inside herself at his words. He hadn't felt such indignation at her similar plight three years ago. "What will they do this winter, Marcus? Go on to the Willamette?"

"Munger wouldn't know what to do with it if McLaughlin gave him half of Vancouver."

"Would Mr. Lee take him in?"

"Why would the Methodists want him? It takes more than a call to preach to make a mission worker. Munger came out expecting the indians to be standing in line waiting for him to convert them."

98

"If we wrote to the Board we might get him an appointment—"

"For crying out loud, Narcissa! Ain't we got enough trouble with the ones the Board sent us? Those two children haven't got one thing to offer this mission. And the problem isn't just them. If the word gets out back east that we're taking them in there'll be dozens more of these starry-eyed dreamers straggling in half dead before another year's past. We don't dare take them, that's all."

They had to keep the Mungers in the end. Henry had been firm against it, reminding them of the Board's directive against joining with independents and making themselves liable for unapproved activities. But Henry hadn't been able to turn the Griffins away when they came begging at *his* door.

The Mungers had shivered and whined through the harsh winter, the boy complaining at having to finish the little room in the new wing; ranting that he'd follow the indians right into the mountains and make them listen; hurt at Marcus' gruff, "Not before you finish this room, you won't."

With terrible, accidental timing Carrie Munger gave birth to her baby one year to the day of Alice's death. Narcissa had had to put that out of her mind while she helped care for the girl.

—only she hadn't been able to look at the baby—

Now as she crossed the yard Asa came flying out of their room carrying the chamber pot. There was an awkwardness in the way he hurtled himself around the corner of the mud block wall that spoke of furious frustration. Narcissa felt some sympathy for this frantic young man who'd crossed a savage continent to save indians only to end up emptying slops for a child bride. Asa Munger's patience with the nesting process had barely stretched over the time required to make the room livable; the outside was in disorder still, with dobes piled helter-skelter around the door.

The heat trapped the smell of drying diapers inside the room. Carrie looked up from nursing the baby as Narcissa's shadow fell across the floor. The girl's hair was stringing worse than ever; her eyes, small to start with, were swollen almost shut from crying. She held the baby tight against her breast; it was a wonder it could breathe.

"Do you need anything, Carrie?"

"We've got food, if that's what you mean." The girl's resentment was like a thorny hedge around her, yet it was hard to keep from feeling sympathy. She looked so young—a child trying to feed an infant and not even knowing how to hold it—

"Is the baby feeling better?"

"I guess so. He wakes up in the night and fusses, like, but he shuts up when I feed him."

"And how about you?"

The child face dissolved into a mask of misery, seeping tears. She wiped her nose on the baby's blanket. "Asa's after me all the time to get the place cleaned up, but I'm just too tired."

She'd have to have help. "You start clearing off the table, Carrie. I'll see if Mrs. Compo can come work this afternoon."

The girl got up obediently and placed the baby on a tumbled bed. "I keep asking Asy to help, but he says he didn't come through those mountains to take on woman's work; he came to convert heathens."

"I'll send Mrs. Compo," Narcissa said again and hurried to the house.

The rooms still held some coolness. She drank a little milk and went to the bedroom. The least effort, emotional or physical, left her exhausted. She lay on the bed—a real bed with a coverlet pieced by Mrs. Hall—and

100

thought of the times she had begged and cried for this house. Now it was finished, and it was no more to her than the cabin had been: a shelter—an empty place—

Marcus and Mrs. Hall had driven themselves to finish the house and get her away from the cabin. They'd plastered and whitewashed the walls; painted the floors. And Mrs. Hall had braided rugs for the bare spots.

But a house couldn't shut out the pain of Alice's absence. The bitter memory of the winter mocked her now. Those first months she'd forced herself to a furious pace, trying to forget, until now she could not control her reactions. Her body demanded rest but her mind continued its relentless activity.

All last winter she rode with Marcus wherever he went; she could not stay in the empty rooms without him. She went with him when the calls came from the Cayuse camp, day or night, even if she was sick each time she entered the longhouse.

The winter demanded its victims from the indians like some insatiable god; and as the Cayuse died, Umtippe's frustration boiled and burned in his eyes. The old *te-wat*, sensing the chief's growing disillusionment with the alien doctor, grew bold in his opposition to Marcus' treatments. With each confrontation her own fear expanded.

She walked the length of the lodge choking on smoke and the smell of the dying; standing while Marcus knelt in each rude cubicle to listen to raspy breathing through a dark chest scaly with grease and dirt, braving outbursts of opposition from Kalakala, hideous in his paint and skins.

Marcus argued against her coming with him to the camp. "Look at you, nothing but skin and bones. Stay away from there. I can take care of myself."

He tried to slip away from her when they came for him in the night, but the slightest disturbance brought her awake instantly, and she paid no attention to his arguments. Finally he had turned on her, accusing her of seeking out this terror to avoid the other, deeper terror: the memory of Alice's drowning. "Alice is dead. She's going to stay dead. And you can't spend the rest of your life scaring yourself out of your mind to keep from thinking about it."

She'd stared at him in the early morning light, hating him—hating him—for making her see what she did not want to see. . . . But she did not follow him after that. Something stopped her at the door when he went to the Cayuse, and she waited, alone, until he returned.

He had made her face up to her own lack of courage, but he hadn't been able to do as much for himself. His efforts to escape the reality of Alice's death seemed as obvious as hers had been; he was whipping up fury at Henry to camouflage his rage that life would dare tamper with his happiness.

He'd always been the one to try to smooth things over; now it seemed he looked for straws to add to the flames of contention. Before, he'd refused to listen to one person talk against another. Now he encouraged William Gray's efforts to stir up a quarrel against Henry's ruling that the Board hadn't voted for William to establish a new station—only to explore for a site for one. A year ago Marcus would have set William straight fast enough. But Henry was a ready-made target for his own bitterness. He'd never really forgiven Henry for the voting to oust them from Waiilatpu, even if the order was rescinded.

When the others voted against them, Henry explained Marcus' outburst as jealousy and shame for her, and his explanation went clear back to the night at the Seminary. She hadn't believed it at first, but Asa Smith and Cushing Eells had both confirmed that Henry *had* detailed the unpleasantness between them from first to last; had declared he built Lapwai as far as possible from the Whitman mission to put himself out of her reach—

Narcissa longed to weep, thinking of it, but no tears came; she'd used up her crying for the rest of her life this past winter. She acknowledged her father's warning now; he had seen the resentment behind Henry's promise given that dark afternoon to never refer to the incident, before her father would give even token consent for her to marry Marcus and go west with him and the Spaldings.

But it had been so long ago—so unimportant to her— so pale, compared to the flood and fire of desire Marcus had brought to life in her. How could she have known that Henry could carry humiliation at her refusal to marry him buried inside himself until it became a compulsion to destroy her?

—because she had let him kiss her years ago—only that.

They had walked back from the Concert Hall to the Academy across a frosty field under a sky crackling with cold stars; Henry ahead of her, hunched over against the chill; and the echoes of the music throbbing and circling in her. And he'd turned suddenly and she had walked into his arms—

It was like being kissed in a dream. Henry's hands were inside her coat, cold through her dress; his lips were fire feeding on hers—forcing hers—and she felt the music beating through her answering the beating of his heart.

He'd held her there, like that, until someone called from the gallery. He had jerked away then; had given a cry of anger and dismay, gasping her name under his breath while she fumbled her coat around her and tried to clear her mind of the stars and the kiss—

Next day he came to her, eyes smoldering, his tongue thick, to insist they marry at once.

She looked at him as if she'd never seen him before.

"Henry," she said, "I couldn't possibly marry you."

And that was the truth.

But he raged under his breath, his passion turned to shame; he had condemned her to hellfire for refusing to allow him to atone for a sin to which she had tempted him. He had dared her to deny that his illegitimacy was the real reason she was turning him down . . . .

He still believed those things, in spite of everything. Her refusal was the blade he'd carried inside him, keeping the wound as open and raw as it had been that day she'd said no. Now he had something else to blame her for. Marcus, enraged at Henry's talking to the others of this private matter, had given them the choice; either Henry would resign from the Mission appointment, or he would!

All the others had brought their own complaints against Henry, then. He listened them out, his eyes on his Bible, saying nothing until Walker called on him to answer.

He stood up slowly and talked to them, Marcus said, the way he talked to his indians: as if they were spoiled children he could shame out of their naughtiness by ridicule. "So all I have to do to regain your favor is to give each of you what you ask. All right William; I vote for you to start a mission at the mouth of the Yakima. And I'll take the cow back from Conner and you can lead it home when you go, Asa. As for you, Marcus, I apologize for talking of unmentionable matters. If you'll reconsider your threat to resign, I promise never to refer to these affairs again."

"And you believed him, Marcus?" she demanded. For she hadn't. Henry had broken his promises before.

"No," he admitted, his voice tired. "But I had to accept his words at face value or leave the mission, and I can't do

104

that. You know it as well as I do."

He couldn't leave of his own accord, she thought now, but he might be forced out again if he continued his attacks on Henry. There was no use trying to rest. She went to the open door and looked out at the mission grounds, seeing the years stretching ahead for Marcus and herself, as dry and empty as the buildings baking in the sun.

She cut a few of the dusty zinnias and walked to Alice's grave, Trapper pushing through the dried grass, sending grasshoppers bursting from the brittle stalks in clouds, and sat down to rest under the trees. She'd brought Blake's poems with her, but left the limp leather book opened on her lap, recalling the little shop where she'd bought it that year she'd taught in Butler. Her father would have disowned her if he'd discovered her reading Blake while she was living at home. An uneducated madman, he'd called the controversial poet. She'd been careful to keep the book well hidden. She wondered if her father had ever known—

The rhythmic thuddings of a galloping horse drummed into her memories. She sat up, listening. they came from the mountains to the south. It was too early for Marcus to be coming in unless there was trouble. She hurried toward the house. Trapper loped ahead of her now, ears pointing, tail alert.

She waited beside the mill shed, shading her eyes against the glare. She could see the rider now, covering the ground like the wind. It wasn't Compo or the kanakas. This man was big. The hooves made a steady thrumming now. And there was something familiar about the crouching rider pounding down the trail. A wild cry shrilled out as he leaped the dry canal, pulling to a lunging halt in front of the house, calling, "Hey you, doc! Doc Whitman! You all in there? Come on out here, you hear now?"

Narcissa ran, forgetting the heat, calling, "Joe! Joe! I'm down here," as she ran. She stumbled on the lumpy ground, caught her skirts out of the way and ran on, Trapper barking at her heels.

He caught her in his opened arms; swung her high, his big laugh filling the afternoon.

"Oh, Joe!" It was all she could manage. "Joe—"

He set her down and held her away to see her. "Well now, Mam," he said in the old teasing way, "sure didn't think you'd be so unhappy to see old Joe Meek you'd start bawlin' when he rode in." But there was that in his voice that had nothing to do with humor. His hands slipped down her arms gently, as if they been waiting for that touch the past four years.

Narcissa stepped back, drying her eyes on her skirt. "Let me look at you, Joe."

His eyes shifted away from hers. "I'm afraid I ain't much to see right now, Mam."

It was frightening to see him like this, in a ragged calico shirt and dirty buckskins; an old felt hat, mended with a piece of wire, slapped on the back of his head; heavier, as if the years had taken his youth and left him someone else's spirit.

What had happened to Joe to change him from that wild young Mountain Man who'd escorted them to the Rendezvous site? That first time she saw him she'd looked up, up, at a rollicking giant of a man with impudent black eyes and a whimsical mouth, and long black hair flung back any which way off his forehead.

Who was this stranger?

"I didn't mean to cause you a fright," he said, bringing her back to the present.

"Come to the house, Joe, and tell me about yourself. Marcus will be here soon."

He talked like the Joe Meek she'd known. "It don't seem possible," he said, staring around the new house. "It *ain't* possible, by glory! A place like this, all painted and polished, out here a million miles from nowhere." He glanced at her and away. "I suppose you got a passel of younguns around here to fill it up?"

There was stark silence while she tried to answer. Joe turned, frowning; started toward her. "Our little girl drowned last summer, Joe—" Saying it out loud like that for the first time.

"Damn me for a clumsy coyote, anyhow! I got no more sense nor a jackass!"

"It's all right, Joe. You better get out there on the porch. I hear Marcus coming."

The two of them shouted and wrestled like boys until she ran them outdoors. "If you want supper tonight you *get*, both of you."

They sat outside after eating, trying to find a breath of air. Marcus was cross-legged on the ground facing Joe, who lounged against the wall, his long legs jackknifed behind his circled arms. "You're a long way from beaver country," Marcus said.

"Beaver's no concern of mine no more. We ain't made enough to buy possibles these last two year. Wasn't hardly a Rendezvous at all."

"Why'd you come this way?"

Joe sat up as if steeling himself to spread bad news. "Old Joe's givin' up his wild ways, Doc. I'm ridin' down to the Willamette and I'm gonna stake me out some land and build me a house for my family and get civilized."

—his *family*—

She felt a stab of—almost of jealousy. She'd been thinking of Joe, by himself, the way he'd always been—free. Deep in her mind she'd believed she laid first claim to his loyalty. "Where'd you leave your family, Joe?"

He picked up a stick and scratched in the hard-packed earth. "Right behind me. You recall Newell? I'm drivin' a wagon for him. We been cussing them through the mountains all the way from Fort Boise. Fella named Wilkins is drivin' t'other one."

"You *drove* wagons from Boise?"

"They're comin'. McKay told me where to find you all; when we got close I figured to ride on ahead."

"How many wagons, Joe? How soon will they be here?" She felt her shoulders tightening. Joe was different— But *families*—

"Tomorrow sundown, I figure. There's just the three wagons. Newell's got his woman, and there's my wife and two little ones."

"We'll ride out first thing in the morning and help them in," Marcus said, but Joe shook his head.

"No need. Virginia can drive a wagon a sight better'n me. I'll wait here and git my visitin' done. We'll be movin' right on to the valley; we got to get cabins raised before the rains start."

She settled back slowly. They'd only be here overnight, then. But *Virginia,* he'd said. Not Mountain Lamb . . . .

She was the first woman they'd seen on horseback since they'd left Liberty Landing until they'd arrived at Rendezvous. She would be a chief's wife or daughter. She did not wear elkskin.

Later she'd asked Captain Stewart about her. He glanced at the girl and back to her. "That's Joe Meeks' Mountain Lamb," he said, and there was surprise in his voice, as if she should have known this. "She's supposed to be the most beautiful woman in the Rockies . . ."

Narcissa wanted to ask if he'd found a white girl this time, but Joe was talking man talk now, his stick making trail maps on the dried ground. And Marcus' words leaped with excitement, like a creek full of trout. "You know what it means, you bringing those wagons on from Boise, Joe? Settlers will be pouring over those mountains—"

"It's too late this year, I reckon," Joe said, "but look out for next."

"I got to get more land under cultivation next year. I got to get the indians to help instead of taking off to the hills in the spring."

"Marcus thinks we'll be responsible for everyone who comes through the Blues," she said.

"By the time they get this far they'll need supplies. If we have them, they'll get them from us instead of from McLaughlin."

"Why shouldn't they go on to Vancouver?" she questioned as she always did.

"These will be American settlers, and HBC ain't going to make them too welcome when they start coming in here by the hundreds."

"Don't exaggerate, Marcus—"

"They'll come by the hundreds, won't they, Joe?"

The whirr of insect wings deepened the following silence. "I don't doubt you're right," Joe said finally. "I'm beginnin' to get a fenced in feelin' already."

Her own sadness reached out to Joe's. What would happen when he tried to take off his moccasins and put on shoes? He'd lived wild so long— His way of life was changing. But could he make this change? Wouldn't it be for him a slow death—a dying that brought no peace?

On the surface Joe seemed the same. His stories followed nose to tail, as they had at Rendezvous. His laughter came bouncing through the window next morning as he worked with Marcus and 'visited.' But it seemed to Narcissa he was trying too hard, determined to show the image of the wild young Mountain Man while the older, heavier Joe Meek kept getting in the way. The truth, she thought, was that Joe was afraid—

She and Mrs. Compo made pumpkin pies and cooked beans with salt meat to get ready for the wagons. They stored melons and cucumbers in the pantry in buckets of water to keep them cool. She started Mrs. Compo on the churning before it got too hot to work out the butter.

—I miss the girls, she thought, as she always did whenever she was getting ready for company. She shouldn't have let them go away like that—

But how could she have done anything else, after she'd found Maria sitting at the table that morning, head bowed, lips moving, looking so pitifully thin and ill . . . .

"Aren't you well, Maria?" she'd asked, shocked out of her own dull pain. Maria's arms were like sticks; her shoulder bones made wings under the dress.

The girl raised her wet face. "I must go home."

"But you can't leave—"

"Please," she begged. "I must leave here." The thin hands beat softly against the table, like captive birds beating against a window. "I cannot stay here."

"Why not."

"I am wicked," Maria cried under her breath. "I let Alice die—"

Blackness began closing in as Narcissa listened to the girl. Dimly she heard the whispered confession. "The baby fell into the river. My fault. . . ." And dimly she heard the soft murmuring of the Catholic prayer, "Holy Mary, Mother of God, pray for me—"

She heard herself shouting, "Stop this, Maria!" and she was shaking the girl, while the urgent whispering went on and on. "Holy Mary, pray for us now—"

"Mother Whitman!" Margaret was trying to loosen her hands from Maria's shoulders; her eyes were wide, her face frozen.

Narcissa groped for a stool and sat down. "Margaret, what's

wrong with Maria? What's wrong with her?"

"She wants to go to her family."

That same morning Marcus sent for Pierre Pambrun. He came immediately. After talking with Maria he came to her. "Madame, truly I believe it is necessary for Maria to return to her mother now."

"It isn't Maria's fault about—about the baby."

"I know. But Maria—she does not know yet. If she believe this thing is true, then it is true for her."

"We've tried to make her understand. We don't blame her."

"Some time she will understand, but perhaps she will be old woman before she finds the truth of this important matter."

He turned to leave; came back. "Madame. What of Margaret McKay? It will be lonely for her here, without Maria." Would you allow it that she come to visit Maria?"

"Is Margaret unhappy also?"

"Non. Non. But she is young girl, and it is good for young girls to be with young people. If you allow her to come we will keep her until they return to school. When summer comes they will be happy again; they forget this shadow on their sun."

What else could she have done but let them go . . . .

Joe came into the kitchen in the afternoon.

"I thought you and Marcus went to round up horses," she said, checking to see if the bread had risen enough.

"There's a chief passin' through got a sick wife, and old Splitted Lip across the river sent for the Doc. Me, I seen enough sick injuns to last me till Doomsday. Figured I'd follow up the smell that's been teasin' my nose all mornin'."

"The pies are for supper, Joe. You sure the wagons will be here this evening?"

"Before dark, for sure."

He sat then looking down at the table. It wasn't like Joe to sit quiet. Narcissa was about to ask if something was wrong when he blurted out, "I got to ask you a favor, Mam."

"I'll help if I can."

He talked with his face turned away. "You know I got a little gal now, about so high." He held out his hand just below table height. "A mighty sweet little doll, but she's growin' up wild; wild as a partridge; and I don't want her turnin' out like these wenches I see hangin' around the forts, waitin' for some man to get drunk and roll dice for them."

"Joe, that's a horrible thing to say! You don't have to let your little girl grow up like that."

"No Mam. That's what I keep tellin' myself. No matter how hard it is to think on, I got to get her settled some-wheres so she can get the kind of looking after a little girl needs."

—He wants to leave her here! she thought. She must be the age Alice would have been, and I *can't*—

"Mam—" His eyes pleaded; angry that he had to beg, but begging all the same. "You'll take her?"

What words would soften the affront to Joe's pride if his favor—one of the few he'd ever asked in his life—were turned down? He would shrivel up before her eyes.

—*but how can I*—

"Joe—"

A sharp, bright light flared and disappeared in his eyes. His face closed to her.

"Joe," she said quickly, "I'm proud you want me to take your little girl." She caught a glimpse of the defenseless man inhabiting Joe's body before he stood and rasped, "I thank you then," and ran from the kitchen.

They were all waiting at the fence when the wagons

rolled to a stop near the house. Narcissa had eyes only for the one with a woman driving; an indian woman. She waited where she was for Joe to bring his wife to her. Virginia was no Mountain Lamb. She was short; her eyes wide set and heavy lidded in a round, soft face; her coarse black hair bound with a blue kerchief. She carried a baby in its board.

As she talked with Virginia and Mrs. Newell, also indian, her attention was on Joe lifting his little girl from the wagon; holding her against him in a long, helpless embrace before letting her down to the ground. There was nothing in the child to remind her of Alice. She was tall for her age, and thin; more like a boy than a girl, dressed in buckskins and moccasins with a calico shirt for a top. Her hair, cropped across her forehead, hung straight and black down her back. Her eyes were black and bright as Joe's.

Narcissa knelt beside her. "What's your name?"

The child's eyes were level with her own. "I am Helen Mar Meek." The name was given with great dignity, as if that told all there was to know about her.

I suppose that's enough to ensure her acceptance anywhere in the mountains, Narcissa thought. She felt Joe's eyes on them, but when she looked up he was busy at the wagon.

Helen Mar followed Joe like a shadow as long as he was there, but she didn't cry next morning when he galloped after the wagon as it rattled off across the flats. That night Helen climbed into Marcus' lap. Glancing up from her sewing Narcissa saw wet tear lines on her face.

"Marcus—"

He drew the child closer; she turned her face against his shirt and he held her like that until she went to sleep.

As far as Narcissa knew it was the only time the little girl cried. She had one time of pain for herself on

113

Saturday. "You must have a bath today, Helen," she said and went on about her work. Missing the little girl she went to the door and called her, and Helen answered from the creek.

Narcissa stumbled down the path and stood beside the water, her mind a confusion of images: a white dress plastered against baby legs—water dripping from long blond curls—

There was a movement in the water. The child slid through the stream like a fish and stood up, long hair streaming, eyes sparkling.

Narcissa reached for her frantically. "You mustn't come to the river by yourself, Helen!"

"You said to take a bath."

"But not here. In the house. I'll help you."

Maria and Margaret returned home the first week in September. Marcus took the afternoon from field work and worked on reports to the Mission Board while they waited. Helen Mar, dressed in a starched red pinafore, was told to play quietly and not get dirty.

The little face framed by the long black braids tied with red ribbons was solemn. "Is it the Sabbath already?"

Narcissa laughed. "It's a celebration. Your sisters are coming home today. You be a good girl while I finish my cooking and we'll go pick some flowers for them."

She asked the Compos and Mungers to come in the evening. The girls helped her by dusting the good china plates. The men sat on benches in the big room, talking weather; Helen Mar watched the Munger baby playing on a blanket. Mrs. Compo was busy keeping little Paul from underfoot.

She'd thought to let the young children eat their gingerbread on the floor, but Marcus wouldn't have it. "There's room at this table for everyone." He lifted Paul to his

114

father's lap and held out his arms for Helen Mar. He asked a brief blessing. As she lifted her head she caught a flash of movement of Maria's hand from forehead to breast, and across. She would have to speak about that to Maria. They couldn't permit it—

Asa Munger ate his gingerbread with the gulping bites of an adolescent. He'd quieted down some; helping Marcus—helping Carrie—

"I'm sure glad you girls decided to come on home," Marcus teased. "It's the first time we've had cake for—"

A sound on the porch rose suddenly to an uproar. Before anyone could move the kitchen was crowded with indians shoving into the main room. Narcissa's cup clattered against the saucer; hot tea splashed her hand. No one moved—no one spoke— These were strange indians bunched in the doorway.

Marcus sat Helen Mar beside Narcissa as Pierre Pambrun stood up, slowly. Charles Compo handed Paul to his wife and moved to where they stood. Asa Munger crouched over his plate, his fork lowering slowly from his open mouth. Fear held the group motionless, the only sound the whisper of the Munger baby's breathing, grown suddenly loud.

The stillness was shattered then by a violent outburst from the leader, a wiry, dark-faced man, braids looped low under his war bonnet, naked except for breech clout and moccasins. Margaret leaned to whisper to Maria, "It's Tamahas."

"You know him, Margaret?" she breathed.

"He has his people at the Fort. He rode out this morning as we left."

What did this Tamahas want of Marcus? He leaped without warning, shaking his humped war club, screaming at Marcus. Narcissa started up; Pierre Pambrun touched her shoulder, his eyes never leaving the chief's face. She sat down.

Compo translated in a soft voice, but Tamahas punched and thrust with his club, spitting his angry words. Marcus stood stiff as starch, bending his head from one side to the other to escape the menacing weapon as Compo's monotonous voice repeated the diatribe. "Tamahas says you have murdered his wife. She has died from your treatment; he demands your life for hers."

The familiar terror rose in her, stronger than the indian smell. But Marcus faced the chief down as coolly as if he was refusing the loan of a horse. "Tell the chief Tamahas I treated his wife the best way I knew. Remind him I warned she was not to be moved. Tell him I refuse to accept responsibility for his wife's death."

Before Compo finished the message Tamahas leaped forward, fists raised above his head clutching the curved club, screaming further imprecations.

"Tamahas insists you are responsible for his wife's death since you are the *te-wat* who attended her illness."

"Inform him I am not a *te-wat;* I am a medical doctor. I warned him I could not help her if he refused to follow my directions. Tell him he is being dishonest."

Tamahas shook his head rapidly.

"He says it is you who are being dishonest because you promise to pay the indians for their lands and you have lived here more than four of your years without paying."

Now anger was in Marcus' voice. "Tell Tamahas I will not talk land prices. Tell him again I refuse to listen to charges he's made against me."

Tamahas stomped his feet, enraged, on hearing the translation; he responded with another tirade. This time Marcus did not wait for him to finish. To Compo he said, "Offer him tea."

Compo raised his voice above the frenzied shouting. Tamahas chopped off the flow of venomous words; his

116

eyes narrowed; he grabbed the cake from Helen's plate and threw it on the floor. "My wife dead. Dead! You give tea for wife?" His voice slipped to a thin, embittered crying. "This wife dead. Dead. Dead." There was startled silence. Tamahas peered at them, his face rigid now as if trying to deny the moment of revealed weakness. His followers broke into chorus."Tea! Tea! Tea!" they chanted. Marcus pointed toward the kitchen and Tamahas was swept through the doorway by his own men.

A convulsive movement circled the table. Narcissa lifted Helen Mar to her lap as Mrs. Compo sat Paul on the bench; Asa Munger ran to the kitchen as Carrie ran for the baby. She should be out there helping Marcus with the tea, she knew, but she was shaking like a cottonwood leaf. She laid her face against Helen Mar's black head and waited for the fear to recede. Beside her Maria and Margaret stared through the kitchen door, waiting with the patience she'd seen before in Indian women.

Eventually the invaders jostled their way outside, but whether it was an hour or ten minutes Narcissa could not have said. Over and over like a cold wind challenging her peace of mind she heard the angry, anguished cry of Tamahas: "This wife dead. Dead. Dead."

Fall gave way abruptly to sharp winds and frosty nights; too soon, for harvest had not been completed. Marcus ordered Narcissa to stay inside but when he went to the fields she took her turn at digging garden vegetables for storage.

It was inevitable that she caught la grippe. The girls watched fearfully as she struggled to control the cough tearing at her throat. But she could not stay inside. Winter had sent warning of its intentions; they would need the potatos and beets and carrots before spring, and there was no one else to help.

She sat at night huddled by the fire, wrapped in a shawl. Once in bed she crowded close to Marcus' warmth while her blood sludged its way through her in icy waves. She strained her eyes mending by candlelight; pushed herself from daybreak until bedtime paying no attention to Marcus' protests.

One night, dozing restlessly, she sat up with a feeling of apprehension, as if something of great consequence was working in her thoughts just out of reach. Finally, reluctantly, she lay back and drifted into a troubled dream . . . .

She wandered in some tumbled, shadowed land where alien forests crowded to the sky. Marcus plunged ahead of her along a narrow path, drawing away from her with each step. Alice ran back and forth between them, never quite reaching either of them. But each time she called, the baby came running only to turn at the last minute and run again to her father.

She heard movement behind her but the path was a tunnel and she could not recognize her followers. Then Umtippe's naked men sprang out of the underbrush brandishing their clubs and pointing their stolen guns, screaming their wild slogans; while from the forest rose the dismal chants of their women.

She shouted for Marcus but no sounds came and he went his way not knowing they were threatened. She was afraid to move for fear Umtippe would find her alone on the path, yet she could not stand still. Those coming behind would overrun her at any moment.

She edged up the path thinking her heartbeat would betray her. But the indians gathered around Umtippe shouting a harangue; and although he used the Cayuse she could see the lighted words with her mind's eyes: THOU SHALT NOT . . . BEAR ANY GRUDGE AGAINST

THE CHILDREN OF MY PEOPLE: BUT THOU
SHALT LOVE THY NEIGHBOR.

And Tamahas raised his hands and the men began a
heavy chant, each singing a different word, and Tamahas
sang in a tragic, golden baritone, "My—wife—is—dead—"
on a descending scale.

Suddenly the followers were upon her, shoving and
shouting for her to make room. She glanced over her
shoulder to see Henry and William and Eliza and the
Smiths—

She fled, sceaming, straight toward the indians; but
they in turn ran screaming before her; and the missionaries came running from behind, as if they were all playing
a macabre game of Follow The Leader through the
menacing forest.

—it was then she discovered Alice was missing—

She came to herself sitting up in bed, struggling against
Marcus' hands. She had lost the eerie dream on waking,
but its pieces floated just beneath the surface of her mind
in fantastic kaleidoscope of shadow and light; she
trembled from weird currents of premonitory dread that
flashed across her consciousness. She could not bring herself to close her eyes again until daylight cleared the
shadows from the room's corners.

The ground froze to iron during the nights now and ice
stayed in the shadowed places through the day. The cold
penetrated the heaviest clothing. Marcus came in from
work with his face and wrists bitten raw by the wind. The
last leaves had long since been torn from the willows.
The cottonwood skeletons cast pencil marks of shadow
over Alice's grave. She went there as soon as she was able
to walk after her illness, but she gained no peace from
standing exposed to the wind whistling through empty
branches and tumbleweeds blowing like unbalanced

baskets against her feet. Going back to the house, it took all her strength to breast the gusts flapping her skirts against her legs.

There was no need now for Marcus to warn her to rest. She hardly found strength to move from the chair by the fire. Time dragged; her eyes stung in the meager light. The spectacles Marcus had ordered in the fall could not arrive before spring. There would be no commerce across the snow-covered continent before the first of May.

The kanaka boys stayed into early winter to help with the butchering. Narcissa was forced to sit listening to the frantic squeals of the pigs and the commotion as the men sharpened their knives and put the barrels of water to boil.

Marcus gave her orders to let Mrs. Compo and the girls do all the work, but she knew that by afternoon she'd be up to her elbows in pork. She couldn't trust the winter's supply of meat to two young girls and an indian. So she sat on her stool while he got Mrs. Compo to washing sausage crocks, and set the girls to grinding. When he went outside she worked cutting and trimming. By evening they had the first two carcasses jointed, the lard in heavy tubs, and the ribs roasting in the iron spider. Her back ached unmercifully.

Next morning her throat was raw again; she burned with fever; her head was heavy. The pale winter light stung her eyes like acid. Breathing became an agonizing effort of will.

She dozed, propped on pillows, aching from head to heels. But she could not quiet her rampaging thoughts. It was time to start the school, now they had a room. Marcus would not listen to her worries. "It can all wait. Sleep now."

But it had waited too long—She tried to throw the covers aside and the weight of the blankets was like the weight of the sea. Her arms were of stone. She gave up then and slept.

Narcissa opened her eyes slowly, carefully, feeling light and warm and at rest; fearing to move lest she disturb the pleasurable peace by lifting a finger. Behind the window glass snowflakes big as daisies floated down in a thick curtain, white on gray.

There was a movement at the foot of the bed. Marcus stood there. She watched him as she had watched the snowflakes. She said his name but he did not answer. She was very frightened and tried to push herself up against the pillows, but weakness had dissolved her bones while she slept.

She held her eyes open as the room darkened. She seemed to be floating above herself, no longer a prisoner of her body's heaviness. She saw the house and the girls and Marcus through a curtain of silence. She was held to her body by the merest thread of communication.

People came and went in the room but she could not hear them; could not cry—could not feel—

I can't be dead! If I were dead, Alice would be with me. God had made that promise for those who believed. She had come to the Lord when she was nine years old . . . .

Light was everywhere; covering the branches of the trees, brilliance striking down through the leaves so the clumps of grass around the boles were golden too; the heads of the converts as they walked to the river crowned with light; the water itself running gold on that Sunday afternoon. When she was lifted from the water by the preacher's hands she'd felt herself streaming with light, inside and out—

And I've kept His commandments since. He wouldn't dare not keep His word to me.

121

But Henry was there by her bed, his eyes burning like coals in the dark. She struggled to sit up. "I have kept His commandments. Tell him, Henry—"

He lifted his head and his voice was like a shout;
For the commandment is a lamp; and the law
is light; and reproofs of instruction are
the way of life; to keep thee from an evil
woman; from the flattery of the tongue of
a strange woman—

"Not that, Henry! You said that before, on the trip, when Captain McLeod was there."

Let not thine heart incline to her ways;
go not astray in her paths. For she hath
cast down many wounded; yea, many strong
men have been slain by her. Her house is
the way to hell, going down to the chambers
of death—

She wept in her prison of darkness. *You're wrong, Henry! You're wrong—!*

But Henry had gone, and in his place Tamahas looked at her with contempt and spoke with contempt:

"Why are you afraid of Cayuse, white woman doctor? You come to help, you say; only to teach and help."

"Yes. Yes."

"You help your husband to kill my people: little children, old men—" he stumbled "—wives. They died from sickness you carry with you. You steal from Cayuse people. We starve; our children and old people starve, and you eat the grain of our fields and do not pay for lands—"

"We save those we can save; help those we can help. We never promised to pay. We have nothing with which to pay. We do not steal your lands. You steal from us."

"We take what is ours. It is the only way we can get that which you have taken."

"NO! NO! NO!" She threw her arms around her ears

122

and shut her eyes against his accusations.

At least I haven't taken other gods; nor made graven images; nor bowed down to idols; nor taken the Lord's name.

But those were the easy ones. *What about Remember the Sabbath?*

An unpleasant laugh roused her. What was William doing in her room?

"You broke the Sabbath time and time again coming across the trail," he said.

"Only when it was necessary, William."

"Well, God didn't say, 'Remember the Sabbath whenever it's convenient for you;' He said, Remember the Sabbath and keep it holy."

Anyway I've honored my father and my mother.

And there was her father, reciting his objections to her marriage . . . .

"Have you lost your mind completely, Narcissa Prentiss? You've always been a stubborn, muddle-headed female. But to marry a man you've only seen twice in the past year, and take off like a gypsy across thousands of miles of wilderness that hasn't even been mapped—"

"I'm old enough to know what I want to do with my life, Papa."

"A toddling baby could manage better. You're thinking to spend the next six months living butt to belly with a man who's been running after you for eight years, and both of you married to others."

"That was all over years ago."

False witness? Coveting? Am I guilty of those, too?

And Mary Walker and Sarah Smith and Myra Eells and Mary Agusta Gray had gathered in the shadows to chant:

*Jealousy is cruel as the grave; the coals
thereof are coals of fire, which hath a
most vehement flame—*

—all of them. I've broken all of them. But I didn't mean to! Can I be condemned for breaking unintentionally?

She heard someone screaming; light sprang up behind her eyes. Marcus was holding her, saying, "You're all right now, 'Cissa."

So she was alive. For what it was worth, she was alive. She went to sleep with his arms around her, and when she woke her mind was clear. She was in her bed, alone, and the snow had stopped falling.

For weeks she lay without strength, uncaring. Her body, come so close to dying, was having trouble remembering how to live. But her thoughts flowed clear; events and people were like sheets of glass moving back and forth across her mind; she saw past and future simultaneously, superimposed on the present. Time was around her like air; a week was gone in an hour; an hour expanded to a year.

It seemed clear now that she had wronged others and herself. Christ instructed His followers to turn the other cheek, to carry the Golden Rule one step further, and love your enemies as your friends.

But how?

Did you get up in the morning and say, Today I will love everyone, no matter that they hate me? No matter that they want to destroy me? Could you go on forever turning the other cheek when your brethren hurt you? Would love protect you when savages were lifting their hatchets to your head?

1841

In early spring word came from Lapwai that the Smiths were in trouble at Kamiah. Marcus reacted with unusual belligerance. "Why can't the others go? Walker and Eells are closer than we are. Why is it everytime someone stubs his toe I have to make a two-week trip to rub some salve on it?"

"It might be serious."

He prowled the room like an angry bear. "What can I do? I can't hardly keep Umtippe away from our own door. How am I supposed to pacify some chief I don't even know?"

"You'd better pack your bags."

"Who will take care of you?"

"I'll be fine. I won't worry about a thing."

"You can worry about me getting through the snow after I cross the Clearwater," he grumbled, and went to rummage for shirts and underwear. "Where are my saddlebags?"

He drank a cup of tea with her before he left. "I still don't know why I'm traipsing off up there," he said. "Ellis is a peaceable chief. What's Smith yelling about?"

"Henry's letter said Ellis had rough-handled Asa."

"The fool had no business ignoring his agreement with the Spokanes. Ellis told Asa he could settle up there if he wouldn't break the earth. The indians worship the earth as their mother. To dig in the ground is to wound their mother. I heard Ellis tell Asa if he ever broke ground he'd be digging a hole for his own grave. So why did the fool decide to spade up garden space?"

"What harm did it do, a little piece like that?"

"The point is, Smith broke the agreement." He looked out at the cold flats. "For two cents I'd advise the Board to sell the property to Jason Lee and send us somewhere else. There must be heathen in the world more anxious to be christainized than these."

She was shocked by his statement; afraid of his mood. "We couldn't give up the missions after all we've gone through to build them up."

He turned suddenly, frowning. "Why can't we? What are we doing here, anyhow? How many indians have we converted? Instead of getting friendlier, they're getting uglier."

"But this is our home."

His eyes moved to survey the room, "A mud-walled house full of homemade furnishings and a few out-buildings. It's cost me five years of hard labor. Alice's life went into this house. And yours might have easy enough."

"That's why we can't leave," she said. "We'd be torn in half if we deserted Waiilatpu."

His mood had not improved the afternoon he returned and found Narcissa walking back to the house from Alices's grave. "What in thunder are you doing out in this wind?"

"You've been gone over two weeks, Marcus. It's good to walk outside."

"It's February, not June. Get back in the house now."

"Was it really bad at Kamiah?"

126

"Yes and no. The indians were as gentle as moths by the time I got there. Henry couldn't go, by the way; Eliza's sick."

"She's well now?"

"Yes. But Sarah Smith can't get out of bed more than two or three hours a day anymore. Things ain't right up there. They're living in a hut I wouldn't put pigs in. Asa's got nothing to do but brood on his troubles, and Henry ain't helping it any."

Henry— Always Henry— "What's he done now?"

"He quibbles over every little thing Smith asks for; but he's spending money like water at Lapwai, and forcing the indians to work whether they want to or not."

It was all starting over again, she thought, the fighting and the hurting. Eleven of them here in the middle of nowhere, surrounded by indians wishing them dead, and they spent their energy tearing each other to pieces.

He took up his complaint again while Narcissa got supper on. "Smith thinks Henry is losing his mind."

"That's a terrible thing to say, Marcus. Henry's always been quick to fly to pieces. He gets carried away with his own arguments till he's storming around. But he isn't insane and you know it."

"He's worse than he used to be. He's like a madman when things don't go his way. Smith says he's using the whips again."

It wasn't fair! To have her new-found peace threatened so soon—

"His indians are turning against him," Marcus kept on. "Henry promises in that high-flown style of his that prayer will bring them whatever they ask for. If a chief wants a new coat he prays for it and expects one to fall around his shoulders while he's still on his knees."

"But things were going so well for him—"

"His indians don't understand beans about farming.

Henry tells them if they'll plant and harvest they'll never be hungry again, which is pure foolishness, because there ain't enough ground at Lapwai to support the Nez Perce; and even if there was, indians don't work like whites. It was a game to them at first, digging ditches and making mud bricks and hoeing corn. When they began to slack off Henry threatened them with hell and damnation. Now he's using something more earthy to persuade them. It's slavery, 'Cissa. And even the indians know it."

"But if he's breaking down he can't be held accountable."

"Smith thinks he should be."

"What can be done?"

"Smith's already done something. He's turned Rogers on him since he's been staying at Kamiah. They've even been writing letters to the Board condemning Henry up and down. They've got William doing it, too."

Narcissa was sick; angry and sick. If the Board found out there was trouble, they might hold up supplies while they investigated.

"Smith's sent a fifty-two page letter of complaint that I know of. What the devil is Greene going to think when he gets that? What are my little notes going to count for, against that? The blamed fools!"

"Don't curse, Marcus. Does Henry know?"

"He didn't mention it. It might be he just don't believe it, though. What time I was there he was ranting about the indians."

"Are they dangerous?"

"Old Joseph is still behind Henry, but the young chiefs are getting wild. Some of them came to the school and threatened Eliza a while back. She locked the doors, but they stayed outside for hours, holding her prisoner."

Narcissa felt the old terror invading her, shaking her. "Did they harm her?" The indians had always respected

128

Eliza—

"No. They stripped themselves and stood at the windows, shouting outrages and threatening to burn the building to force her out. Old Joseph came in time to prevent that, thank the Lord."

"Where were the men?"

"Held prisoner; forced to watch. Henry said he had no doubt if they could have broken in they would have attacked her then and there and forced the men to look on while they did it."

The air seemed cold. The settling dusk made the house seem small and insubstantial. What if Umtippe's young men decided to come here—

"Old Joseph don't know how long he can keep them in hand. Henry's been like a demon ever since it happened."

"Let's have our supper and forget the unpleasant things for a time," she said, laying out the plates. "Call the girls."

But before they could sit down at the table Compo called from the porch, "Come, please, doctor. The Munger man is crazy." He stands in the middle of his table, waving a knife; the baby is terrified, but he will not allow the mother to attend to it."

They found Asa Munger sitting at the table, his shoulders rigid, staring straight at the wall. Carrie caught her breath when she saw them and released her tension in a spate of words. "Asy's sick, Mrs. Whitman. He thought I was the indians. He kept yelling that he was going to make them listen to his preaching and he'd kill any that moved. And it was me he was pointing the knife at."

"It's all right now, Carrie." Narcissa soothed the rumpled hair. "Doctor will take care of him."

But the girl could not stop her hysterical report. "Ever time I tried to get up to take care of the baby he'd jump down and put his knife against me—right here—and I was afraid to even breathe—"

She took the girl's arm firmly. "Hush, Carrie. You'll wake the baby again."

Marcus glanced up from grinding a powder. "Take her to the house." he ordered. "Wrap the baby good; he's soaked. I'll give Munger something to keep him quiet tonight. Charlie Compo can sleep here to watch him."

Narcissa waited to eat her supper with Marcus when he returned. "We've got to send the Mungers home, 'Cissa. That boy's bad sick."

"I know."

"The HBC train will be coming through any time now on their way to Rendezvous. I'm sending word to Walla Walla that the Mungers are going east with them. They'll be able to find passage back to St. Louis with the Caravan."

"Can Asa stand the trip?"

"I doubt he'll even know what's going on. I'll give Carrie something to quiet him down in case he needs it. Where is she now?"

"Asleep."

"Good. That's where we belong, too."

The blankets were like ice. Marcus held her against him, rubbing her shoulders until her shivering subsided, but the new trouble buzzed in her mind; she turned this way and that trying to get comfortable.

"You can't do a thing about Munger," Marcus said in the darkness.

"It isn't just that," she said. "It's everything. Is it going to go on like this for the rest of our lives?"

She waited for his answer; waited and waited—and suddenly her heartbeat was a loud drumming. Finally, faintly, he said, "I keep telling myself things will straighten out, but—"

He stopped, just like that, in the middle of a breath; and she was afraid to break the silence.

She carried the unfinished sentence inside her for weeks like a warning. She tried to finish it, but she couldn't, anymore than Marcus could. It was an ominous tunnel to the future, and she sensed something frightening waiting ahead of them . . . .

As if to confirm her uneasiness word came again from Kamiah: there was real trouble now. Marcus was plowing in the southwest field, a quarter mile away; too far to call—too far to run. A cluster of young indians lounged at the corral fence watching a new colt's faltering efforts to stand.

"Go for doctor," she cried to the nearest; "over there."

They all looked at her with mocking eyes, pretending not to understand.

Her fear turned to rage. She reached for the nearest. "Go bring the doctor! Do you hear?"

The boy smiled insolently. She pulled at the dirty shirt and shouted, "You do as I tell you!"

She felt the others crowding close; smelled their anger under the indian smell. The boy jerked away; his shirt tore; she pulled her hand back from contact with the naked brown flesh as if she'd touched a snake. Her eyes met his and she gasped at the hatred she saw there—as if fire leaped from his eyes.

"—I'm sorry—" She ran across the grounds and stumbled into the kitchen, slamming the door and leaning there, her breath sharp in her lungs.

The Nez Perce who'd brought the message looked up from his food. "Trouble happen?"

She jerked her head up and down. "I shouldn't have done that," she breathed.

There was a heavy knocking. She jumped aside. Johnny

Mungo, a hired man, pushed inside. "You hurt, Mrs. Doctor? What happen with those Cayuse?"

"Where are they now?"

"Running. Like bad, angry indians. To the camp. They hurt you, Mrs. Doctor?"

She shook her head impatiently. "I'm all right, Johnny. "Go get Doctor. Fast. Tell him there's bad trouble at Kamiah."

They came in a wagon from Walla Walla: Pierre Pambrun driving, Asa Smith beside him with Mrs. Smith in a bed in the back, and Rogers slumped in a corner of the box. Sarah Smith's face was a skeleton mask of yellowed skin over bones, her eyes completely circled with dark rings. She felt like a sack of sticks under her clothes when they lifted her down.

Narcissa had beds ready. The sick woman dropped back against a pillow and looked up at her with eyes as sad and hopeless as death.

"I couldn't stomach the food," she said. "Dried peas and salt meat and the like—I just couldn't get it down, seems like. I got along on milk till the indians stole the cow. After that I just couldn't eat no more."

"I'll bring you something now, " Narcissa said. "You rest."

"That's why Mr. Smith was plowing the garden, because I was hungering for vegetable soup." She closed her eyes. "I haven't been able to sleep, neither."

Cornelius Rogers was asleep when Narcissa came back from caring for Mrs. Smith, sprawled on the bed like a tired little boy. The shadow of his beard heightened the impression, as if he'd sneaked into bed without washing his face. He breathed heavily through lips bright and tight with fever. She straightened the blankets over him and went to the kitchen where the men sat around the

132

table.

"Why didn't Henry come with you, Marcus?"

"They're all down with the fever at Lapwai." Asa Smith's voice shook. "Two of Joseph's men brought us to the Fort." His head dropped to his crossed arms.

"Let's get him to bed, too." Marcus and Pambrun carried Asa Smith to the pallet in Roger's room.

"I'll be all right—" Smith mumbled as they helped him from the room. "Just—"

Marcus eased him down to the flat bed and covered him gently while Pambrun looked on, his eyes filled with sadness.

"That poor man; he has lived with the fear of death for weeks," the Factor said as they sat again at the table.

"Do you know what happened, Mr. Pambrun?"

He shrugged. *Non.* I do not understand this. The indians at the Fort do not speak of trouble among the Spokanes. Joseph's men do not know of trouble. Truly, I believe it is the fear in these people that makes them see danger in every shadow. Chief Ellis is not a warrier."

"But he threatened Mr. Smith not more than a month ago."

Pambrun's eyebrows raised with a jerk. "Only when Mr. Smith broke his agreement with the Spokanes. I do not believe we can hold that against Ellis."

"Then the indians aren't dangerous?" She watched his face closely.

"I did not say that! I speak only of Ellis. These others— Umtippe and Tamahas and Tillikay—these ride with the young chiefs of the Nez Perce if they are called. They all want trouble. Stikus came to the Fort five—six weeks ago. He say the Cayuse are unhappy. They make trouble if they can." His black eyes were piercingly direct, as if to make sure she got his warning.

Marcus, rejoining them at the table, spoke bluntly of the

flight. "There wasn't any trouble I could find out about. They'd had some stealing, like we all have. Smith was scared as a spooky horse after that ruckus with Ellis. He just broke and ran."

"They are against going back then?"

"Dragons couldn't pull Asa Smith back up there. He's leaving the mission as soon as Sarah's able to ride."

"Where will they go?"

"He's planning to talk to Lee. If there's something for him at the Methodist mission, he'll stop there. Otherwise I expect he'll try to arrange for passage on the next HBC ship to Owyhee."

"We can't blame them," Narcissa said after a moment. "What good were they doing up there?"

Marcus' eyes were harried. "What good are any of us doing?" he said, and stalked from the room.

Two sick people in the house kept Narcissa moving fast; but the thing that drove her day and night was the need to answer Marcus' angry comment with some affirmative proof.

—Marcus was giving up—

The thought would sneak up on her at odd moments, and each time her bones seemed to turn to paper. Her strength was dependent on Marcus', and his on hers; if one lost heart they were both finished.

Asa Smith wandered around the mission grounds waiting for Sarah to be well enough to move on; a puppet, for all the interest he showed. When Narcissa spoke he looked at her with blind eyes, almost as if he didn't remember her.

—she could not endure anything like that for Marcus—

Sarah was coming along now she had food she could keep down and a safe bed. But Cornelius Rogers was desperately ill. He tumbled in a fever, his face flaming, the covers thrown aside. Marcus dosed him with the medicines he had. There were moments when he seemed to know where he was, but most of the time he fought back when they helped him, delirious.

He was thin as a shadow but conscious the day the Smiths left for the Willamette. Narcissa couldn't help overhearing the goodbyes, cooking supper there in the kitchen beside the sick room.

"You're not returning to Kamiah, Smith?"

"I wouldn't go back there if Moses himself took me by the hand and led me there," Smith cried.

"You going to settle in the Valley?"

"All I know is I'm going to be somewhere civilized this winter." He hesitated. "If you want I'll wait a few days—"

There was a silence. Narcissa waited for Rogers' answer along with Asa.

"Don't wait, Smith," he said finally. "No telling how long it'll be before—" He left the sentence hanging there, and she thought impatiently, Before what?

"You going back to Lapwai?"

"That's the one thing I won't do. I've had enough of Spalding to last me till doomsday."

"You going to stay here then?"

"I don't know if Whitman could let me stay without permission from the others. And that won't come easy."

I ought to get Smith out of there, Narcissa thought, but she did not move. Eavesdropping or not, she had to know what they were saying about Henry; had to hear it for herself.

"Spalding ain't going to like losing his printer, and him with the only press in the Territory," Smith said.

"A man only threatens me once with a whip."

"It'd be better to stay here than to try to get along with Spalding, I'll say that for sure."

"For sure," Rogers whispered. "but the Doctor may not want me here either, after—"

Maria came from Sarah Smith's room then. "Tell Mr. Smith Mr. Rogers needs to rest now," Narcissa said, and the girl ducked around the curtain without knocking.

She sensed trouble they did not know about. Rogers' thoughts were really no concern of theirs. It was his reference to Marcus that bothered her, implying secret knowledge.

They were up at dawn next day. The Smith's were going overland to the *dalles*. Sarah turned on the porch and looked at Narcissa for a long time; saying finally, "I can't thank you—" and went to where the men waited to help her into the wagon.

Asa looked at the ground. "I'll return the horses and rig as soon as we're settled, Doctor."

"When you're finished with them. We'll want to hear how things are going with you."

"God bless you." Asa got into the wagon with some difficulty. They followed Compo, who would lead them to Stikus' camp. One of the chief's men would take them from there to the Valley.

Narcissa watched them out of sight, feeling an unexpected sense of loss. It wasn't that she would miss the Smiths personally, she thought, wrapping her shawl tighter against the wind; it was because their leaving diminished the total strength; with their going the mission was smaller, weaker, measured against its enemies.

She walked softly going into the house, as if those enemies were all around her. She didn't wish to call attention to herself.

As Narcissa stepped into the kitchen Maria slipped out of Roger's room. She stopped; light and shadows flecked her eyes like small birds startled into flight. "Mr. Rogers called," she offered finally.

It was wrong. All wrong. Maria never volunteered

information. She watched Maria closely for a few days, but what she was watching for she never shaped into conscious thought.

Marcus was in the mountains most of the time during May and June, working on the new mill. The Cayuse had gone into the mountains too, and Waiilatpu was all but deserted.

Cornelius Rogers was out of bed finally, so thin his bones showed through. He wandered about as Asa had done but without being so withdrawn. He did small chores as he felt like it, in the house as often as out.

He was a strange young man, she thought, with his brown eyes brooding one minute, bursting with light the next. He'd read for hours, then talk her to death with what he'd read. He'd gone through all her books twice over. She had loaned him Blake's poems and his mind caught fire from the wild splendor of those verses. He leaned on the kitchen table while she made preserves, his tongue running away with his thoughts, trying to put his admiration for Blake into words.

"Well, Blake, he writes about the universe as if it was his own back yard; as if he'd grown up with flower beds full of stars, and the clouds for grass."

She was uncomfortable with his intensity, as if he were admitting her to some intimate private place. She knew what he was feeling. But he shouldn't expose his thoughts so to a stranger.

"Are you sure you know what you're trying to say, Cornelius?"

"I'm sure. I just can't get it into the right words is all. You take that poem about 'Tiger, tiger, burning bright—' Doesn't it sound to you like he saw how beautiful a tiger was, and nobody paying attention, and he just had to magnify it so the whole world could see it at once? The forests of the night must cover half the world. And if a tiger was that big, wouldn't the gold in his coat and the shine in his yellow eyes look burning bright?"

She let the spoon ride the bubbling jam. "There's more to it than that, Cornelius. Blake's tiger is a symbol for the fascination evil holds for us; he's asking if God made evil as well as good, since evil is so often beautiful—" She watched him closely. "Haven't you read poetry before? Of course you have."

He stared up at her. "Not anything that sets you on fire the way Blake's does. Now that verse that goes, 'With sweet May dews my wings were wet—"

"I haven't time now, Cornelius," she broke in, rescuing her spoon. "Why don't you help the girls for awhile? They've been hoeing since we got the clothes out this morning."

His strength wasn't really up to such work. He stayed in the house that afternoon while she worked with the girls in the garden. The sounds of his violin swept out to them there: a fervid, pagan music. She looked toward the house, frowning. Where had a preacher's son learned music like that?

She asked him when they went back to the house. He brought his eyes to meet hers as if coming back from a journey of centuries. "I was trying to describe the tiger—"

She felt a startled recognition; the music *had* been a magnificent tiger, stalking the forests of the night. She looked at him suddenly, searchingly. He was no more a missionary than Pierre Pambrun, or John McLeod.

She had an irrational thought then: that Cornelius Roger's imagination might become a threat to all of them. Was this what Henry had sensed and opposed when he turned his sarcastic wrath on Rogers? She shivered. It would be crushed out of him soon enough. Cornelius might think he could cage his free-soaring thoughts, but one day—one day— they would break loose and carry him away with them like a runaway balloon—

What in the world was she thinking? She had been like that when she first discovered Blake. It's finding a new world just beyond your fingertips, she thought; being young, you have to reach for it. Once in awhile you barely brush it with your outstretched hands, but it goes— It goes away and you're left staring after the wonder and the magic.

She straightened and went to her mending. He can keep his mind down out of the clouds if he tries, she told herself. I learned to.

In late afternoon she walked to Alice's grave. The trees were noticeably taller this year; their leaves cast speckled shade on the thick grass. If it hadn't been for the weathered markers no one would have guessed the graves were here.

Except for Hind's. When she had come in the spring she had seen with sharp, premonitory pain that the ground had given way there. She had had a mental picture then of Alice's grave, the next spring or the next, dropped suddenly, outlining the shape of the small box—

She moved abruptly, putting the thought out of mind. The buildings drowsed in the sun. She sat in the coolness and looked at them, half-dozing. Soon it would be time for the animals to be fed, and they'd raise a racket loud enough to be heard at the Cayuse camp; but right now she could almost hear the hawk gliding through the sky out to the west, it was so still.

When Maria came outside again she followed the girl with her eyes as she scattered the corn among the suddenly raucous chickens with wide sweeps of her arm. When it was gone she slipped into the shed for the eggs. They had a good flock now from those three hens Thomas McKay had given them. The rooster Marcus bought later lorded it over the bunch of them. They'd have fryers in another two weeks. She smiled, thinking of the letters from home, full of worry that she and Marcus were living here without any comforts. She'd seen many a farm in New York that hadn't nearly as much to offer.

A little breeze swept down from the foothills carrying the sound of a dog's barking. Narcissa roused herself. That would be Trapper racing along with Marcus. She got to her feet slowly. She hadn't intended to sit so long. But she did not hurry, walking back through the summer afternoon. Supper was ready except for warming. The water in the irrigation ditch flowed clear. She watched the undulations of mint and cress growing half submerged along the edges, like delicate lace; stooped carefully, breathing the damp smell of summer, and picked a few sprigs to nibble as she walked on, the taste sharp on her tongue.

She paused in the yard. Marcus was coming across the flat at a steady lope, a toy rider come to life against the full-grown dimensions of the landscape.

As she turned back to the house a blue-clad figure raced across the yard, a bird in full flight. Cornelius Rogers called, "Maria! Maria, wait!" He was standing in the door of the shed as if he'd stopped short there against his will, watching the fleeing girl with an impotent urgency. Narcissa's suspicions surfaced again then, sharp and clear. Had Maria been in there with Cornelius all this time? It shouldn't have taken so long for her to gather the eggs.

That night at table Narcissa watched Maria and Cornelius, aware of awkwardness beneath their behavior. Maria was silent as usual, but nervousness showed on her, as if moths were beating their wings under her skin. Cornelius kept pulling his eyes from Maria's face, but always they turned back to her; he lost track of the table talk and fidgeted with his food.

She must find out what had happened in the shed

between them. She and Marcus were responsible for Maria here. Should she tell him? But tell him what? Thinking about the scene aroused a vague embarrassment in her. But what had she seen, really?

When Narcissa went to the kitchen to check on the dishwashing she found Margaret working alone. Maria had disappeared. Nor was Cornelius anywhere about. When she asked Margaret where Maria had gone, the girl shrugged without looking at her.

She walked out into the yard. It was a night young people would feel a need to be alone together, she admitted, filled with a heady summer perfume, a young moon turning the buildings to castles. But not for Maria— Not for Cornelius— She walked toward the shed, listening. They were out here together. The night air carried the feel of love to her, enveloping her like beating wings— like the scent of honeysuckle—

—and what if she found them together—?

She half-turned to go inside; a movement caught her attention. There, in the shadows at the end of the house: Cornelius bent over Maria, sheltering her; cradling her; crying her name softly, "Maria— Maria—" his voice heavy with love; his hand a pale blur moving gently— gently—against her hair. Narcissa could feel his longing as if it were herself there in his arms—

She held herself motionless, scarcely breathing. She must get away from them, lest she be touched and burned by their passion. But as she backed, step by step, from their hiding place, her searching foot struck a stone, sending it like a shot against the wall of the shed.

Cornelius' voice repeated her name, "Maria—?" with caution now; with fear.

Narcissa abandoned her place in the shadows; ran to get away from that painful intimacy, no matter that they heard. Maria would never forgive her for spying. Never.

She sat on the outside bench to gain control of herself. If she hadn't run would they have known she had been listening?

—but if she had stayed she might have heard more—

There was no dodging the situation now. Cornelius couldn't take an indian wife, like some trapper. The Mission Board would never condone that. As for Maria—

She stiffened suddenly. They were coming onto the porch. She waited in silence as Cornelius gathered Maria into his arms once more. When he released her Narcissa called, "Maria, come here please."

They turned together. "Mrs. Whitman—" Cornelius started toward her. "Not you, Cornelius. I wish to speak to Maria. Please wait inside."

Slowly he obeyed. Slowly, resentfully, Maria took a few steps in her direction.

"I didn't mean to spy on you tonight," Narcissa said as steadily as she could manage, "but since I did see you I can't ignore what has happened."

There was no answer.

"I only want to help you, Maria."

"Help me?" The girl spoke with mocking pride. "My mother is Crow indian; my father is Canadian. What can you feel that I have felt? What can you say to help me?"

"Maybe I can help you see that this is wrong, what's happening between you and Mr. Rogers?"

"Oh? This is halfbreed problem, *non?* You could never know what it is to be *half* anything. You are all what you are."

Maria had never been like this before: bitter, unapproachable. "Maybe I could understand if you told me."

"If you wish. I will tell you that halfbreed means you are only half as good as white, because you are half white. If you are beautiful, you are only half beautiful; if you are strong, you are only half strong. But if you are bad things, you are two times bad, because you are white bad and indian bad. If you are cowardly you are two times cowardly; but if you are brave you are only half brave. All good things you are half; all bad things you are two."

The girl's directness shook Narcissa. Yet if what she said held truth, it was only partly true. "You are too young to be talking this way, Maria."

"I am woman. White girls remain children until they marry. Indian girls are women early."

"But you've lived with us, Maria. We've brought you up as our daughter—"

"And that is supposed to make me white child, instead of indian woman? My father thought that would happen when he sent me here. Sometimes he feels his white blood strongly. But already, before I come to you, the men at the Fort looked at me—talked at me—and I knew already, then, what they said."

"Surely not, Maria—"

"An indian girl is taught from a baby of man-woman things. It is white child who grows to woman and knows only to hide herself from man."

"I don't wish to hear this," Narcissa said. "Doesn't it bother you at all that you're hurting us by behaving this way?" Accusing when she should be patient—

Maria did not answer; the seconds dragged on and on. Narcissa wiped her eyes, swallowed her pride, took refuge in rejection. Perhaps Maria was incapable of feeling gratitude or sympathy. She was indian—

"What do you expect us to do?" she asked finally.

"I have not thought of what you will do. Only of what I will do."

"And?"

"I go to Walla Walla tomorrow."

It was a disturbing answer. What would Pierre Pambrun think if Maria came running home for no reason;

and by herself? Or would she be alone? She hadn't meant to make the girl leave Waiilatpu.

"How can you, after all we've done for you?" The plea slipped out in spite of herself. She had had no intention of revealing her hurt.

Maria touched her fingers in the darkness. The contact, unexpected, burned like a live coal dropped on her skin; Narcissa jerked her hand away instinctively.

"I did not want to come back here to live," the girl said then, softly, sadly.

"Why did you?"

"I did not know how to make my father understand that I could no longer live here. He is white, and he admires Doctor very much."

Not herself. He admired *Doctor*. "I'm sorry you've been so unhappy here," she said stiffly.

"I have not been unhappy always. The first year I was a child playing in sunshine in summer. I did not feel at home here after Alice was dead. When the letter came for Margaret McKay and me to return to Waiilatpu I did not wish to come. I did not wish to feel what Richard felt before he went away. I did not wish to grow to hate what I am."

—but that wasn't the same at all—

"I will go early tomorrow, before it is light. I will tell no one I am leaving. I will tell my father I return because the priest comes soon." She hesitated. "And I will not tell Rogers."

Narcissa tossed and turned in the night, listening for Maria's leaving. She hadn't meant to drive her away. She had not told Marcus of the episode; had convinced herself that Maria was making idle threats.

She was roused from a troubled napping by Helen Mar shaking her arm. "Mother! Maria has runned away! She has runned away!"

"Who told you that?"

"Margaret."

Narcissa sat up in bed, pulling the little girl against her, trying to quiet her cries. "Maria hasn't run away. She went home for a visit. Sh-h-h— You'll wake Father."

Marcus raised up, half awake, his gray hair spiked in all directions. "What's happened?" He lifted Helen Mar into the bed with them. "Tell me now."

"Maria runned away."

"You're having a dream, baby. Maria's right in there in her bed. Come on now. I'll show you."

"Marcus—"

"Well, ain't she?"

"Maria left in the night."

The way he looked at her she might have said Maria had been swept from the face of the earth.

"She went home last night."

"Well tell me. Hush that crying, Helen Mar Meek, so I can hear this."

Before Narcissa half finished her story he was pulling on his clothes. She heard him calling Rogers awake in the other room; heard the two of them go outside. What was he saying to Cornelius? What she had said to Maria, she supposed, and felt a kind of sympathy for the two of them. They couldn't be allowed to continue this romance, but she didn't want them hurt.

"Mother Whitman?"

She looked down at Helen Mar's wet face.

"When will my sister come back home?"

"Maria isn't your sister, Helen Mar—" She stopped abruptly. Helen's black eyes were accusing.

"You said she was my sister."

Fear touched her then; for Helen Mar and Maria *were* sisters in a sense; half white, half indian. This same unhappiness could come to Helen Mar a few years from now. What if a son of Henry's should look at her with love; and what if, then, Henry said, "No! You are not good enough."

But it wouldn't be the same! It wouldn't be the same at all! Helen Mar had been raised as their own child; *was* their own in all but name. She would be white in every way by the time she was grown.

The round indian eyes stared up at her, unwavering; the bronze skin gleamed against the white ruffled night dress; the heavy black hair fell straight.

"*Will* Maria come back?"

"I don't know, baby," she admitted, putting her arms around the little girl. She laid her face against Helen's hair and the feel of her in her arms was no different than when Alice had cuddled against her. Where was the truth of this matter? She felt shattered inside, remembering Maria's sadness when she'd said she was going. It was as if Narcissa had crushed a jeweled Easter egg in her clumsiness with the girl.

She found Marcus in the kitchen, his face dark as the sky outside. "Rogers didn't know she'd gone," he said. "He insists he's going after her."

"He's still weak, Marcus."

"He's getting his things together anyway."

"You have to stop him."

"You want me to tie him up? I can't keep a grown man from doing whatever he wants to."

Rogers pushed into the room carrying his saddle bags, his face closed tight against them. "Can I borrow a horse, Doctor?"

Marcus' mouth tightened. "I'm not going to be a party to any of this."

"All right then." Rogers brushed past him to the door. "I'll walk if I have to."

"Wait, Cornelius." Narcissa ran after him. "Please

146

wait."

He turned on the steps and looked up at her. "Haven't you done enough with your interfering?"

"You can't throw your life away for a girl like that."

"What kind of girl would *that* be?"

"She's an indian, Cornelius."

"And how does that affect my loving her?"

"It hasn't anything to do with love—"

"What do you know about it?" he cried. "You're old. You've forgotten about love, so you try to make me believe I don't know what love is. Well, you can't!"

He was hurting her deliberately for the hurt she'd done him. "I remember!" she cried. "I know what you're feeling. But it isn't love. It's—desire. It's being young, and wanting . . . . It's just *wanting*.

"That's enough for me."

"You going to be like these trappers out here, Rogers?" Marcus called from the door. "You aim to take that girl until you're tired of her and—"

"No! I aim to marry her! I aim to stand with her and have a preacher marry us, till death do us part!"

"It'll be a priest you stand in front of if you marry that one," Marcus said. "A Catholic priest in a black skirt making crosses in the air. Is that what you want?"

Rogers threw his head back; tears made streaks to the corners of his mouth. "What difference does any of this make if I love her?" He ran then, across the yard and into the meadow, and the dark sky seemed to swoop down to cover him as he ran.

"Come on inside." Marcus pulled Narcissa into the kitchen. She stood where he released her. "What are we going to do."

"I'll have to get word to Henry and Elkanah Walker."

"But what then?"

"We'll wait and see."

By noon a downpour pounded the earth like hammers. Narcissa pictured Cornelius slogging through the knee-high grass, wet to the skin, his face streaming. "Do you think he really tried to walk to the Fort, Marcus?"

"No. I think he cut a horse out of that herd in the north pasture. He may have a sore rear end when he gets there, but he won't have sore feet."

"Would he have been able to ride out the storm if he caught a horse?" '

"How in thunder would I know?" He put down his book and removed his spectacles. "Why don't you forget it now? We can't do a blamed thing until the others get here."

Her nervousness had drummed at her all day. Now her voice broke. "He's still sick. You know what will happen if he spends hours in this rain."

"He's young. He'll make it all right. As soon as Henry and Elkanah get here we'll do something." But he came to her and put an arm around her. "What else could we have done?" he asked. And she had no answer.

A rider brought word from Pambrun before the others got there. Marcus talked with him on the porch while Narcissa waited, ready for bed, for him to bring her news of Cornelius.

"Pambrun wants me to come to the Fort," he told her. "Rogers is sick again. He's afraid to keep him there without proper medical care."

"I'll go with you—"

"Will you bring Maria home?" Helen Mar begged. Margaret listened without expression.

"I don't think Maria wants to come back just now, baby; but we're going to bring Mr. Rogers home with us. He's ill."

"If Mr. Rogers comes back, Maria will want to come too."

148

The air was still damp, but clean now. Narcissa remembered that day four years before when they'd started for the Fort and had been turned back by heavy rains. She almost wished for another storm like that. Anything would be better than the meeting ahead with Pambrun.

She was rocking with fatigue when their horses paused on the gravelly flats beside the Fort. "It always looks the same, doesn't it, Marcus."

"May not be the same this time. I have a notion our welcome won't be as warm as it's been in the past."

"Mr. Pambrun won't believe we ran Maria off."

For answer he kicked his horse lightly and they galloped on to the gates. It occured to her, later, that this was the first time they'd approached a building since they left St. Louis that someone hadn't been waiting to greet them.

The chickens and turkeys in the courtyard announced their arrival with loud clackings. A dozen indians lounged there, but they had seen no lodges near. Pambrun, come to investigate the noise, ran suddenly to greet them. "I did not know you had arrived. My apologies, Madame. Please come to the house."

"How is Mr. Rogers?"

"He is very sick man. I do what I can for him; and Maria does what the Doctor has told her before, but he is very, very sick man."

Narcissa hesitated. "How is Maria?"

His quick glance touched her face. "She is well."

They could hear Rogers' heavy breathing before they went into the breathless cubbyhole. It smelled hot, as if the fever in him had burned up all the oxygen in the room. Marcus knelt with his head against Rogers' chest.

Maria had slipped from the room when they entered without a greeting. Narcissa felt an urgent need to escape from the thick air. Perhaps she could find Maria; explain she hadn't meant to hurt her—

But Maria had disappeared. Pambrun followed her to the big room, and sent his wife for tea. She was uncomfortable alone with him, feeling the same need to set this unhappy situation straight with him as with Maria.

"Mr. Pambrun," she said abruptly, "I'm sorry for this."

"Of course, Madame."

"Has Maria told you what happened?"

"*Non.* Maria says she has returned to be here when Father DeMers comes, but the good Father will not be here for another month. It is the young man who tells me what has happened, only his words are hot with fever and I cannot be sure he says what he means to say."

"They insist they love each other."

"And is that not possible?"

"Mr. Rogers insists he wants to marry Maria."

"Then it is the marriage that is not possible?"

"You know it isn't possible! It would be the worst thing that could happen?"

Marcus came into the room rolling down his cuffs. "He's hardly getting enough air to keep him alive. Is there any way we can get a fire going in that room, Pambrun?"

"To be sure, Doctor. We will bring an iron spider filled with coals. That is enough fire?"

"I need to get a kettle steaming. It's the quickest way to open his lungs.

The hours in the saddle had jounced Narcissa so she ached all over. She leaned her head against the wall while she waited—

"Madame?"

She opened her eyes quickly.

"You are very tired, *non?* You would like to rest?" He led her up the steep outside stairs. When he left the attic storeroom she slipped off her shoes and fell onto the bunk, dropping at once into a deep sleep.

She was nagged awake by an insistent need to go to the outhouse. She fought against this intrusion of her senses into the comfort that cradled her, but she could not deny the urgency once she had acknowledged it. She sat up, groping in the windowless room for her shoes.

"What's the matter?" Marcus' sleep-heavy words startled her.

"I have to go outside."

The new day was just beginning to lighten around the edges. The yard fowl were coming awake. Outside the stockade a dog barked, but half-heartedly, as if still in sleep.

She had no desire to go back to the loft after visiting the outhouse. She sat on the bottom stair and watched the faint pink streaks of light nudge up over the mountains and unroll into magnificent clouds of salmon and gold; for a few minutes the world was bathed in illumination that turned the walls to flame-colored barricades. At that moment a rooster blazoned out his reveille and the Fort awoke.

Pierre Pambrun came out on the porch and stood looking over the courtyard, feet wide apart, hands planted on his hips. She got up quickly. "Mr. Pambrun—"

He came to her, his hands smoothing the wild brush of his hair. "*Bon jour,* Madame Whitman. You slept well?"

"Oh, yes. But I couldn't stay in bed."

"This time of day is too good to waste on sleep." He pulled a clay pipe from his waistband. "You will permit—? A pipe before breakfast clears sleep from the head so a man can face the day."

He found a packet of sulpher matches in the same fold and pulled one across the rough wall. It exploded into sizzling flame. Narcissa jumped, still wary of these lucifers, though Marcus carried a few of them when he travelled alone.

"Do not be startled. The odor is the most dangerous thing about them." He puffed the tobacco alight and looked at her through the smoke, a question in his eyes.

"I must talk to you, Mr. Pambrun."

He nodded. "About Maria and the young man."

"What's going to happen?"

He gazed out at the courtyard, in motion now as the animals stirred with the waking day. "M'sieu Rogers has said he desires Maria for his wife."

"Cornelius Rogers is only a boy."

"He is plenty old to be a husband."

"But we cannot allow this marriage!"

"And why not, Madame?" His voice was soft.

"You know the reasons as well as I. He's too young to know what he's doing. This marriage right now would ruin his whole life."

"Because Maria has indian mother?"

She hesitated; stepped closer to him. "Yes," she said, "that, and—"

"There is something else?"

"Maria is Catholic. Mr. Rogers is a Protestant missionary. Surely you understand that a marriage between them wouldn't be acceptable. Your priests don't even recognize his religion."

"My own thinking is different from the priests in some things. Years and years I have spent alone, listening to the rivers talk; hearing what the forests say. The grass on the plains whispers to a man when he is alone; the stars in the heavens have something to tell him if he will listen."

He tapped his pipe out against the wall and thrust it into his waistband again. "I have come to believe, Madame, that *le Bon Dieu* is a big God to make all this big world; and that He would not have time to worry about all the little differences that keep our minds busy down

152

here. I think if He did not love His children with brown skins He would not have made those; and I think, also, that He is not so much concerned with how we worship Him, as that we do."

His black eyes were mild, yet somehow demanding. While she struggled to bring her thoughts into order Marcus came out to the porch and it was too late to say more.

It was just as well. By the time they left Walla Walla it had become clear that Pambrun would not help them break up the romance.

Narcissa shifted in the corner of the wagon bed to ease her aching legs. There were hours of travel still ahead before they reached Waiilatpu, but at least the sun had gone down. She might be able to sleep now if she could get comfortable.

From the pallet on the wagon floor Cornelius Rogers mumbled. She leaned closer but the jarring of the wheels bumping over open land made hearing impossible. He'd slept heavily most of the day from the laudanum Marcus had given him. He had pushed at their hands while they carried him to the wagon, shouting for Maria, begging Pambrun not to let them take him back to the mission. When he was lifted into the wagon Maria had come running to throw herself across him like a limp bird, whispering, soothing him, begging him not to weep— Narcissa had held him down with a blanket around his shoulders, and him crying all the time for Maria to rescue him, while Marcus whipped the horses across the gravel flats and the Pambruns looked on, their silence an accusation.

But even Pambrun had agreed it was necessary for them to take Cornelius back to the mission. Marcus couldn't stay at the Fort this time of year to care for him, and he needed a doctor's attention. Narcissa had tried to

153

explain to him why they were returning him to Waii-latpu; but, half out of his mind, he'd confused her words with those she'd called to him that day he'd run away. Once they had him home Marcus should be able to make him understand. It would have to be Marcus, she knew; Cornelius would never listen to her again.

He moved restlessly, moaning. Narcissa touched his forehead, lifting her hand quickly from the burning contact. She felt for the canteen. His mouth would be dry as dust from the fever. She leaned over to help him drink, but he turned his head impatiently and the water ran onto the blankets. As she sponged it up with a towel, he sighed and let his hot face fall against her hand, rousing an uneasy compassion in her. It wasn't fair to take advantage of his illness to win the unequal battle.

But what else could they do? They had a duty to him, above compassion, above friendship, to keep him from ruining his life. He was too young to know that every man his age felt this temptation. Marcus said it was natural—boy bursting into manhood, demanding recognition; that he'd be grateful, later on, that they had kept him from marrying now.

—but would he—?

He was mumbling again, his voice heavy. Narcissa put her ear to his lips to catch the ragged phrases, sliding down a little to ease the cramps in her legs.

"... man ... give substance—of his house—"

Did he know what he was saying? His eyes were closed. She moved away, painfully; his litany began again. "Behold ... my love ...."

There was nothing she could do but make the unconscious gestures of comfort. She touched his face; smoothed his hair. And too swiftly for her to escape he rolled his head to her shoulder as a child would do, his arm flung heavily across her, and she was lying in the dark, his head

154

cradled against her like a child's—like a lover's—

" "—*thou has ravished my heart—my sister—my spouse—*" She recognized *The Songs* now, and was held by the consuming passion of the poetry. *"Behold thou art fair, my beloved . . . Thy lips art like . . .threads of scarlet . . . . Eyes like . . . pools of Heshbon—"*

Her face flamed; her mind flamed. She could not listen to this outpouring from a man whose barriers were down. She tried to pull away; his fingers dug into her thigh; held her there.

"How fair art thou, O love, for delights—" he crooned. *"How beautiful . . . thy feet, the joints of thy thighs . . . like jewels . . . ."*

And his hand moved gently, rhythmically, along her leg. Not even the ministers voiced the love songs of Solomon, and here was Cornelius Rogers lifting them straight out of his heart for—Maria—lying in her arms—

"Thou art all fair, my love . . . . There is no spot on thee . . . .

—if she moved and he cried out and Marcus turned—

He found her hand and fondled it against his face, singing against her fingers his confession of imagined love.

—imagined? Or remembered—?

His head moved against her breast, his face like fire through her clothing. *"Thou hast ravished my heart—my sister—"* he breathed. *"Thy breasts are like young roes—"*

She tried *not* to see Maria, young round breasts and slender legs, all one bronze color from head to foot. She imagined the two of them lying on the pallet in his sick room. Like this—

Narcissa struggled suddenly, pushing herself to a sitting position, fighting away from his groping hands, as the ardent whispers changed to pleading.

Marcus stopped the horses. "Everything all right?"

155

"He's been raving, Marcus. I can't quiet him."

He felt Roger's face; tucked in the blanket and straightened, a weary shadow in the dark. "I can't do anything more until we get home."

"I want to ride up front now."

It won't be comfortable with no back to the seat."

"I don't care." She scrambled along the wagon bed and climbed over the seat. "My legs hurt."

—and my mind—

The heavens spread above them, prickly with stars; the prairie flats stretched around them, a shadowy vastness that encompassed the world and she felt smaller than a grain of sand. This was a night to support Pambrun's Big God. He would have to be big as space itself to embrace the sufferings of all the creatures on this earth, she thought. Or are we flattering ourselves to think God has time for all the petty troubles that plague us? In the back of the wagon Cornelius Rogers still mumbled his pleas. Did it really matter to God that he burned with love for an indian girl? Where, exactly, did God's Word forbid love between the races?

Her mind reeled. Somewhere God had promised to keep His eye upon the sparrow, but could He? With the world crawling with living creatures, *could* He—?

Well, He could light the stars by millions, flung out across the night sky forever. Was this a visualized pattern of God's power to count His children here on earth?

Once home, Narcissa knew a constant worry that Cornelius would remember somehow that she had heard him talking that way. If he did he gave no indication. They managed to keep him in bed four days. The fifth morning he was gone, and the wagon with him. Marcus refused to go after him again.

At the end of the week Henry came, haranguing over Roger's defection before he was out of the saddle. They could not even get him to sit down and eat; he paced the floor, his voice rising as he flung himself about.

He had faced Rogers down at Walla Walla before coming to Waiilatpu. "I made it plain the Directors would have no choice but to release him unless he came to his senses in a hurry."

"Do you think there's a chance of that?"

"Not with Pambrun putting up a fortune to tempt him to marry the girl."

She couldn't believe that of Pierre Pambrun! That was selling Maria!

"You're sure of this?" Marcus demanded.

"Pambrun showed me the paper. It's written there, plain as truth: Rogers gets twelve hundred dollars as soon as the marriage takes place." He leaned on the table to glare at them as if they were at fault. "I told Rogers he was selling himself! I told him Elkanah said it would take a lot of love to hide the indian habits, once the heat wore off."

—but that wasn't the way to reach Cornelius! He'd never listen to criticism of Maria—

"I pointed out she's a halfbreed and a Catholic, barely able to read and write."

Narcissa felt a stab of anger. What did Henry know of Maria's education? She'd been teaching the girl for four years now.

He caught her expression. "No offense, sister; but we all know the indians are only capable of learning the rudiments."

She heard Maria in her mind saying, If you are good, you are only half good; but if you are bad, you are two times bad— Was Maria right, then? Was *anybody* right in all this?

Henry began his pacing again. "Rogers never should have been allowed to go to Pambrun in the first place."

This time Marcus stiffened. "I doubt if even you could have kept him from going, Henry. Did Rogers give any indication that he might change his mind?"

"His answer to everything I said was, 'It doesn't make any difference. I love Maria.'"

Love again. No matter where she looked, how she pushed her thoughts and examined her conscience, they came back to love.

—stay me with flagons, comfort me with apples, for I am sick of love—

The *Songs of Solomon* again, she thought; and fought down an impulse to laughter.

Henry and Marcus finally accepted Rogers' leaving as final. She couldn't believe they'd seen the end of the affair. It hung over her for weeks like a hawk circling a chicken pen. But nothing happened that they heard.

The indians were unstable too. Their movements did not follow the time-honored pattern of spring-leaving; fall-returning. Small bands hung around the mission, begging or stealing, but always refusing to work. The new fences seemed to infuriate them. They knocked down whole sections as fast as they were raised. Marcus raged when he found the broken posts. Horses disappeared; cattle were 'lost'. And they were helpless.

In late summer the Cayuse began to come down from the mountains. Dusty bands passed Waiilatpu daily, and there was a noticeable belligerence about them that added to Narcissa's worry. They didn't wave and call out to Helen Mar hanging on the fence as they had in past years. After the first day she called Helen to the house when the indians were passing.

Marcus made a fast trip to the Fort in September. The afternoon he was due back she walked with the girls to the top of the hill to watch for him. The landscape was summer brown now; the tall dried grass rippled in an invisible wind like an ocean bleached of its color. The sky was heavy with clouds rolling and tumbling across the sun. It would be raining by morning.

"Mother! Look!"

Helen Mar pointed to the northeast. A chill raced down her arms; she edged closer to the girls. The prairie was moving with tiny figures riding, walking toward the Fort. The indians were gathering but they were giving Waiilatpu a wide berth. She turned and saw others riding down out of the Blues and to the west; a divided river flowing around an island.

She would never have known they were near if she hadn't climbed the hill. Marcus was riding home against the flow of that river—

"We must get back to the house, girls." Narcissa hurried them before her down the hill. And it seemed the wind rose, the sky darkened, in the time it took them to cross the meadow. Her head was throbbing by the time she heard Marcus' horse come into the yard that evening.

"What's happening, Marcus?" There was no keeping the fear out of her voice.

He touched Margaret's shoulder and lifted Helen Mar in his arms. "It's the priest, DeMers. I told Pambrun he was keeping the Cayuse upset by letting the priests come to the Fort, but he says he can't refuse them the hospitality of Walla Walla, that he has no control over the movements of the indians; that he can't stop the Fathers from holding services."

Helen sat on his lap. "Did you see Maria?"

"Yes, Baby. I saw Maria. She said to give you a hug."

"When is she coming home?"

"It's time for bed now." Narcissa spoke sharply, "Margaret, you help her."

When the girls were out of the room she turned to Marcus. "Did you talk with Cornelius?"

He nodded.

"Does he show signs of changing his mind?"

"No. He's all but married to Maria now. He's working with Pambrun. He's gone, 'Cissa, and we might as well give up to it."

The indians were back by the end of September, riding defiantly with loud talking; circling the mission before going on to the camp. There was an ugliness about their insolence more frightening than anything they'd done before.

Marcus was increasingly impatient with her complaints. "They're always riled when they've been listening to the Catholics. They'll settle down when winter comes and they need something to eat. This year they'll be civil or they'll starve. I'm through fooling with them."

Narcissa was almost happy to see winter come, as if the hot tempers of both Marcus and the Cayuse would be cooled by freezing weather. She tried to start lessons again but her students did not return. She accused Marcus of forgetting to send word.

"I sent Compo," he growled when she asked him. "If they ain't here, it's because they don't want to be."

Her fear of the indians was on the rise again. She brooded that her girls no longer trusted her. Was it because of Maria? She felt the presence of that unhappy affair in their lives again—unresolved; menacing.

William Gray brought them news of Pambrun's accident. "Pambrun's been thrown from a horse," Marcus said, stripping off his dirty shirt. "He's hurt bad. Get my bags ready."

"You're going after the way he's acted?"

He didn't bother to answer. "Put in plenty of clean rags if you have them. I'll need bandages."

—of course he would go. Pierre Pambrun had helped them time after time, whatever he'd done about Rogers. He couldn't be blamed for wanting the best for Maria. It was a responsibility weighing on all fathers in the Territory.

That day at Vancouver when Dr. McLaughlin had asked her to instruct the Indian wives and children, she had seen it then.

"How far do you wish me to carry this instruction, Doctor?" she'd asked.

His eyes had been shadowed with pain as he spoke of his daughter and conceded that in spite of her favored position here in the wilderness, and the probability that she would marry one of the Company officers who came and went at the Fort, she still might be subject to ostracism if ever her husband returned to the centers of civilization.

He had grieved over the possibility that his beautiful child might feel prejudice from his own peers under certain conditions. "I could not bear that—" he had said, his voice revealing his deep concern. "I cannot have her hurt because of her parentage."

A quick pity had touched her then for this man—bigger than other men, all-important in an empire that covered half a world—responding to his anguish for his mixed-blood children. Was it fair now to resent Mr. Pambrun's feeling the same concerns for Maria? Pambrun loved his children with the same fierce, protective devotion Dr. McLaughlin had revealed to her then.

How could they blame the Walla Walla Factor for knowing a similar anguish? The difference, of course, was that there had not been a personal involvement for her in the matter of Eloisa, as there was with this of Cornelius and Maria.

The three days Narcissa waited with William for Marcus to return were tight with tension. For once she was glad to have him there. He was someone to talk to. He was secretive about what he had been doing at Walla Walla, but she was grateful for his company, nevertheless. When, the second afternoon, he was accosted by indians, Narcissa was as frightened as if it had been Marcus who was attacked.

"Those young bucks are getting too big for their britches!" He leaned against the wall, breathing hard. "There's one that'll think twice before threatening a white man again."

"Are you hurt?" She tried to examine the cut on his face but he pulled away. "I ain't hurt. But that Cayuse has an almighty sting on his forehead."

She was frantic. The girls came running and she turned angrily. "Margaret, take Helen and stay in the other room until I come!" She ran back to William. "Now tell me!"

He was watching through the window as he talked. "I was in the shed going over some harness when I looked up and there was this young buck, cocky as the devil himself. I asked him what he wanted. He yanked the bridle out of my hands without a by-your-leave. When I ordered him to let go he jabbered something and grabbed my arm. And then I let him have it with the reins I was holding. I cut him right across the eyes. He let out a yelp like a kicked dog and jumped back, snarling in Cayuse, threatening me. But he didn't leave, and I gave him another lick. He ran then all right, screeching at the top of his lungs."

Narcissa was stunned. William hadn't had time to

think of what could come of this! Maybe Marcus would know what to do when he got back, but she doubted it. He was as helpless before attack by the indians as anyone else.

But his news, when he got home the next evening, overshadowed theirs:

Pambrun was dead.

Narcissa could not imagine the little man still, unspeaking, eyes closed against the life they had mirrored so imaginatively. William brooded over the story. "I suppose Rogers will marry the girl quick as he can now."

"It may speed things up all right. A family needs a head in this country. There was talk, after the funeral, that they'd be moving to Vancouver right away."

"He's in the ground already?"

"There wasn't any use waiting. It'd take two days to get someone there from Vancouver. Mrs. Pambrun wanted it done right away."

"Who conducted services?"

"I said a few words. And Rogers."

Marcus, conducting a Catholic funeral?

"I don't know that I would have been so charitable," William said. "After all—"

"Pambrun was my friend. The way I looked at it, it wouldn't hurt him none in the eyes of his priests to be buried by a protestant. It wouldn't be any more than if he'd been laid to rest without a service at all. And it made me feel better."

Remembering Pambrun's words on the subject, Narcissa thought he would have felt better too had he known.

So they were blown into spring on a wind of unrest. The weather grew milder. The departure of the Pambruns for Vancouver, and Rogers with them, was a quieting influence. Finally the affair was settled. Rogers and Maria would be married as soon as they arrived at the

Fort.

The new Factor at Walla Walla was Archibald McKinley; a long-time member of the HBC officers, but Scotch Presbyterian. Now they could hope for less encouragement for the priests moving into the Northwest like flocks of complacent blackbirds. They're alike, Narcissa thought, seeing Marcus and McKinley together; stocky, solid men with plain faces dominated by sensitive eyes. You could look at either of them and recognize his worth.

Their only disagreement was over the Cayuse. "I tell ye, mon, ye're a fool to be stayin' oot here by yoursel' i' the midst of these savages; they're feelin' ugly. One day they'll take offense at some wee bit o' nonsense and come at ye like the furies." McKinley joggled his ferocious eyebrows. "Get oot, Doctor; get oot o' here before ye regret it—"

"You don't really expect me to leave Waiilatpu to them, do you? They're trying to scare me off. And I won't leave."

"I guess it depends on whether a mon cares more for his pride than for his hair," McKinley said. "As for me, I'd gie 'em the place. There's thousands of spots bonnier than this one. There's thousands of sinnin' indians too, waiting' to be saved. Let these keep their bit o' swampy land."

"You aren't changing my mind." Marcus grinned. "I know you'd like to see me run off so you'd have first chance to trade with the settlers coming this year."

"Weel, there's thot o' course. But it's the savages I'm chiefly concerned aboot. It's nae just this scurvy bunch. The Nations are boilin' and stewin'. The Company has ears all over the Territory, remember. It's no laughin' matter."

"I appreciate your concern, McKinley, but—"

"Look at the bonnie lass there," McKinley continued,

his voice fierce, gesturing toward Margaret studying by the fire. "What if Umtippe decides he'd like her to wife? All he has to do is come for her."

"I think he'd better not try it!"

"How're you plannin' to stop him, Doctor."

"I don't think Umtippe would risk Tom McKay's wrath by harming his daughter."

McKinley sat in cloudy silence.

"You know I have to stay," Marcus added finally.

McKinley gve him a long, steady look. "Aye," he said grudgingly. "Aye, ye'll be stayin', but take care."

The thought of coming settlers crowded the indian threat out of Marcus' thoughts. He set to his plowing, having persuaded William to stay on temporarily. With Compo they worked to break land for crops to supply those who would be arriving in the fall. No one questioned Marcus' certainty that they would come. He *knew;* and his faith was such that, imperceptibly, he brought the rest of them around.

He was able to coax some of the Cayuse to help him get grain and corn and potatoes planted. But the conflicts that developed were sharp and terrifying.

Tamahas and Tilhoukaikt brought their lodges early in the spring and joined Umtippe's wild young men in taunting the workers. Groups of riders would bear down on fields on their painted horses, leaving broad trails through the greening crops. Time after time Narcissa would hear the shouting; would run to see Marcus shaking his fists and threatening them off his land.

Annual meeting was early, at Lapwai. The latest indian trouble had roused strong reactions. As usual Marcus and Henry saw the issue from opposite viewpoints.

"The Cayuse resent the land going under fence," Marcus

165

said. "They say the land belongs to them."

"Maybe they have a right to their claim," Henry argued. "Crops for the missions are one thing; crops to sell for profit are another."

"I've never sold a pound of grain for profit, Henry!"

"You're doubling your acres to have supplies to sell to settlers you say are coming."

"They're coming all right. And I'll have supplies for them, at cost. There'll be no profit."

"Brother Whitman." Elkanah Walker rose slowly, as if to avoid hitting his head on the ceiling. "I've studied the orders from the Mission Board, and there's nothing in them about setting up trade stations for travelers."

"You want me to deny hospitality?"

"If you must give it at the expense of your mission, yes," Elkanah said, chewing thoughtfully.

"When you antagonize the indians over the land needed to raise extra supplies you're jeopardizing the work of all of us," Eells added.

Marcus faced them all. "You agree on this among you?" Elkanah nodded in time to the movement of his jaws. "You want me to refuse these people when they come down out of the Blues?"

"You haven't the right to stir the anger of the indians at the expense of the missions," Henry broke in.

Out of his anger Marcus drew the one charge they had avoided. "You're adding fuel every time you take a whip to one of them, aren't you, Henry?"

There was an awkward silence. Henry turned away without answering them, and the arguments raged again. Marcus, trying to pressure Walker and Eells to his side, put into words the second unpleasant secret they harbored among themselves.

"You're going to have to line up somewhere, ain't you? Or are you planning to write some letters of complaint

166

about me to the Board, like the others you've sent?"

Henry was back into it then. "What letters of complaint?"

The others refused to look his way.

"Tell me! What letters? What complaints?"

It came into the open then, with Walker making a shamefaced confession. Henry was unbelieving. "Marcus, you knew of this and said nothing?"

"What good would it have done? The letters had gone before I knew of it."

"I deserved the opportunity to defend myself, didn't I?"

Marcus had no answer. He's already regretting his quick words, now it's too late, Narcissa thought.

Henry walked out of the room. In the silence Eliza stood with a rustling of her heavy skirts and crowded past. The terrible arguments! Every year they spent the Meeting quarreling, and on the last day patched up some compromise to get them through another year.

Narcissa stood up before she had time to think better of it. "What's the matter with everyone? There are exactly eight of us left, among thousands of indians who would just as soon kill us as look at us. Why do we keep fighting each other?"

The men stared at her; Elkanah Walker cleared his throat.

"I know," she rushed on, "women aren't supposed to speak in meeting. Well let me tell you I'm tired of spending one week out of every year fighting. No wonder we can't make friends with the indians; we don't know anything about friendship!"

Her footsteps drummed on the bare floor as she fled. She ran along unfamiliar paths, looking for someplace to hide.

—she wanted to go home; back home to Steuben County, a continent away; where she could walk down a street and say 'Good morning,' without someone finding fault with the way she said it—

Marcus was in their quarters when she came back an hour later. "Was anything decided?"

He shook his head.

"Why don't we go back to Waiilatpu, Marcus?"

"Now?"

"Right now. We can't do any good here, after the way I spoke out today." He made a motion of protest. She put her arms around him and leaned against him. "Don't bother to smooth it over for my sake. We're just different from the rest. I don't know why; I don't know how; I don't even know who's right. We just don't fit in with the way they think. So let's go home."

They were two days back at Waiilatpu when a troop of soldiers came riding into the mission yard, the morning sun glancing from their buttons. The Whitmans waited on the porch. "United States Army!" Marcus shouted. "I told you they'd be sending troops from the States! They know this is going to be United States territory some day. I told you!"

And Narcissa was touched by a throat-filling pride as the men stopped in the yard in formation. They carried mail from New York, reinforcing her impression they'd ridden straight from there to the mission. Actually they were completing a continental tour of exploration. From here they would return to Washington to report directly to President Polk.

For Marcus the soldiers were a sure sign of government interest in the Oregon country as American territory. His questions to Lieutenant Wilkes were blunt; he read into the answers an assurance that the United States was readying a claim to the northwest. He harbored a secret conviction that they were scouting for a permanent station near Waiilatpu. He worked harder than ever once they'd gone.

He wrote to Lapwai and Tshimakain trying again to win the others to his plans for making Waiilatpu a way station for the settlers coming down from the Blues at the end of their journey across the continent. The letters only strengthened Henry's opposition. Marcus was going beyond the instructions of the Mission Board, Henry insisted. It wasn't fair for him to have all the tools at Waiilatpu.

Marcus stormed at their stubborness. "We can't get the message to the indians until we get settlers here and establish claim to the Territory. As long as McLaughlin calls the tune from Vancouver he'll do everything he can to keep the indians from listening to us. He told us so, that first night we saw him. Henry's afraid Waiilatpu will outgrow Lapwai; that we'll become better known, with all the immigrants going by here. Walker and Eells don't even know what's going on—"

"You think you're going to change their minds, Doctor?" William shook his head. "I doubt it myself."

Then, in early August, a wagon creaked down from the foothills. They left breakfast on the table and waited at the fence while Marcus threw a saddle on the big gray and galloped to meet them, Trapper at the mare's heels.

"Can't be settlers," William said. "One wagon wouldn't come by itself."

Where *would* a wagon come from down that trail except from the East? Fort Boise was the nearest settlement in that direction. And HBC men didn't drive wagons.

It looked like a woman on the seat. A young woman— Narcissa started toward the wagon and thought she heard a baby crying.

Dust boiled up as Marcus came on ahead. "Remember Jim Bridger? The trapper I operated on that first summer I came West? Well, it's him; and he's got the Mungers with him."

Carrie sat looking straight ahead, her knees spread a little so her skirt made a hammock for the baby. She had a rag tied over her hair. Her face was burned brick red around her puffy eyes.

"Where's Asa, Carrie?"

"Curled up on the floor of the wagon, looking into space."

"Did they miss the caravan?"

"There wasn't a caravan this year, Marcus. There wasn't a rendezvous. Joe was right. Beaver's done forever, and there's no need for a caravan now."

"Then they made the trip for nothing?"

"Yes."

The wagon stopped. Jim Bridger jumped from the wagon, landing silently on moccasined feet. His long hair appeard almost white against his sunburned face. He lounged in front of her lazily as if he leaned comfortably against a tree.

"You'd be the Doc's woman," he said, appraising her from blue eyes fringed by long fair lashes.

"Yes, Mr. Bridger. Is your wagon the only one?"

"Yes mam."

"Excuse me while I help Carrie—"

The girl jerked her head around then, as if recognizing safety at long last. She gathered the baby to her and put her face against him. "Mam, we couldn't go home. There wasn't nobody to take us."

The children crowded to see the baby and there was a strange child among them. She was dressed as Helen Mar had been when Joe brought her, in trousers and a boy's shirt; but her hair curled in soft brown waves about her face, and her black eyes were narrow and long; tip-tilted.

"You'd be the woman here, I reckon. The Doctor's woman."

Narcissa smiled. "Yes, I am. But how did you know?"

"Old Joe Meek, he told and told about you ever time he got the chanct. Reckon you must be the only lady with sun-colored hair in the world, to hear him tell it."

"Well Joe Meek didn't tell me about you. What's your name?"

"Maryannbridger."

"Mr. Bridger's your father?"

Yes'm. Jim Bridger, the best damn trapper in the Rockies."

She frowned. "Mary Ann, we don't use that language here."

"Huh?" The black eyes met hers, blank and flat as shoe buttons.

"Sometimes men talk that way, but not young ladies. Margaret, take Mary Ann to the house with you and Helen Mar."

But Mary Ann hung back. "Missus," she said over her shoulder, "is my pa coming too?"

"He's coming," she said, her voice gentle, but the child kept looking over her shoulder.

Her own eyes lingered on the trapper: slim, handsome even. Had any of the Mountain Men escaped this trap of indian families?

Carrie limped to the house. "I sprained my foot a few days back. Asy wandered off and I was looking for him and stepped in a hole. It's been a bother to me, having to look after the baby and all."

"How is Asa, Carrie?"

She didn't have to look for Carrie's tears; they were there in her voice. "He don't even know us any more. He thinks he's in Pennsylvania; don't even know he's got a wife and baby—"

It was later she realized the full implication of Jim Bridger's arrival with the Mungers. There had been no rendezvous. There had been no caravan to serve as guide for wagons. Her eyes sought Marcus. There would be no settlers this year . . . .

Jim Bridger went on to Fort Walla Walla after two days. And he left Mary Ann behind to 'git some schoolin'.

1842

It was the next fall before they came. Late in September
Dr. Elijah White—small, handsome, immaculate—rode
in with three young men to announce the eighty-odd
immigrants with eighteen wagons would be arriving by
mid afternoon. Marcus' long wait had not dulled his
excitement. He blustered like a whirlwind, picking a
camp site, checking supplies, moving cows from one pasture to ready it for the train's stock.

Narcissa felt her own pride as the settlers neared the
mission. The house was polished from ceiling to floor;
crops were almost harvested; the animals were fat. The
girls looked like dolls in their gray and white checked
ginghams with red ribbons in their braids. She and Marcus could hold up their heads, meeting the newcomers.
Even Mary Ann wore a dress. It had been a struggle to get
her into skirts. Housebreaking, Marcus had called it.
More like trying to put petticoats on a swallow. And as
for shoes— More than one Sunday, seeing the little girl
neat and starched, Narcissa had congratulated herself on
achieving the impossible, only to spy a bare toe curling
from beneath the long skirts. She moved to stand behind
the girls at the fence as the first wagon stopped. She
wanted no misunderstanding about Helen Mar and Mary
Ann and Margaret. They were Whitman children, and

she would allow no thoughtless snobbery toward them.

The Cayuse who had gone to meet the train trailed the wagons like a dark shadow. The ones left in camp gathered at the mission to watch silently. They came to count the travelers, she knew; counted and added and subtracted the food and land these people would take from what they had left.

Narcissa held the girls back, but in the end she was the one who could not hold back. When the women dismounted, bonneted and gloved, it was like seeing her family gathering for some holiday; she ran to the nearest and embraced her as if she were Jane come after all this time.

"Mrs. Whitman," the woman wept, "you don't know how I've looked to this day—"

—but I do know! I've waited on both sides of this day; waited to get here and waited for you to come—

The children, caught up in the excitement, were running and shouting. Narcissa gave up all attempt at order. It was a moment of pure happiness. What was the harm in letting the heart take over?

She led the women to the house, knowing their eagerness to be inside walls again. Marcus had tables set up in the yard to serve refreshments. They'd stored melons in buckets of water in the store room all day to cool them. The men were carving the big red wedges loose and stacking them on platters.

As Narcissa showed the women through the house she kept an uneasy eye on the preparations through the windows. Marcus was inclined to be too generous. She'd die of embarrassment if they ran short of ripe melons, this first time people stopped.

She was bringing the last guests to the tables when Marcus sent William to the patch for more. "Be careful not to get the ones we've doctored."

174

She noticed the quick curiosity in Dr. White's manner. "What's that?"

And Marcus explained too much. "It's the only way we can keep the indians from stealing the melons. We dope a few big ones with calomel. They always go for the big ones. Makes them sick without hurting them, and they make a wide path around the patch for the rest of the summer."

Dr. White hadn't said anything, but Narcissa was uncomfortable that he'd heard that.

She was undressing for bed, so tired she could hardly take the pins from her hair, when Marcus came in from settling the travelers in the east meadow.

"'Cissa, you'd better read this." His face heavy— His voice heavy— "It's from David Greene."

The letter was to the point. In view of the trouble in the Oregon missions, the Spaldings were relieved of their appointment and ordered back to the States. She and Marcus were ordered to remove to Tshimakain . . . .

"But we can't go to Tshimakain! Who"ll look after Waiilatpu?"

Marcus' voice was carefully blank now. "Lapwai and Waiilatpu are to be closed."

—to receive this news today of all days, when Marcus' faith was finally proved—

"*Why,* Marcus?"

"Those letters they've written about Henry. Walker and Eells are going to be all-fired disappointed when they find that after all their trouble to get rid of Henry, they're going to be stuck with me."

"But those letters were written two years ago. Since William's withdrawn everything is going fine."

"The Board doesn't know anything except what the letters said, though."

"They wouldn't want us to leave here now, when everything's beginning to work out—"

"I've sent Compo to meet Henry; if he misses the Lapwai party he's to go on to Tshimakain. I want everyone to know what they've done with their tattling."

Dinner next day was an ordeal, with special guests from the train there, and their minds and hearts full of the orders from the Board. They'd hardly had a chance to talk about it, with the house full of strangers. These settlers would be moving to the Willamette after a rest. They didn't dare talk, for fear the news would leak out to the Methodists. They suffered and worried privately, talking in snatches broken off in mid-word when anyone approached.

Narcissa had the impression Dr. White knew of their trouble, in spite of their secrecy. He had the relaxed manner of one who eases his way through life by personal charm, but when others were talking he watched Marcus and there were questions in his eyes, as if he recognized a man under pressure.

She would have enjoyed his company any other time. She couldn't help wondering if the rumors they'd heard were true. Marcus had judged him well-qualified even before White's trouble with Jason Lee. He didn't put much store in stories of White's drinking and his involvement with women patients.

The Doctor was a fine-boned man, clean shaven except for the small moustache that followed the line of his upper lip. And many a girl must have envied those lashes. His eyes were clear and light, and seemed to see farther into a person than was comfortable, but there was tolerance in them, she thought. Sometimes as he listened his mouth would drift into a wistful smiling that made him look much younger than he was.

If there'd been trouble with his women patients it seemed likely they might have started it. Whatever had

176

happened, Jason Lee had sent Dr. White on his way last year. Still he must have impressed someone in Washington; he carried an appointment as Agent for Indian Affairs in Oregon Territory. And he'd succeeded in leading the eighty-three settler wagons across the continent with little trouble.

It was late the second evening before Henry and Eliza arrived. They got the children fed and into bed while Marcus led Henry aside and had him read the letter. By the time she and Eliza joined them they had gone through the same hopeless arguments she and Marcus had covered the night before.

"What can we do?" Henry's uncertainty was somehow more unnerving than the news itself. Narcissa couldn't remember him ever asking that question before.

"We have to inform the Board that the situation has changed completely since those letters were written."

Henry bit at his lower lip. "Even if we can get a letter on the HBC ship—"

"A letter won't do! They can pass over a letter. I have to go in person. If we leave here the Catholics will take over before the dust settles. McLaughlin will be here helping us pack if he hears we're pulling out. The settlers will slow down to a trickle if they can't get supplies here to get on down river."

"It'll be next fall at the earliest before you can get to the States, and another year before you get back. Who'll take care of things here if you're away two years?"

Narcissa hadn't even thought of Marcus going East, and it seemed settled already. She should have thought of it. Of course he would go back and defend his mission. But she'd be here alone.

Marcus paced, ruffling his hair as he went round and round the table. "There's three men asked me already about hiring on for the winter."

"But it will take too long," Henry insisted. "If they cut off our credit how will we live?"

"It'll take six months at least to close out the missions. I intend to be in New York before then to stop them."

'You can't get across the mountains until the snow melts next spring."

"I can if I cross before it comes down this fall. If I leave here tomorrow I can catch the HBC Fall Express to Fort Hall. They ride hard. I'll have a good chance to get through South Pass before it's snowed in. After that it's just steady riding to St. Louis."

—but did *Marcus* have to be the one? Henry had been ordered back. Why couldn't he make the trip and explain? But no, Henry couldn't do that. He would seem to be pleading for himself. Marcus could plead for all of them.

Henry kept his eyes on the floor. "You haven't got half a chance of making it through the Rockies before winter—"

"Well I'm going to try, Henry, if it's only a third of a chance. Somebody's got to get back there. I'm willing to do it, and no one's going to argue me out of it."

Henry stood up slowly. "All right, I'll see that everything's settled for winter before I go back to Lapwai. But I think you should wait until we hear from Tshimakain if you can. A matter of this importance should bear signatures of consent from all of us."

"I suppose so—" Marcus conceded. "It'll take me a day to get ready. They may be here by then."

"You can't go by yourself, Marcus."

He frowned; nodded. "There's a guide came with the train might be willing."

The morning Henry left for Lapwai Narcissa waited on the porch while he went to bring his horse around. It was still dark. Eliza and the children had returned to Lapwai days before; Henry had stayed on to get the settlers started down river. Now he was leaving too.

She blinked in the lantern light as if it were the sun stinging her eyes. She couldn't seem to clear her mind. She'd made breakfast for Henry with her ears ringing, hardly able to hear his last minute instructions. She had slept hardly at all since the train arrived. The commotion had been constant, the yard and house alive all day with people coming and going, asking questions. She'd not gone to bed at all the night Marcus left. He had tried to get her to sleep but she wouldn't leave him.

"We'll be apart long enough, Marcus. I won't waste what time we have now."

He and Asa Lovejoy had left before dawn a week ago. She'd stayed in the yard long after the horses, with Trapper trotting along beside them, had blended into the darkness.

Since then she'd been busy with letters to send to the valley and with getting Carrie Munger ready to leave again. Carrie hadn't wanted to go. "I get the feeling like it ain't no use, Mrs. Whitman. Asy's going to die. I know it. It might as well be right here."

"If you give up now you'll never get home, Carrie. You can travel to the valley with these people and catch the HBC ship when it sails. Once he's back with his family Asa may improve." She hoped that was not a lie. And if it were, Carrie would be better off with her family than out here with strangers.

"I'll go if you say so," the girl said, "but it won't be any better."

The Mungers had gone with the settlers the day before. Henry would soon be on his way. Today she'd get a chance to start cleaning up.

She heard the horse's clopping in the dark. One thing you could say for Henry, he didn't waste time. He appeared in front of her, the light from his lantern giving his eyes a blind look like the eyes of a statue. He wavered there; she tried to concentrate on what he was saying—

"You'll be all right," he said from far away, "and I'll come as often as I can. Geiger is a good man. I've sent word to Rogers to see if he'll come back up here for the winter. Compo and his family will move down from the mill in a few days. You have nothing to fear, but in case of trouble, send word to McKinley. I'll stop there and leave word with him that you're alone."

She nodded and the movement sent Henry dancing like a shadow in a fire. If he didn't go on and let her get back to bed she'd fall. But he stood there for what seemed like hours; reached out to press her hand; finally climbed into the saddle and rode away.

She walked unsteadily to her room and lay down in her clothes. Her mind was filled with a rushing sound, like water falling somewhere—

—and in that sound she seemed to hear Henry as he turned away saying, "Bless you, Narcissa."

—Henry had never called her Narcissa. Not even that time at the Seminary. He'd called her Miss Prentice, even that night.

Mr. Geiger was a plain, silent man who seemed lost inside his clothes. He took his meals at the house, and slept in the room the Mungers had used. Narcissa was so bone tired she hadn't even the strength to miss Marcus, except at dusk when everything grew quiet and the girls were in bed and she felt the night coming down. Then his absence cut sharp; then she was cold no matter how high the fire blazed. The house was too big; too empty.

On Sunday Mr. Geiger came to breakfast wearing a wrinkled white shirt and a string necktie. She felt uneasiness about him. When the girls went to freshen up for services he said, "Mrs. Whitman, is they always this many indians wandering around the place?"

She went to the window; saw groups of Cayuse lounging near the barn, talking together, watching the house. "It isn't unusual for them to gather like this," she said. "They're probably looking for things the settlers threw away."

"At night too? I heard them moving around in the dark. Trouble is, I can't tell if anything's missing. Would you know what to look for?"

"I'm not sure."

"We'd best take a look."

There were Cayuse on the north and east of the house too. They seemed not to notice as she walked by with Mr. Geiger. She couldn't tell if things were missing. "We've sold so much to the train it's hard to know."

"Think I'll sit up tonight and watch things," he said carefully.

More Cayuse had come while they were in the sheds. As they walked back to the house Narcissa felt their eyes, although they seemed to ignore the two of them. She bit hard on nothing. They were putting her to the test. They knew Marcus was gone; knew Henry had gone—

And she had to do something to show she was not afraid. "The best thing is to try to pull their attention from whatever they have on their minds," she said, trying to keep her voice steady.

He nodded.

"Do you play a musical instrument, Mr. Geiger?"

"Harmonica," he said. "Jew's harp."

"Do you have them with you?"

"You mind me asking what you're thinking, Mam? I doubt I can keep their minds off mischief with a Jew's harp."

"I'm going to hold Services, Mr. Geiger. They always come for Services when Marcus is here. I'm going to pretend that's why they're here this morning. Maybe I can make them think so, too, before it's over."

"I'll be right back."

With the girls trailing they walked out to the east flat. She saw a few of her school girls in the crowd; maybe she could get them singing—

But the indians didn't follow them to the meadow. They stayed in their little groups and watched from the mission grounds. She felt naked as she covered the box and laid her Bible there.

Mr. Geiger smoothed his harmonica. "We gonna wait for them?"

Should she send word that Services were starting? Marcus never did. They could start the singing. That should bring them closer. But then what? If Henry was here preaching they'd come fast enough. The Indians admired a man who thundered and raised his fists and proclaimed the power of God. They would only laugh at a woman—

"Mr. Geiger," she looked at him quickly, "could you preach a sermon?"

He fumbled with his mouth organ and cleared his throat, blinking. "Well, now, Mrs. Whitman, that's not in my line. It takes a special calling to deliver a good sermon."

"They'll laugh at me if I try it," she said, "but they might listen to you. I've seen them sit for hours while Mr. Spalding preached. He's a strong preacher though; he uses his voice and his arms."

He looked at her helplessly. "I know what you're saying, Mam, but truly I don't know if I can do it. I ain't a talking man."

"Could you read something?"

He watched the indians beginning to move in a body out onto the meadow. "I could *try* mighty hard, if you

182

think I should."

"Let's begin the singing then. Do you know *Faith of Our Fathers?*"

He whacked the harmonica against his palm.

"Then play it loud."

The girls sat cross-legged on the grass, their faces sober. There was no use trying to fool them; these children had been raised on trouble and were watching her intently, awaiting her signals.

"Girls, sing out," she ordered. "Sing loud." She nodded to Mr. Geiger.

He cradled the harmonica at his mouth, bent over, as gently as he would have held a kitten. The music seemed to sparkle on the frosty air. They sang the first verse and started the second, but the girls had forgotten the words. "Sing louder," she sang to the music, and they shouted the words they knew.

A few of the Cayuse were edging out now: women and young children; some old men in ragged coats and blankets.

"Once more!" she cried, hoping they could finish. Helen Mar was out of breath. She felt her own voice weakening. But she sang! She sang!

And while she sang she scanned the Psalms with frantic purpose. One of the warlike ones would have to do.

> *Why boastest thou thyself in mischief, oh*
> *mighty man? . . . Save me oh God, by Thy*
> *name, and judge me by Thy strength. Be*
> *merciful unto me, oh God, be merciful*
> *unto me . . . . Deliver me from mine enemies—*

It would have to do. The center of the crowd was wavering—breaking—following the first brave ones. If Mr. Geiger could hold them with a sermon, this might work—

A troop of young braves sat their ponies near the fence, gesturing angrily after the advancing crowd. She motioned to Mr. Geiger. "Number fifty-nine," she breathed, "and read it loud."

She sat down, tucking her skirts under her; they'd all catch their deaths from sitting on the soggy ground, but they'd better have colds than indians threatening.

Mr. Geiger was mumbling the first lines to himself, trying out the phrases.

"Mr. Geiger! Begin!"

And as if steeling himself to meet some terrible fate, he threw his head back.

Deliver me from mine enemies, oh God; defend
me from them that rise against me. Deliver me
from the workers of iniquity, and save me from
the bloody men.

He glanced at her. She nodded encouragement and he continued:

For lo, they lie in wait for my soul . . .
awake to help me . . . awake to visit all the
heathen.

He glared at the Cayuse sitting their horses across the field; threw his arms up suddenly, held them there, reading the next lines under his breath. Mary Ann's eyes danced.

"Don't you dare laugh, Mary Ann Bridger! I'll spank you hard!" And the girls, alert to danger, went still as mice.

They return at evening. They make a noise
like a dog—

The young braves rode away from the fence toward them. Mr. Geiger raised his voice. "Like a dog—" he repeated. he began to pace, grabbing the words from the page as he could,

Because of His strength will I wait on thee;

184

for God is my defence—
The seated indians rustled around to stare at the horse-
men bearing down on them. Narcissa's breath caught—
held. Not even these young hotheads would ride down
their own people!

At the last minute they split around the seated indians;
pounded up to the altar box; reined up short, shaking
their fists at Geiger and muttering.

But Mr. Geiger was a man transformed; caught up in
his own eloquence. He returned the fist-shaking, bel-
lowing:
> *—scatter them with Thy power; bring them
> down, O Lord of our shield.*

The young men crowded their horses forward. Geiger
did not give ground.
> *Consume them with wrath; consume them, that
> they may be not! And let them know . . . .*

He stumbled; his eyes searched the page frantically and
flicked back to the indians;
> *And let them know God ruleth . . . unto
> the ends of the earth!*

And he began walking straight toward the riders.
"Now git!" he roared. "Git out of here and let us finish
our Services in peace!"

Narcissa stared, not believing what she witnessed. He
was an avenger; a rabbit turned fierce as a lion, facing
these savages down. And winning. For they were backing
their horses step by step; they whirled and raced for the
river, leaping the fences and pounding pell mell across
the fields.

Mr. Geiger came back to the box; seemed to sag all at
once. He dropped to his knees with a thud. "Let us pray."

Automatically she began the ritual, "*Our Father, which
art in heaven—*" Mr. Geiger's voice groped to catch up;
raced ahead. They ended the prayer breathless.

Narcissa stood up then, and the girls, too. Behind her she heard the indians rising. She went to Mr. Geiger.

He looked up at her. "Are they gone, Mam?"

"Yes."

He got to his feet then like a bundle of old clothes picking itself up from a corner. He watched the retreating indians. His breath blew out of him in a loud sigh. "Did I do all right?"

Narcissa was exhausted by the morning's tension. Dinner over, she went to her room for a nap, warning the girls not to go outside. It was a day to be careful.

At dusk the yard was deserted. She and the girls went to gather eggs and feed the chickens. They found Mr. Geiger sitting in the shed, his rifle beside him.

"You think they're coming back, Mr. Geiger?"

He didn't look away from the river. "I got this scary feeling like they might try to sneak over here after it's dark."

"Come get something to eat while it's still light."

"I'm not hungry, thank you Mam."

A shiver dusted her arms. Mr. Geiger seemed so inadequate to be standing off Umtippe's warriors by himself.

"Shall I bring you something?"

"No, Mam. Just you take the young ladies back inside. It's too cold for them out here."

As she left the shed she said softly, "Be careful, Mr. Geiger."

"Don't worry, Mam. If they start coming tonight I'll just preach at them. That'll scatter them fast enough."

She sat reading after the girls were asleep. Her nap had taken the edge off her weariness, leaving her nervous, unsettled. Her attention wandered. She tried to write to Marcus but her mind was alert for the sound of indians. If Trapper was here he'd set up a growl like a coyote the minute an indian crossed the creek.

Her eyes grew heavy as the time dragged by but she sat on in the kitchen. Mr. Geiger might need help . . . .

. . . she jerked awake, roused by a heavy knocking. She had fallen asleep at the table. The room rocked as she got to her feet. The knocking sounded again, louder—

"Just a minute, Mr. Geiger," she called. The bar was heavy. She worked at it; lifted it—

The stench struck her the moment the door cracked. She crowded against it, trying to replace the bar. But she hadn't the strength. The smell of indian clogged her throat like burning oil; the door opened against her weight. A hand slipped through; a brown muscled arm was thrust into the opening and she slid backward on the painted floor, pushing and screaming—

—and was thrown back violently as the door crashed open; found breath to scream once, "Mr. Geiger!" staggered, trying to run, trying to escape that savage—that *thing*—with his eyes glinting in the dim light, his mouth showing white teeth opened as if to bite.

She flung herself toward the parlor door and hit the wall. Immediately the indian smell was around her—over her—like a blanket. Her face was mashed against a sweaty shoulder; she was against the wall with the hot weight of that monstrous body upon her—

The smell of the naked skin stung her nose. *I can't stand this— I can't stand this—* She struggled to twist her face free; pushed and scratched and fought, but could not move, held by an arm like lead across her and the strength of that swollen body thrusting—thrusting— A rough hand tore at her skirts; tore at her petticoats; flung her finally backwards across the table, pain bolting from her back to send her whirling upward, upward on a pattern of bursting light . . . .

She tried to breathe and seemed to be swallowing air in chunks; light came back to her in blocks: fading— brightening—fading— She was on the floor, a shadow looming over her. Screams formed in her throat and fought with her breathing—

"Just lay there a minute till your breath comes back, Mam."

It was Mr. Geiger. She sat up. The room whirled but she held herself upright and it quit its drifting and she could see others there.

"You girls get back to bed," she whispered. They weren't to know what happened— Almost happened—

But Helen Mar threw herself on her lap and held on around her neck. Mary Ann and Margaret crowded against her too, and Margaret kept asking in a scared, high voice, "Are you all right, Mother? Are you all right?"

She managed to quiet them. She sat on a stool and smoothed her hair and slowed her breathing. "Get in my bed, girls. You can all sleep with me tonight."

They went unwillingly, looking back nervously.

"I'll be right there," she promised, "after I talk with Mr. Geiger."

His face was grim. "Speaking blunt, Mam, I got here just in time. I guess I dozed off, it being so still; but all of a sudden I come awake with this prickling feeling at the back of my neck, and I seen light blazing out through the door. I made it here in about three jumps. And there he was—" he gulped. "I didn't dare shoot; I just swung out and cracked him one on the back of the head, enough to send him staggering out the door."

She was swept by a shuddering reaction; her teeth chattering, her hands shaking. She was too weak to sit on the stool—too weak to stand—

"Mam, you able to lock this door behind me and get to bed?"

She managed to nod.

"You do it. I'm going out, and you ain't to open that door for nobody till you see it's me or someone you know for sure. Understand?"

She managed to get to her bed; and lay shivering with her arms stretched over the children. Margaret woke her. "Mother, someone is knocking."

She stumbled to the kitchen window to see Mr. Geiger nodding consent for her to open the door. He got a fire burning and set water to heating. "I sent word to the Fort," he told her.

Mr. McKinley came with three of his men. He talked with Mr. Geiger before coming to the house. Standing, then, he announced gruffly, "Get your things ready. I'm moving you and your family back to Walla Walla."

"I'm not sure I can make the trip," she said, still weak— still sick—

"Ye canna stay here!" His eyes were fierce under the heavy brows.

"You believe there'll be more trouble?"

"That I canna say," he said. "But I'm certain there'll be trouble if the Doctor returns and finds I've let something happen to ye. So gather whatever ye'll be needing. We'll leave i' the morning."

There was so much to be taken care of before they could leave—

"I've taken the liberty of puttin' Mr. Geiger i' charge here. And I've suggested to Mr. Compo that he move down here at once, and the young man wi' him. There'll be three good men to handle matters."

Narcissa huddled with the girls in the back of the wagon covered with ponchos to shut out the drizzle blowing ahead of the wind. Their clothes were packed around the sides of the wagon box; everything else was left behind.

She was burning with fever by the time they reached the Fort. Mrs. McKinley and her daughter waited on the gallery. They helped her to bed, and she lay in the little room that had been Rogers' when he was ill, and shivered in the cold, and tossed with the fever, and cried weakly for Marcus.

—a year, at least, before he would return—

1843

The world dripped dismally as Narcissa picked her way along the muddy trail bordering the river. A cold wind was stripping leaves from the trees as an angry child might, in fits and starts. Across the meadow she could see the Methodist mission buildings, solid and prosperous. Mrs. Lee would be worrying, thinking it a duty to keep her in sight every waking minute for fear she would tire herself. Ever since Marcus left she'd been at the mercy of kind-hearted people who worried about her. Sometimes she had to get off by herself, even if only to sit beside a muddy river swirling and pounding from nowhere to nowhere.

A year of living in other people's homes had sharpened her need for privacy needle fine. Whether or not she heard from Marcus she was determined to leave for Waii-latpu within the week. He would be coming any day now, or he would not be coming at all. And if she were compelled to spend another winter alone, it would be in her own home, not in some other woman's. She sat on a boulder, careless of her skirts, and watched the tumbling water. The Willamette rolled heavily, chocolate brown, swelling and dipping, growling a reminder that once winter settled in it would be impossible for her to get back to Waiilatpu before spring.

There was always a river, it seemed, keeping her from what she wanted. From the day she'd left Steuben County she'd been plagued by rivers. She thought back seven years, when she'd stood on the banks of the Missouri in the rain, bored with waiting for the trip to begin; tired of Henry and Eliza; thinking that if she could just get across that river, everything wonderful would come to her. Just for crossing that river . . . .

It hadn't occurred to her that those unpleasant days at Liberty while they waited for the DIANA would be typical of the rest of the journey. She'd supposed that the crowding, the minimal privacy, the all-but-intolerable lack of opportunity to be alone with Marcus, were inconveniences that would somehow straighten out once the main journey got underway.

She pictured herself as she was then, standing on the old tree roots on the muddy bank of the river day after day, staring down the channel and *willing* the boat to be there. As if she could cause it to appear by the intensity of her desire to be gone from the wretched place; done with the rain and the discomfort and the forced intimacy compelled by their sharing the tent with Henry and Eliza. But she had never sighted the steamer.

Her father had called St. Louis the jumping-off place for nowhere. He hadn't known about Liberty Landing. They'd been warned by the man in the Fur Company office what to expect. He was only trying to be helpful when he urged them to catch the steamer readying to leave then, instead of making the trip cross country in the spring mud. He was obviously thinking of Eliza and herself. He'd had no way of knowing that the boat that was to pick them up at Liberty would be delayed, and that they would go cross country from Liberty whether or not they chose to.

Nor did he know that Martha Ann Satterlee would die there while they waited. None of them could have known that although, looking back, she realized Marcus must have suspected. Even their separations later along the trail were foretold by having to split the party, some of them staying behind with the sick woman, the rest going ahead in an effort to persuade the caravan to wait for them.

She'd been sick of it long before they traveled on: the whiny women and the moldy, crowded tent; the muddy campground and William's complaints. Somehow they'd pushed ahead and caught the fur brigade, mostly because of her insistence they must not go back to face the "I told you so" of her father, and from townspeople who saw her as thinking she was too special for the common lot of them.

She sighed, remembering all the turning points. What would have happened if, instead of pushing forward to catch Fitzpatrick's train, they'd gone back home from Liberty? Would they have taken a second chance to come this way? Would they be raising a child in some easten town—a living child of their own?

Well, she'd crossed the Missouri and a hundred rivers since, and found problems waiting on the other side of every one of them.

"Mrs. Whitman—"

She hadn't been able to sneak away after all. Jason Lee came riding along the path, the sound of his approach blotted up by the soft ground and the noisy river.

"You've a message from the Doctor; a rider just came from Vancouver." The letter was new looking. Marcus was home then; if it had traveled from back east the trip would be showing on the outside.

She opened it too fast, tearing one corner. "He's meeting me at the *dalles,* she told him, reading. "I'll have to make arrangements at once."

"I'm traveling to Wascopum early next week. We'll send him word."

She didn't want to wait a week before starting home! She hadn't seen Marcus in over a year— but she had no choice. There wouldn't be an earlier passage.

They started the trip under threatening skies which withheld rain until they portaged the *cascades*. There the storm flailed them; the wind howled down the gorge of the Columbia in gale force, knocking them about on the slippery rocks and whipping spray over them in sheets.

In the boat again she went over all she had to tell Marcus. The year had seemed unending, living it; it would take days of talking to make up for the separation.

She'd had just the two letters. One, from St. Louis, told of the terrible snows in the mountains; how they'd struggled through arm-high drifts for days and come out on the California trail near Taos, in Mexico. And that they'd had to kill Trapper.

The other was written from her parents' home, a short page saying the Mission Board had reacted favorably to Marcus' report, and that he was bringing his nephew Perrin back with him. At fourteen, Perri would be a help. And Marcus would need plenty of help. Waiilatpu had looked tacky when she was home in the spring. The Cayuse had been rooting around the place like scavengers ever since he left. It was a miracle they hadn't destroyed everything after the way Dr. White had come pounding back up river with that band of volunteers to investigate the attack on her . . . .

He'd arrived at the *dalles* the same afternoon they brought her to the mission there. She was tired of talking about the incident; ready to put it out of her thoughts— *having* to put it out of mind or go crazy thinking about it.

Dr. White didn't know beans about the Cayuse. They were like children when they were caught in trouble; they wanted it forgotten as soon as possible, afraid vengeance would fall on the tribe as well as the guilty ones. Now White was planning to gallop into their camp like thunder and threaten Umtippe's people with frightening punishment.

"It was only one man, Dr. White," she insisted. "Don't stir up the whole tribe over it." She knew if she wanted to see her home again the matter must be dropped.

He was standing, jealous of the time spent talking. "But we can't ignore incidents like this! All the tribes are restless; we need an example. The only thing that keeps them under control is fear of punishment."

—but it was *her* home that would be destroyed if he roused the Cayuse; *Marcus'* work that would be wiped out—

"Threatening them may make it worse."

"I know we won't get the guilty man. Tamsuky will never admit it—if it was Tamsuky. I'm hoping the Cayuse are frightened enough to sign the laws the Nez Perce have adopted. I've called a meeting of the Cayuse chiefs. If I can get the older ones on my side they may be able to influence the younger ones to see reason."

Thinking of Umtippe and Tamahas and Yellow Serpent— angry, vengeful, all of them—she doubted his success. Stikus and Tilhoukaikt would go along with him, but their camps were small; and the excitable, war-hungry braves followed the other chiefs.

If she had been able to travel she would have gone with him and talked with Young Chief of the Walla Walla's, who had taken Lakit for one of his wives. She had not been able to convince Dr. White; he was like a hound after rabbits.

"I'll send you word of the outcome." At the door he

stopped for a moment. "I almost forgot. One of my deputies would like to see you if you're well enough."

"Do I know him?"

Dr. White smiled. "I gathered so from the way Mr. Rogers spoke of you."

They'd heard nothing at all of Cornelius since he and Maria had left Walla Walla. They would be married now; probably there was a child on the way. Another life of unhappiness begun. But maybe it would not be so for Rogers' child. The mixed blood children carried the most important names of the Territory. It was possible they would be absorbed into the settlers' families and their descendents not realize—

But would it be right? How could she ever be certain?

He hesitated in the doorway. He was different, she saw at once. He'd found himself, whatever road he'd taken; he had the look now of a man who knew where he was going.

"Have things worked out for you, Cornelius?"

"Yes," he said. "But not the way I thought." A look in his eyes sent a warning to her not to question.

"You're married now."

"About a month ago."

Why should it shock her so to hear him say this? She had known his intentions.

"How is Maria?"

"She's at Nisqually; married to a trapper from up there."

They faced each other over a long silence. "It's best, Cornelius," she said finally. "I'm sure you've made the right decision."

His mouth twitched. "Don't give me false credit, Mam. It wasn't me decided it. Maria wouldn't marry me after all."

Her sense of relief vanished. It wasn't finished for him

at all! Perhaps it would never be finished for him.

"Does your wife know about Maria?"

"Not from me. I guess her family heard the stories going around; it's all anybody talked about for weeks. But I figure it's done with; part of my life that doesn't concern Satira."

"What have you done since you left Waiilatpu?"

"I worked the summer for Lieutenant Wilkes, interpreting. Since me and Satira is married, I've been helping at the Methodist mission. Her father is the preacher, Dr. Leslie. They let me go off to come with Agent White." He stumbled. "If I'd only known there was real danger I'd have come when Spalding sent for me. The way I figured, it was just another trick to get me back up there."

His confession touched her deeply. It bothered her that he had been saved by default. But Maria had recognized the truth of the matter, and she found some comfort in that. It seemed some kind of proof that what they'd been doing these past years had not been total failure.

In February she received news that Cornelius Rogers and his bride drowned in an accident at the falls of the Willamette. She brooded for days after. Just as Cornelius managed to get his life in some reasonable order, he had to die! There was no security in this voracious land except what a person could find within himself. They all lived here at the whim of nature.

On Christmas day Dr. White reported the Cayuse had refused to support the Nez Perce laws; their mood was growing uglier all the time. Narcissa was disappointed to tears. The Perkins and the Lees were kind to her, but she had been away from her home too long. The children were waiting at Walla Walla. She had the feeling that if she didn't get the family together again soon they would be scattered forever.

But Dr. White vetoed any notion of her returning alone to the mission. "The Cayuse are in a turmoil because the Nez Perce signed the laws. They fear being crowded off their lands. They are convinced for some reason that Dr. Whitman went east to bring back an army to destroy them."

"They've accused us of wanting to run them off for years."

"They're desperate now. You must believe me when I say it's out of the question for you to go back there by yourself."

"But I won't be there by myself! I'll have the children. Mr. Geiger and the Littlejohns are there. And the Compos."

"Mrs. Whitman, there's been more violence you don't know about. Three days before I got to Waiilatpu they burned the grist mill. Geiger and Littlejohn couldn't hold them off. The men have sent their families to Lapwai." He took her hands, his eyes sad, his mouth grim. "Promise me you won't try to go back alone."

And she had agreed, with reluctance.

Letters from Waiilatpu reported the indians were still convinced Marcus was returning with an avenging army. The missionaries at the *dalles* grew panicy as the news spread. The Reverend Perkins wrote to Dr. White begging him to do everything possible to calm the fears of the indians.

By April the tension was wire-tight. Mr. Geiger wrote the indians were gathering at Waiilatpu—more than two thousand, he'd guess, already—for the meeting with Dr. White. Rumor had it the Nez Perce were being drawn over to the side of the Cayuse. Word came that a young Nez Perce chief had been sent to buffalo country east of Fort Hall to persuade the tribes there to cut off the Whitman party.

Every passing traveler was bombarded with questions about the indian situation. Narcissa finally stopped listening to the talk. She had made up her mind to go back to Waiilatpu when the weather cleared. She didn't want to know of trouble that might prevent her going.

The spring express for Montreal carried encouraging news. The Nez Perce had sent a delegation to Dr. McLaughlin to discuss the imagined war the whites were planning against them. The Governor had told them bluntly that he did not believe the Americans were making such a war. His word was accepted where others' were not and the tension eased off.

Spring bloomed early. Narcissa made arrangements to go home, refusing to listen to objections. She stopped overnight at Walla Walla, and went on the next day to Waiilatpu, taking the girls with her. She found no tension at the mission. Peace seemed to have arrived with the spring sunshine. Mr. Geiger had cleaned up most signs of last winter's depredations. He was already plowing, and to her surprise there were a few Cayuse cultivating plots. But only a few.

Now more than ever she doubted the wisdom of the indian meeting. She had discussed it with Mr. McKinley. "The Cayuse are quiet now. Can't you make Dr. White understand it would be best to leave them alone until Marcus gets back?"

"It's ma understandin' McLaughlin has strongly advised the Doctor against such a meeting already."

But Dr. White appeared at Waiilatpu early in May, and there seemed little point in trying to talk him out of his plans. He and his party went on to Lapwai, to return a week later with five hundred Nez Perce. The meeting would be held. There seemed no reason to refuse when he asked her to represent Marcus.

It was a bright day, with clouds fluffing the sky in great mounds. She rode with Dr. White and McKinley and Thomas McKay, and the two Methodist missionaries. Trailing them like a magnificent comet's tail were the Nez Perce in ceremonial clothes; the chiefs splendid in shoulder capes encrusted with buttons and quills, war bonnets streaming feathers down their backs. Their lances rippled with ribbons. Copper discs hung around their necks reflected the sun in dazzling flashes. Narcissa's apprehension eased a little when she recognized Old Joseph at the head of the band. He was a man of gentleness, of honor; he would do everything he could to soothe the unruly ones among the Cayuse and the Walla Wallas.

For five exhausting days then, the indians debated Dr. White's laws under the cottonwoods near Umtippe's camp. The Chiefs listened with concentration while Dr. White read the eleven laws; leaned forward as each was interpreted by Thomas McKay. They then talked among themselves before questioning the doctor. Yellow Serpent was the chosen voice.

"And are these laws from heaven?" he demanded.

Dr. White nodded emphatically. "Laws of all civilized countries have God's approval."

Yellow Serpent, nodding, spoke in Cayuse, with Thomas McKay interpreting, softly, slowly, "My heart is glad that this is so, since many of my people are angry when I have had them whipped for crime, saying God would send me to hell for it. Now in these laws, approved by God, half the crimes are punished by whipping. I am happy knowing whipping is pleasing to God."

Narcissa looked quickly to Dr. White. This wasn't the intent of these laws! But the agent made no rebuttal, and she hadn't the courage to interrupt.

Umtippe rose next, black eyes defiant. "You have said the laws will be the same for white and indian," he challenged. "Now! If indian steals, he will be lashed." His mouth worked in anger. "Tell me! If white man steals, will he be lashed also?"

Dr. White's eyes veered from the speaker. "The laws say the whites who break them will be punished. Is there a vote?"

A deep bass hum of disapproval rose from the Cayuse like a cloud. Thomas McKay stood with the lithe grace she remembered from the trail, and spoke softly, in Cayuse first, then in English. "I have been a wanderer through your country for many years. I have mingled with you in bloody war and profound peace; and I have stood in your midst surrounded by plenty, and suffered with you in seasons of scarcity. You know me. I come now at the call of the great chief, the chief of all the whites as well as the indians, whose children are as numerous as the stars in the heavens. Will you hear and be advised? You will. Surely you will hear. These are good and just laws, and will help prevent trouble for you all. Hear them and adopt them and live in peace and security."

He sat down in a movement smooth as water flowing, and McKinley, face bristly as a thistle, lumbered to his feet, growling above the soft flow of McKay's interpretation, "Ye ken, all o' ye, thot I've lived among ye for some years. We've had nae trouble to speak of; and the laws the doctor wishes ye to adopt will keep it thot way. I know this much: Boston, French, and King George all think as one on this matter; and the Cayuse and Walla Wallas should be one with the Nez Perce, who've already voted to accept."

And Dr. White took his turn again. "The laws are good laws. They will benefit all of you; the indians will feel their protection as well as the whites—" He waited then, hoping for the vote.

But an ancient chief rose from among the Nez Perce.

Red Bear—Bloody Chief—heavy Sioux bonnet almost hiding his wrinkled face; gray braids looping beneath the feathers. "I speak today; tomorrow perhaps, I die. I am the oldest chief of the Nez Perce. I was the high chief when the white brothers Lewis and Clark visited me and honored me with their friendship. They told me it was better to be at peace; they gave me flag of truce; I have never again fought the white man. They talked of this day; the Nez Perce have long looked to it and prepared for it by sending three of our sons to Red River school to be ready. We have chosen one of them as our high chief under these laws. If the Nez Perce can do this thing with honor, the same can be done by the Cayuse and Walla Wallas. Now. I can say no more. I am quickly tired. I ask you to think and remember the days of war. Now we can know peace and order."

The Cayuse were impressed by Bloody Chief's words. Quickly, two more Nez Perce chiefs spoke for the laws. And just before the vote Old Joseph rose and urged the Cayuse in strongest terms to accept them. When all had finished the vote was called again.

Dr. White gave them no time for reflection after a narrow victory. He proclaimed a feast for all, including the women, for which cows had been butchered and a cart loaded with wheat, salt, and corn.

Riding back to the house Dr. White said, with evident satisfaction, "Well. It took five days, but we got what we wanted. Now maybe they'll stay quiet for awhile."

"It's a domned good thing ye brought Joseph wi' ye or ye'd no hae put it through," McKinley said. "It was his votes carried th' day for ye. The Cayuse ain't any more in favor of them now than five days ago. Dinna forget that."

"They'll honor the signing, though?"

"Aye, as long as ye honor it yoursel'. But I'm telling ye, mon, th' first time some drunken clown kills a brave or rapes a woman, ye better be prepared to hang him high as a dead goose."

Both men insisted she go back to the Fort. "Ye're invitin' trouble by stayin' here by yoursel', woman," McKinley warned.

"I think the danger's past now. The Cayuse will soon be leaving for summer hunting."

"There's nothing to stop them coming back any time they please," Dr. White said impatiently.

"That paper is good just as long as Umtippe and Yellow Serpent want it to be; no longer," McKinley said, "And if ye've no regard for your own life ye might a least gi' a thought to the lassies. Are ye wantin' to see them murdered i' their beds because of your stubborness?"

"I'm not leaving." And she would say no more.

They might have avoided the argument. The infection that had plagued her since Alice's birth flared, aggravated by the days of hard travel; she woke in the night torn with pain, barely able to call Margaret. Dr. White gave her laudanum.

McKinley was waiting by her bed when she awoke. "I'll no mince words, Mam. Ye're gravely ill, and I'll not be takin' th' responsibility for lettin' ye die here. I'm takin' ye to Walla Walla and from there to Vancouver."

She shook her head weakly.

"And I'll no be swayed by woman's tears. Ye're in need of medical help, and ye canna get it closer than Vancouver. White's already on his way. We'll make ye a bed i' th' wagon, and I'll take ye down river mysel' i' th' boat. We're startin' at once."

"I won't leave the girls—"

"They're comin' to Walla Walla. I'll send them on to Vancouver by express next month. Now I'll listen to no more talk."

They made the nightmare trip down river in three days,

Mrs. McKinley caring for her in the boat; making broth for her in a cooking basket with rocks heated in an iron kettle in the end of the boat and thrown into the water in the woven pots to heat it to boiling.

The rocking motion sent sickness through her in thick waves; she cried when she was conscious, and didn't care. At the rapids, they tied her into the boat and let it ride the current; Mrs. McKinley rocking beside her; the river hurtling over them in choking swells, throwing the canoe into the cliffs and back to the other side of the narrow passage. At one terrifying rapids the ropes snapped. They were flung like a chip about the cauldron that boiled among the rocks until Mr. McKinley went into the water and fought the boat to the quiet water beyond the *chutes*.

Narcissa spent a month in the big bed at Vancouver, the days hardly more than the opening and closing of her eyes. Sometimes she would lift heavy lids to see Dr. McLaughlin's great white head bent over listening to her breathing. Other times she had glimpses of Mrs. McLaughlin rocking beside the bed, knitting.

She bribed pain to stay away by lying very still. The fat posters supported a pale yellow canopy and it shed a soft sunshine over her hands lying on the blanket. They were very thin. She wondered if her body was as thin as her hands.

One morning she cared enough to ask Dr. McLaughlin, "How many days have I been here?"

He smiled. "Over four weeks."

"You've been very kind—"

"You are a dear friend and I'm grateful I was able to help. My regret is that you did not come sooner. Dr. Barclay says this is a condition of long standing." He hesitated. "Does Dr. Whitman know?"

"He's had so much on his mind—" She looked away. "It

was a slight complaint. I thought it would go away."

"I shall see that Dr. Barclay writes a full report for him. It will be easier for him to keep an eye on you, knowing what we've dealt with here." He stood up, straightening her pillow. "Rest now."

The weather had warmed by the time she was able to walk about the Fort, reminded time after time of the weeks she'd spent there while Marcus explored for the mission site. Making her way to the great log gates through the busy courtyard, trying to sort out the mixture of accents from the trappers and traders and Hudson's Bay Company officials, she looked out over the river flats. The channel was broad and full now, carrying at the moment a native canoe, painted and carved, which reminded her of that grotesque vessel they'd seen on their first trip here.

The muddy road curving up from the river landing had not improved much in the years since she'd been here. She recalled having walked up the slope between Marcus and Pambrun, unsteady after days in the boat; past the rows of small houses fencing in a large painted building beyond a young orchard of apple trees, grown now and snowing blossoms on the wind.

She had first seen Dr. McLaughlin as he stepped into this same opening in the walls, larger than life against the courtyard activity; the height and strength of him of a size, surely, to control the wilderness he commanded. Flanked by his smaller companions, he'd seemed a titan in his elegant clothing. And he still presented a commanding appearance, with his silver hair and magnetic eyes, which changed color with his emotions.

The awe she had felt when he bowed over her hand as he greeted her had been replaced in the years since by respect—even affection. His unfailing courtesy and interest in their welfare in spite of philosophical and political difference of viewpoints spoke well for his character.

The courtyard had sounded like a pen full of guinea hens as they followed him past shops and stalls and people to his home. Narcissa turned to look at the governor's mansion now, trying to see it as she had seen it then—a miracle after all those months of wilderness empty of buildings except for the isolated forts. It had been the marigolds, she thought, that had made her catch her breath—

Inside, of course, it was heaven to see polished floors and painted walls and gleaming furniture again, reminding her of homes of friends and relatives on the other side of the continent. She recalled her first glimpse of Mrs. McLaughlin as she'd looked when the Governor presented her to them that day they arrived—a fascinating combination of primitive and sophisticate. As she was still, Narcissa thought now, still wearing silver bells on her house moccasins with her modish dresses.

She remembered the courtesy with which the Doctor had introduced his wife, his pride apparent when he made the introduction. And that had not changed, either—

She smiled, recalling her curiosity that Mrs. McLaughlin had not appeared at the dinner table that evening and her astonishment that this great man of unfailing consideration would subscribe to the common practice of banishing his native wife to the kitchen; and Eliza's indignation that this was indeed the case. Eliza's refusal to come to the table until the practice changed had not surprised her at the time. As for herself, she had looked forward to the evening meals; and she did now. You never knew who would be sitting beside you— a penniless trapper or one of the important men of the territory like Peter Ogden, Governor of New Caledonia.

She shouldn't have been surprised then, on coming

down for dinner that same evening, to see a priest standing with Dr. McLaughlin. He was a slender man, small and pale in his skirts and shawls, but a priest nonetheless.

The Governor was listening attentively. Narcissa stopped in the doorway, nervous at being so close to a Catholic Father. It had never occured to her that she would ever be in a position of having to make conversation with one.

As he talked the young man made awkward gestures with his hands, as if he were trying to pull words out of the silence. She had thought all priests were old, but this one was hardly past being a boy. He had black hair, brushed close to his head, and dark eyes. It surprised her to notice a faint shadow of beard on his face.

What ought she to do? Dr. McLaughlin would present him, and she would have to be polite. What in the world would she say to a priest?

"Ah, Mrs. Whitman." Dr. McLaughlin had seen her. "Come meet my dear friend Father DeMers."

Narcissa rather enjoyed his company, after the first shock had worn off; but it troubled her that Dr. McLaughlin had given him special attention. It was clear that Father DeMers was more than a casual guest.

A suspicion grew in her mind as the evening progressed: that Dr. McLaughlin had been converted! Mr. Douglas conducted Protestant services here at the Fort now, but the Governor had not attended any of them. Confirmation of her thoughts came the next day when she went to ask about passage home.

"Come in," he urged when she knocked at his office-door, but there was barely room for an extra chair since the addition of an enormous black iron safe embossed with brass scrolls and guarded by a massive lock.

To her questions about passage he shook his head. "Father DeMers is going up river within the week, but that's much too soon for you to make the trip. When you are able to travel I will see you get home safely."

"When is Father DeMers leaving?"

"He'll stay at Vancouver through the Sabbath to hear our confessions and say Mass. He'll leave early Monday morning."

She stared at him. *Our* confessions, he'd said—

His green eyes met hers with understanding. "It is a great comfort for those of us who have been without services of a priest to have Father DeMers and Bishop Blanchet in the Territory. Father tells me more priests will be coming by fall to work among the indians."

"Marcus was right then!" she said with bitterness in her voice. "He said they'd try to take over our stations—"

"Oh, no! You misunderstand me. They are not planning to work near you. One site is planned for the Spokane territory; and one in the valley."

"We have a mission among the Spokanes," she reminded him. "And Mr. Lee is in the Willamette."

He leaned forward, his face close to hers in the small space. "Mrs. Whitman, with all the thousands of souls here to be saved, can you seriously resent the work of *anyone* who comes to help? Isn't there room for all?"

"Not the way the Catholics save souls! The priests bring in a pack of gaudy pictures and teach the indians a few questions and answers; once they've memorized these, the indians are baptized wholesale, hundreds at a time."

"And is that so wrong?"

"Yes! The Catholics are making a game of salvation. They're cheating these poor savages."

"I've heard the same charges made against the Protestant missionaries," he murmured.

"Where?"

"From the indians themselves. They say your preachers

208

promise them great rewards if they become Christians; but when they ask to be baptized, they are refused."

"Because they're not ready for baptism. They have to experience a change of heart before they can become Christians. They look on prayer as a form of magic; they believe Christianity is a means of getting anything they want without working for it. They have to understand what baptism means before they receive its rewards."

"Mrs. Whitman, I can't believe we are so far apart in our feelings on this subject. Surely, surely, there is need for all, of whatever faith—"

She stood up, trembling. "I cannot agree, Dr. McLaughlin. I can never accept the rightness of men who make empty promises to deceive ignorant people for their own ends."

She wrote to Jason Lee asking if she could visit there. The Lees had invited them many times. She would spend the time until she was able to travel to return home as far from Vancouver and its Jesuit Governor as she could get.

Lee's mission had been established long enough to have acquired a feeling of permanence and enough families to make social events a pleasure. The girls learned to play with other children.

But somehow the trouble with Dr. McLaughlin followed her. Margaret had remained at Vancouver. Captain McKay thought it wise for his daughter to stay with Mrs. McLaughlin for the summer; and though he promised to bring her back to Waiilatpu when the school began again, it had seemed a punishment for the break with Dr. McLaughlin.

The high point of her summer was seeing Joe Meek again. She'd hardly recognized him in a black suit and white frilled shirt, but Helen Mar threw herself at him like a whirlwind while Joe's grin fought back tears.

He let Helen go finally and came to her. At the last minute his shyness overcame his delight; he stopped a few steps away. "I look some better than I did the last time you saw me, I guess."

"I can't believe you're Joe Meek." His face was smooth above the white collar; his black coat fit his shoulders neatly. And he wore shoes: black, side-buttoned shoes of soft leather. "It looks as if things are going well for you, Joe."

"Up and down," he grinned. "I'm learnin' to ride with the swells."

"I'm happy for you, Joe."

"And you can tell the doctor I've taken the plunge. I got religion." He nodded at her look of surprise. "That's right. I'm a new man, inside and out; and you know what? It hasn't been near as dull as I thought it would be."

A hail from Jason Lee sent the boats toward a small beach. "We'll camp here for the night. Looks like it's getting ready for a hard rain. We'd better set up before it hits."

She woke in the night to the beat of rain on the tarpaulin stretched over the boat in which she and the girls slept. She lay in the dark and thought of Marcus on his way down river to meet them. Tomorrow he'd be with them. Tomorrow—

1844

From the hill Narcissa let her eyes follow the trail
across the sun-bleached grass and up to the Blues. Already
the far peaks shone crusty with snow. The wagons had
been lagging in all week, and more would come. This
year's train was an army of stragglers; wagons and riders
and indians tumbling down from the mountains in a
broken stream.

Since Gilbert Newton came on ahead of the first wagons they'd known this would be a wretched arrival. He'd
told of early snows from Fort Boise on west; of short
supplies and sickness and two babies due to be born at any
time.

At least the train had broken into small units. It was
easier to deal with a dozen wagons at a time than with
five hundred at once.

She turned her back to the wind, her eyes watering.
Winter was creeping closer every day. They would have
all these people to care for, and how were they to do it?
The Grays had gone to farm in the Valley, leaving only
Marcus and herself—

The settlers with money would buy provisions and go
on to the Willamette. But the ones who'd used enthusiasm instead of common sense to make up their outfits
would get this far and fall apart. It would mean crowded

quarters again; the school closed for the third year in a row to make room. They'd manage lessons for the immigrant children, but the indians would be crowded out. Marcus said the indians wouldn't come anyway, but he didn't know that for sure. They might come this year if there was a place for them.

He'd managed to double his crops by hiring some of the settlers to stay late with him last spring. He'd even persuaded some of the Cayuse to plant again. Something —fear of Dr. White, or lack of help when the mission had been closed a year ago— had made the Cayuse listen to him. They'd been quiet enough through the summer. But what would happen when all the wagons got here?

The indians' alarm over last year's train of eight hundred had quieted when they saw Marcus had not brought an army after all. Would they rise in fear and anger now, seeing double that many settling down at Waiilatpu for the winter, or passing on the Willamette?

She pulled her collar higher around her throat. It was time to get back to start the evening meal. At least there'd be no sick travelers to cope with tonight.

They'd made no decision yet about the Sager children. She stopped by Alice's grave as she came down the hill. If she'd died before Alice, she'd have hoped some woman would want her little girl—

—but how could she care for six children? Plus a five-months-old baby? She'd hardly been able to look after Mary Ann and Helen the past year.

Marcus looked at her soberly when she first brought it up, and discouraged her. Was it because he doubted his own strength to take on the extra load?

"Where can we send them?" she insisted. "The settlers will have all they can do to take care of their own these first years. We can't expect anyone to find room for seven children."

212

"No," he said, "but I might find seven different families who would take one each."

"Mrs. Sager didn't want them separated. You encouraged these people to come out here, Marcus. The Sagers died on the way. Don't we owe them something?"

"*You* almost died last winter, and you aren't able to care for those children now. That's all I know."

Marcus didn't intend for her to take the Sagers. But her conscience wouldn't release her from a sense of obligation to their mother who'd tried so desperately to arrange for them before she died.

The letter sent ahead by Dr. Dagen had been long and persuasive; he knew the size of the task he was asking them to take on themselves. He had driven the Sager wagon since the father's death; and after Mrs. Sager passed on, he had cared for the children by himself, with the help of the older boys.

It would be best to plead for them after they arrived. Marcus woud find it harder to turn away seven helpless children standing in front of him than to refuse a letter from a stranger.

She was bottling apple butter the next morning when she heard the dry rattle of an approaching wagon. She could see only the one from the porch. But that one—!

The team of oxen moved with the deliberate plodding gait of animals spending their last reserves of strength. Two men sat on the seat; no telling how many the tattered canvas top concealed.

She waited on the porch for a rangy man with eyes too young for his face to come close. "Mrs. Whitman?" She thought she'd never heard a voice so tired. "I'm Captain Shaw with the train coming in. You received Dr. Dagen's letter about the Sagers.

Her heart began a faster beating. "They're here?"

"Right out there, Mam. Can you come?"

The little ones huddled like frightened rabbits against the wagon, barefoot; the tallest boy leaning against the wheel, his hand on his arms, had holes the size of flapjacks in his trousers.

She touched his shoulder; he went still as ice. "Are you ill, son?"

The rumpled straw-colored head moved back and forth once.

"What's your name?"

There was no answer. A bigger boy, slumped on the wagon seat now, burst into rasping sobs. She watched, helpless; listened, helpless, to the sounds he tried to hold back with both fists jammed against his mouth. She touched the calloused foot pushing against the wagon frame and managed to whisper, "Don't cry now. You're safe here."

The sunburned urchins, hair cropped short in chunks, could not be sorted at first glance into boys and girls. She knelt beside them. "What are your names?" And they fled like wild things, except for the oldest girl whose leg was wrapped in a filthy bandage trailing a rag from the heel. Her frantic eyes were like fires in her face.

"I won't harm you, child. Call the others and we'll go to the house." She turned to Dr. Dagen. "Can you unload the wagon? I'll take care of the children."

His brown eyes swimming with hard-fought tears showed a gratitude he could not voice. "It will be good for the boys to work now. They will unload."

The oldest sister had gathered the little ones to her. "Don't cry no more, Louise," she was whispering. "This here's the Missus Whitman that Mama told us about. She's gonna help us get settled now. Don't cry no more. You hear? You don't want to get her mad at us first thing."

She lifted the little one. For a second the thin body was rigid; then, suddenly, softened against her. "Let's go find

214

some dinner," she said with difficulty.

What if Marcus absolutely refused to keep them? Captain Shaw was taking it for granted they were staying; and Dr. Dagen was telling the boys about the wonderful adventures waiting them here; and the little one—Louise—was choking her holding on so tight. What if Marcus decided against them?

She wouldn't allow him! This was the family she'd been denied and not even Marcus could take them from her!

Mary Ann took the first steps to get acquainted, sitting down by the older girl. "What's your name?"

"Catherine," she said. "And there's Beth, and Mathilda is next, and Louise is the baby."

Mary Ann's face clouded. "I thought there was a lot of you."

"Well, there's Jonny and Frances; they're my brothers. Francis' name is really Francisco, but he doesn't like it. And then there's—" She looked quickly to Narcissa. "Missus," she said, "what's going to happen to Henrietta."

"Captain Shaw said the Baileys would be along any time."

"I heard some of the ladies say likely you wouldn't care to keep a skinny, sickly baby."

She looked away from the fear in the girl's eyes. "They were just talking. They don't know." She'd *have* to make Marcus see these children couldn't be torn apart.

He stopped in the doorway with a startled expression when he came, as if seven youngsters made a much larger group than seven imagined children. Well, six—

She laughed. "Come meet them."

"Is this all?"

"There's the baby. It's with another family. How soon will they be here, Captain Shaw?"

"Tomorrow, I should think." He hesitated. "Don't expect too much from the little one, though. She's hardly—"

"Captain—" she broke in. "Why don't we discuss it after dinner?" Behind Catherine's back she gestured to the little girl waiting stiffly for the words that would condemn the baby to some other home.

Sometime during the evening meal their resistence broke down. They all ran outside after eating, with Catherine limping along after them.

"At least they eat like children," she said, pouring tea for the men.

"Mrs. Whitman," Captain Shaw said then, "about the baby. The poor little thing's hardly alive. Mrs. Bailey's done the best she could, but she's got a drunken clod of a husband and two overgrown sons who have made it impossible for her to do more than keep it alive—"

"We'll make up for it when the baby gets here."

"If it isn't too late," Dr. Dagen said.

"It can't be too late!"

"'Cissa, are you sure you're able to accept the baby? The others, yes; they're old enough to help care for themselves. But the baby—"

"You can't separate them. They can't bear any more unhappiness right now."

"And what if the baby dies? Can you bear any more unhappiness right now."

"I can stand it better than those children." Her voice broke. "Please, Marcus— I want the baby more than any of them."

He stood abruptly. "Can you handle the cooking and washing and sewing and ironing? Can you, Narcissa?" There was anger in his voice, as if she had no right to force him to this decision.

"Doctor," Captain Shaw said, "I know we're asking a lot of you, but these children are absolutely alone in the world."

Marcus turned slowly. "It's a terrible thing to be alone, Captain. I'm hesitating because I don't think I could endure it. My wife almost died the past winter. I don't want to be alone because she takes on more than she can handle. Have you considered taking them to the Methodist mission?"

"Mrs. Sager was so definite about us bringing them to you I hadn't thought of any other course."

"I'm not even sure the Mission Board would approve my taking them." He walked to the window. "Do I have the right to allow them to stay here, for that matter? We can make the decision to risk our own lives, but can we decide for these children?"

"You've decided for the two little girls already here."

"Their fathers can come for the girls if they need to. These new ones haven't anyone to speak for them in the matter."

Dr. Dagen sat at the table picking at the cloth. "I will speak for them," he said. "I will decide that the risk is small for what they will gain in love and care."

Nobody answered him. "Maybe the boys can go on to the Valley," she offered. "They're old enough to make their own way if they have to."

"No. With Perrin gone with the Walkers we need the boys here. I want the boys." He turned suddenly to Dr. Dagen. "We'll keep them until spring. That will give time to plan for their future."

He came to her then. "Until spring," he repeated.

Twelve families asked permission to stay the winter. For once the weather cooperated. In spite of early snows in the mountains the nights were mild enough for most to live in their tents, leaving the school free for classes.

She was drawn immediately to Alan Hinson, the young man they hired to teach school. His eyes changed color from blue to green to hazel depending on the light and his enthusiasm. His mouth seemed large because he smiled so much. She was happy that he would share the big house with them.

Marcus hired the other men to finish the saw mill. "We've over a hundred dollars in notes left from the beef and flour we sold to pay HBC," he said when she questioned the expense.

"The Board might question that."

"Why? With them to help, we can cut enough lumber to get a decent mill in operation. I'd like to build some housing for settlers here." He looked past her, as if seeing a town around them. "Lots of people would just as soon settle here if they could get started."

She laid aside her knitting. "Aren't you worried about what people will say?"

"Why should I be? I'm not doing anything wrong, am I?"

"I wouldn't want you talked about the way Mr. Lee is."

His eyes twinkled. "The main criticism I heard of Jason Lee is that he married again too soon after his wife died."

"Be serious, Marcus. You know people are saying he's more interested in showing big profits on his station than he is in bringing salvation to the indians."

The lines in his face reset to anger. *"People* are always saying something hateful. People that don't know what they're talking about, especially. Let them talk. They can't hurt us."

"David Greene could hurt us, if he believed them."

He put his glasses on and picked up his book. "I've sent a full report to David Greene."

At year's end she could look back on a fall and winter that showed the mission beginning to catch up to the picture she had carried in her mind since Marcus asked her to come to Oregon; patterned after Fort Vancouver

218

and flourishing in the same way. Lapwai, with its board box buildings crowded along the river couldn't claim superiority now, not even for the school.

Often these days she totaled the sum of her contentment: Waiilatpu prospering, her family in health, and the indians not too troublesome. The buildings were newly painted in the fall, the corral rebuilt with fencing from the mill, and the pig pens moved away from the main buildings. That should be enough to carry her through the rest of the winter.

Settling seven undisciplined children into the routine at Waiilatpu had been a battle, but by now a pleasant monotony kept their lives moving smoothly—morning prayers, breakfast, chores, lunch, school, supper—livened by cut fingers and stubbed toes, Sunday Services, and afternoon holidays when the weather permitted.

She still argued against Marcus taking the children with him to the Cayuse camp. No matter how he assured her the indians were quiet, it frightened her to have them over there. After their visits she'd look at Catherine and the little girls and Mary Ann and Helen and remember the trappers' stories of chiefs who captured white girl children to raise for wives. She'd tell herself Marcus wouldn't put them in danger, but she was beside herself whenever he took them across the river.

And the chronic infection was dragging at her again, worse than before. She hadn't discussed it with Marcus, in spite of Dr. McLaughlin's warnings. He might decide the children were too much for her if she told him now.

She couldn't let him send the children away when they'd just settled into the family. Sometimes, rocking Henrietta, she thought half her unhappiness of the past few years had been due to the ache for another baby. Strange how exactly a little one shaped itself to a woman's arms, no matter how long it had been.

1845

Narcissa couldn't exactly say when the contentment began to cloud. Spring, as if jealous of their peace, was cold and wet; Marcus was like a nervous stallion waiting for the ground to dry for spring plowing.

The indians were restless again. They'd had a letter from Henry warning them about a half breed who'd come with the fall train. Tom Hill had been educated at the HBC settlement at Red River and was spreading wild talk against the missionaries.

He's been telling the Spokanes how, after the first missionaries came to the Delawares, the white settlers followed and ran them off their lands. He argues that the indians here will end up the same way.

"You think Ellis is listening to him, Marcus?"

"I don't know about Ellis. But I'd sure hate to have that kind of talk get down here to the Cayuse."

Then word came from Walla Walla that Yellow Serpent's son had been murdered in California. By white men. Marcus was unnerved by the news, as if the peaceful winter had left him vulnerable to his fears of indian trouble to come.

He made a quick trip to Walla Walla and returned more apprehensive than when he left. "Old Peu-Peu is in a rage." he told her. "McKinley's worried enough to admit it."

"Could Elijah's death have been an accident?"

"McKinley says Peu-Peu is trustable. He said the indians made a deal with Sutter to trade horses for cattle. They mistakenly rounded up some cows belonging to neighboring whites. These fellows stormed into camp while Yellow Serpent was away with Captain Sutter somewhere. Elijah was in charge."

"He was only seventeen years old—"

"Elijah explained they'd have to wait until his father got back, but they shot him then and there."

"That boy—?"

"At least they let him say a prayer before they put a bullet through his head."

He leaned his forehead against the window glass as if to cool his anger that way. "I can't say I blame Peu-Peu for wanting vengeance. I'd be looking for vengeance too if it was Francis or Jonny."

"At least they have the Laws for protection now. Have they called on Dr. White?"

"I don't know if he has jurisdiction in California, but I've sent word he'd better get up here fast. With Tom Hill stirring them up, this is all they need to break loose again."

They waited uneasily through April for Dr. White to take action. The indians that had roamed the mission yard this time last year, benign as sheep, now carried little fires of outrage in their eyes, and she lived once more with fear.

Marcus, on edge, had little patience with her worrying. When she tossed at night he would speak sharply, telling her there'd be time enough to deal with trouble when it happened.

Small incidents increased; the thieving expanded and

young men attacked fences and fields on their rampaging ponies. There was trouble with one boy Marcus caught trampling the winter wheat. The boy returned next day, saying he wanted to apologize, but Marcus, his patience exhausted, refused to see him. A contest developed between them, the boy trying again and again to intercept Marcus as he worked about the mission; Marcus stubbornly refusing to believe in his contrition. This furthered her uneasiness. She had never seen Marcus vengeful.

Robert Newell spent the night with them on his way to the Umpqua. She couldn't help but compare him with Joe Meek. They'd trapped the Rockies together as Mountain Men. Newell had chosen to retreat as civilization closed in; Joe had joined the newcomers and made a good life for himself.

After supper Newell squatted on the floor, indian fashion, his eyes almost shut as he looked up at Marcus in his rocker. "You in trouble with your injuns, Doc?"

The rocking chair stopped dead. "What makes you think that?"

"I been hearing things—"

"Where from?"

"All around. It's whispered through the camps that you're usin' witchcraft against the tribes. Witchcraft and poison. Figured you'd want to have some answers ready, case anyone comes askin'."

"One of Umtippe's crew ate some poisoned meat the men put out for wolves. They were warned, but they're such gluttons they'll take a chance on dying to stuff themselves."

Newell shifted. "Starvation'll do funny things to a man's judgment, Doc. These people got less and less to eat every winter."

222

"Why don't they stay put and raise crops then? They'd rather steal than work, and I'll tell you right now, Bob, I don't intend to sit by while they rob me of what I've sweated to grow."

They sat out a long silence. She had the feeling Newell didn't approve of Marcus' statement. Her anger rose at even this nebulous criticism. Were they supposed to sit back and smile when the indians stole and burned and destroyed?

"What about the boy that died?" Newell asked finally.

"A dozen boys have died in that stinking camp the last three months."

"They're sayin' you put a hex on this one, Doc."

Marcus glared at his interrogator. "Why is it when some young pup tears up something I'm supposed to pat him on the head and tell him it's all right, just because he's sorry?"

"Things might be better if you did. They claim you used magic to cause the boy to choke."

Marcus got to his feet. "Where you hearing this hogwash, Newell?"

The grizzled head tipped back; the narrowed eyes blinked. "Every path I take among the tribes I get the word about you, Doc. It ain't me you need to find a answer for. It's them, when they come callin' for one."

Within days after Newell's visit came a letter from David Greene that set Marcus raging.

We are not sure you ought to devote so much
of your time and thought to feeding the
emigrants, thus making your station a
restaurant for weary pilgrims on the way
to the promised land—

He crumpled the letter and threw it on the fire. "Does he want me to watch these people starve just so we won't be accused of making too much money?"

Marcus was growing inflexible against criticism. "Don't ignore what they say, Marcus. They have the right."

He turned on her. "Why? We built this place from bare earth; we know the situation. Why should they question my judgement about something they know nothing of?"

"They have the right," she insisted.

His mouth was set; he refused to answer.

"Remember Jason Lee was called home for exactly this reason."

That same week one of the settlers brought back word from Walla Walla that the Jesuits were planning to build a mission near Waiilatpu. Marcus sent word to Lapwai and Tshimakain calling Annual Meeting immediately at Waiilatpu.

So the tensions increased; and the lovely winter fell to pieces as it passed, like a snow man dissolving. If only her illness would go the same way—

Dreading the confusion of Annual Meeting, Narcissa still caught herself thinking of the women who would be visiting. She admitted to being hungry to talk with them about the children, and to show them through the house. She'd given up hope that any of her family would come after all this time. The Walkers and Eells and Spaldings were as close as she had to a family now. She would have to substitute shared troubles and pleasures for blood ties. And as usual the anticipation was lost in the continuous squabbling that undermined their gatherings.

Marcus' yearly journey to the valley spanned a miserable six weeks. Heat hung heavy over the mission: they were plagued by swarms of mosquitos from the Cayuse swamps. She'd worked too hard during the Meeting; now, painfully, she was paying the price. Some mornings she could barely pull herself out of bed. More than once she had fallen asleep, exhausted, as she spread the covers, to wake hours after with one of the girls asking directions for getting supper ready.

While he was away Catherine came down with summer fever. She pushed herself even harder, praying she'd get the best of her own illness before Marcus returned. In the spring, he had said— And it was already summer.

—she would not give up the children if she died for it—

But Marcus came back brimming with criticism of Dr. White's handling of the indian trouble. "The fool is fixing to have us all killed with his pussy-footing around. You know what he's done now?"

She shook her head.

"Ellis went down there to ask White to start proceedings against Elijah's killers. Instead White had a big party and ordered everyone in the Valley to come all dressed up; trying to flatter Ellis into forgetting the laws say a white murderer should be punished by hanging the same as an indian murderer."

"Chief Ellis won't be satisfied that easily," she said.

"Of course he won't! And White doesn't even realize what he's done. He's bragging all over the valley that he put down an indian uprising by stuffing the chief full of chicken and dumplings."

"Didn't you talk to him?"

"I told him we were sitting in the middle of a hornet's nest, and if we suffered any harm it would be on his head."

"What did he say?"

Marcus slumped suddenly. "He accused me of over-charging the settlers for supplies. Said he'd had complaints from men who'd had to pay their last dollar for food to get down to the Willamette."

"You must have misunderstood him—"

"No," he said. "I didn't misunderstand." He straightened; forced a smile. "Let's forget all the trouble for now. Where are the children?"

But she had to add one more trouble. "Marcus, Francis went to the valley with the Graysons." .

"He *what?*"

"I tried to talk him out of it, but he wouldn't be stopped."

He sat drinking his tea and looking out the window. "Are the rest of the children unhappy?"

She stood behind him, rubbing his shoulders. "Francis wasn't unhappy, exactly," she said, needing to protect the boy. "He's worried the children will be a burden to us. He wants to get started taking care of them himself."

—and you did say they had to leave in the spring, Marcus—

"No need for him to worry or feel that way. I stopped to see Captain Shaw while I was at the Falls; I told him we'd keep them all." He pulled a paper from his pocket and handed it to her.

Without a word! He'd just gone ahead and let her worry; let the children worry—

"The judge appointed me their legal guardian until they come of age. That way they'll be able to keep their own names."

She couldn't stay angry with him. He'd forgotten, probably, that he'd ever issued that ultimatum.

"I don't know what he will think to hear one of them has run away from us—"

"Write to the judge and explain," she said gently. "He'll understand."

He reached up to hold her hand still against his shoulder. "Why is it the ones you care for most hurt you so?"

—how else would it be? You couldn't be hurt by someone you didn't love—

226

The whole summer was out of balance. Crops planted late matured early, and they never caught up with the steady rush of harvesting. They'd had word this year's train would be early and worked against that deadline to have stores ready.

Francis returned after getting Marcus' letter. In the face of simmering indian resentment it was good to have him where they knew he was safe. As safe as anyone *could* be—

The fear of indian trouble was constant now. Hovering bands of Cayuse watched them work, eyes smoldering at the sight of crops being stored for use by more newcomers. Tom Hill spread word that almost five hundred wagons had passed Fort Hall. She could feel an undercurrent of defiance whenever indians were near. The pleasure of late summer was buried under its presence, like smoke blotting out the sun.

One night they were knocked up by two Nez Perce who were visiting the Cayuse camp. Marcus went to the door in his night shirt while she waited in bed, trying to hear the conversation.

"Tilhoukaikt's got a band of young men stirred up to attack the train," Marcus told her, coming back. "I've got to get word to them."

"Can't you send someone?"

"Go on back to sleep. I'll get Alan up before I leave to keep an eye on things."

She caught his hand but he slipped his fingers loose. "I have to go, 'Cissa. I can't let those people be attacked without warning." He bent and kissed her forehead; wiped her tears with his roughened fingertips. "No crying now. I won't be gone any time at all."

So she was put through the torment of waiting to hear that he had been waylaid by the Cayuse; or that he hadn't reached the train in time. She suffered again through that terrible trip to the States he'd made with Lovejoy; trapped by snows for days at a time; in the end forced to kill and eat Trapper in order to survive. She had thought him safe all that time, and he had starved and frozen his hands and almost died. Now she imagined him prisoner of the Cayuse, beaten and spit upon, as a kind of inverse insurance that he was safe.

He returned after four days. Nothing had happened, except for a few tense moments when Tilhoukaikt found the immigrants had been warned. "Docta! I defy you!" he'd raged. "I defy all settlers and all government!"

She could picture the train circled at dusk, and the indians gathering while Tilhoukaikt stormed.

"I reminded Tilhoukaikt he'd signed the laws," Marcus said, "but he spit on the ground and yelled, 'Those damn laws all white man lies! They no good for Cayuse! Indian be killed; white man not hanged for that. Elijah killed. Nobody be punished. I defy laws!' I warned him if he touched the wagons the government would send armies with guns to kill the Cayuse."

"But nothing happened—?"

"Nope. I set a guard around Tilhoukaikt and kept him in camp that night, and next day I told him we were moving on and not to get in the way. He took his men off and that was the end of it."

—but it was not the end of it. Tilhoukaikt wouldn't forget that Marcus had sided with the whites against the Cayuse. He wouldn't forget—

She pushed herself to get ready for the arrival of the train. Some, under Steve Meek, had turned off at the Malheur trying a short cut to the Valley. Even so three hundred wagons would come by Waiilatpu.

They waited and waited for the train to arrive, making their preparations; waited and waited; and one evening eight wagons limped down the trail, outlined against the dying light. The main party had taken another cut-off—down the Umatilla—to the *dalles*. With supplies left over from an easier passage they could by-pass the mission.

All these weeks of crushing labor to have flour ground and beeves butchered and vegetables ready— All that work for *nothing!* What were they to do with all these surplus supplies?

"White's behind this," Marcus raged. "He's angry that I criticized him about Ellis!"

"Marcus, Dr. White is on his way back to Washington—"

"That's right he is! He's met the wagons and told them to by-pass us. Well, I won't let him get away with it!" He rushed toward the barn.

"Wait for me, Marcus."

He turned back impatiently. She caught at his shirt. "What are you going to do?"

"Load the wagon with flour and take it up where they're turning off. I'll sell it. White's not going to ruin me!"

"They'll say worse about you than they have about Jason Lee."

He shook her hands from his arm. "Get back to the house now. I know what I'm doing."

She was crying when he drove out the gate. Now those who were against him would have proof of their accusations. They'd welcome a second chance to remove Marcus from the mission.

He was hardly out of sight when the children came running to say there were indians on the hill. She waited in the doorway as they marched their horses down past the cemetary toward the house.

—they weren't mission indians—

There were at least two dozen of them, led by a white man. He wore a soft shirt and wool trousers and a flat-crowned hat like the Latter Day Saints. But the rest of them were indians: blankets and leggings and braids.

Narcissa could feel an undercurrent of defiance whenever indians were near. She was mad at Marcus for leaving her to face strange indians alone. It was his business to deal with wandering scoundrels. Instead he was off peddling flour, trying to show up Dr. White.

They sat their ponies near the gate while the leader walked up the path. She had been wrong about him being white. Up close she could see signs of indian: black braids under the flat hat, brilliant black eyes, the way he walked; although his light skin and the refinement of his features told of white blood too.

He stopped at the steps, removing his hat as he spoke. "Mrs. Whitman?"

She nodded. She knew now who he was. She knew—

"I am Tom Hill," he said. "You have heard of me?"

She didn't know what to say to this man who was preaching trouble for them; yet, curiously, she felt no fear now. Something about him prohibited personal violence. He dealt with ideas. His eyes, deep set, sad, drooped at the outside corners. His mouth was sensitive; his nose slender. Except for the braids he looked more like a poet than a rebel leader.

—but he's not, she reminded herself. He's a savage— half savage, anyway—and he's working against us every minute.

"The doctor is away now. Please feel free to wait here until he returns. Rest your horses."

Tom Hill smiled as if he understood her reluctance to deal with him; understood it, resented it, and forgave it, all at the same time.

She decided to send Jonny after Marcus. "Tell him to hurry, Jonny. Tell him Tom Hill is here."

230

They were back by evening. A traveler had given Marcus word that Hill was heading for Waiilatpu. He'd turned back before Jonny caught up with him. He stopped to talk with Tom Hill before coming to the house.

"I've invited his men to a feast tomorrow night," he told her. "And the Cayuse too. "Might as well buy some good will with all this grain."

The feast was held in the indian room. She and the children watched from benches along the wall; Marcus' only condition was silence. There was to be no whispering, no laughing; for who knew what would insult a Chief now, with the trouble blowing hot and cold?

The ceremony began solemnly. Marcus and Tom Hill led the gaudy crowd into the room lit by a glare from the fireplace and flickering candles placed on the window ledges. Immediately the big iron kettles of mush and tallow were set in the center of the floor. There was scuffling and shifting as the indians pushed in close. Tom Hill and Marcus were directly across from their benches, within reach of the pots with their horn spoons.

The candles threw mad, dancing shadows on the walls, as if gargoyles were cavorting, as the indians ate with slurps and blubberings, their arms jerking the hot mush to their mouths as fast as possible. It was like watching some weird feast of witches. The indians, filled to capacity, whacked their distended bellies to produce an undercurrent of hissing and belching and blowing.

Then tea was poured into cups of those that had them; and passed to the others in the indian cup. Narcissa bit her tongue, seeing her precious sugar dropped into the cups in chunks. Marcus' instructions for silence applied to her, also. Beside her Mary Ann giggled softly. Narcissa grabbed her arm and pointed to the door. The little girl ducked outside, hands tight across her mouth. She frowned at the others in warning; the titters could catch from one to the next like fireworks sputtering along a fuse.

Marcus spoke a welcome while the pots were scraped clean. When he sat down, Tom Hill rose—graceful, ominous—and faced the Cayuse chiefs, and raised his hands, and began to speak in the uneven play of light and shadow.

"He's talking Cayuse—" Jonny breathed.

Narcissa was uneasy, hearing the awkward syllables from his mouth. Tom Hill looked too much the white man to be aligning himself with the indians. Why had he rejected the teaching he'd received at Red River? Had he been treated so terribly? There was a look of bitterness about his eyes. But why blame all white men for what a few had done to him?

She understood enough Cayuse to catch the drift of his arguments; the same ones he was reported spreading among the Spokanes and Pend d'Oreilles and Walla Wallas and Nez Perce; trying to settle old scores on an unfamiliar battlefield.

Marcus' face was wooden, but his fists tightened now and again. He couldn't afford to appear worried before this man. Tom Hill would take every advantage; he would use a frightened missionary, no matter how well he'd been received by him.

She and Marcus cleaned up after they'd gone. "Did it do any good, Marcus?"

His answer was slow in coming. "Hill will be a thorn in our side for a long time to come."

"Then why bother to be nice to him?"

"Maybe he'll give us credit someday."

"Part of what he says is true"

"It still don't excuse him stirring these people up. The Cayuse ain't the kind of savages you wind up when you want them to step and turn off when you want them quiet."

So another winter began with the ominous signs of indian trouble. A few immigrants who'd fallen behind straggled in. There was Osburn and his wife and three children; and Tom Summers and family. Marcus hired them for the winter. At least they were lucky in those two. Osburn was a millwright and Summers was a blacksmith. One man, Isaac Cornelius, announced plans to settle permanently near Waiilatpu.

The last were two young men, well-dressed and well-spoken, who'd asked to stay the winter. "I hired Rogers, the big one, for a teacher," Marcus told her. "The other one is too sick to work."

"What is it?"

"Consumption. And don't get that scared look on your face. They're in the end rooms in the wing, and Rogers will take care of Finley. I'm ordering him to bed."

At least they'd have a teacher for the winter. Alan Hinson had gone with the others to the Valley this spring. Rogers— A half-formed wish crossed her mind that he would be happier than the other Rogers had been.

Marcus began to feel more hopeful. "If Tilhoukaikt will just let us alone now we can get a lot done before snowfall. For two cents I'd send Osburn and Summers to the mill this winter."

"Is it safe up there?"

"As safe as anywhere, I reckon."

The indians wandered Waiilatpu like rusty leaves blown on a worried wind. They did not settle in as winter approached. There was constant coming and going. They hung around the barns, haggling for beef scraps when they butchered; begging for grain; waiting for handouts of clothing.

"Where are they coming from, Marcus?"

"I wish I knew."

The winter failed to live up to its promise. Marcus fumed at finding jobs assigned to hired workers half done after he'd ridden both ways to the mill and put in eight hours there with Osburn. Most of the settlers didn't like long hours in rainy weather; the wages were small. Their minds were busy with their own dreams of farming in the Valley. This was Marcus' dream, and a tired one at that.

"You'd think they were made of sugar candy," he'd growl on rainy days. "Maybe we're wastin our time trying to make a waystop here. They rest up all winter and the minute spring comes they're off for the Valley."

"You can't expect them to be interested in the mission, Marcus. This is our business, not theirs."

"They're interested enough when they come in here starving and asking for credit."

His fault-finding made her impatient. "You didn't like it when they went on by," she reminded him once, and went to check on Helen Mar, home from school with another sore throat.

She was grateful beyond words for the extra men at Waiilatpu, nights after the indians returned from forays into the countryside. Dancing until dawn, their howlings filled the sky like wolves' songs. And days when they rode out, painted and naked except for capes and britches, and no one knowing where they were headed, she thanked God for the settlers.

Sometimes the screaming dinned until she wanted to howl and scream herself. She would look at Marcus blindly and shake her head, and he would go to the window and look out at the leaping shadows circling the fires across the river, and clench his fists and say nothing.

The threat of disaster was around them like smoke, ready to smother them. Sometimes, after the dancing, the

Cayuse would come for Marcus and she would beg him not to go—beg him, crying—but he always went, using the one argument she couldn't refuse, "It's what I came here for."

In one way it was a good winter. There was little sickness in the Cayuse camp. But there was hunger. The extra indians had used up the Cayuse food supply. Before the new year started they were everywhere, begging.

Marcus sold them what he could get pay for—usually horses—and gave them what he could spare. During one cold spell he gave them three mutton ewes: they made a feast and were back next day demanding more. The ewes were grazing Cayuse land, they insisted; they belonged to the Cayuse. And grain was grown on Cayuse land; it belonged to Cayuse people—

Still there was only one confrontation. Marcus and Tom Summers were deepening the mill race and heard shouting from the camp. Four riders were plunging through the winter grain. Marcus shouted, but they came on, jumping the fence where the two men stood.

A lead pony carrying grain sacks refused to jump the fence; a brave knocked the rails aside and kicked the animal through the opening, ignoring Marcus' yells.

Narcissa and the older girls were hanging clothes on the fence. They ran toward the uproar. Marcus and Tom were shouting as loud as the indians. Now and then a clear word emerged but nothing that made sense. She ran with her eyes on the uneven ground. Hearing Helen Mar scream, she looked up to see a tangle of flying arms, and like a judgment an ax raised and aimed at Marcus' head.

Her screams joined Helen's; she ran stumbling and screaming, across the muddy ditch; scrambled up the far side praying under her breath.

—*do something, God! Do something*—

Marcus had grabbed the ax and was clearing a circle

around himself. One of the Cayuse had fallen. Tom Summers was backed against the fence, kicking off two of the attackers while Marcus swung the ax like a sword—

Narcissa pushed the girls behind her, looking frantically for a weapon. There was nothing within reach. But as suddenly as the attack began the indians ran for their horses. Marcus and Summers pursued them through the broken fence and stopped there, panting, "When you . . . ask in a civil manner . . . I'll grind your grain . . . ." Marcus' voice gained strength as his breath returned. "And keep those horses out of my fields!" With a wide sweep of his arm he threw the ax after the galloping horses.

Summers came running, all at once conscious of her and the hysterical girls.

"Hush, now," she tried to quiet them. "It's all over." But her voice was as shaky as her knees, and she doubted they heard her.

Marcus walked stiffly to where they were. "What's the matter here?" he demanded. "Are they hurt?"

She shook her head. "Are you?"

"No," he growled, "I'm all right."

"Is Mr. Summers safe?"

"I think so."

Helen Mar grabbed Marcus around the knees, wailing. He loosened her arms. "Stop that now! Come to the house, all of you. There's nothing to beller about."

He walked ahead of them, his head bent. Narcissa was more frightened by his attitude than she had been during the battle. She sent the girls to finish hanging the clothes. Marcus threw himself down on the couch, his arms crossed over his eyes, his mouth trembling. It was like watching the sun fall out of the sky; she lost her own strength, seeing him fight his weakness. She wanted to go to him, and could not. His pride would suffer enough, once he recovered himself. The only comfort she could give him now was privacy.

"If they'd tell me to go, I'd leave," he said at last, his voice colorless as an old rag.

"You don't mean that."

"All I want is for them to demand the mission, so I'm clear with the Board. They can sell it or burn it or give it away for all I care."

"Marcus! Stop this!" She wiped her eyes with her skirt and went to the couch. "You don't mean it—"

He lifted his arms; looked at her from dull eyes. His face sagged; his mouth was still unsteady. "I'm tired, 'Cissa," he said, "tired beyond endurance."

She went to her knees; put her arms round him; lay with her head on his chest. She waited for his will to come back, but he didn't stir, and finally she got to her feet, the way an old woman moves, and left him alone. He didn't stir as she left.

In the bedroom she lay without moving. No matter how they fought this savage land they were beaten back. And no one cared. She had written hundreds of letters to their families and friends, begging them to come and help. Not one had come. Not one—

That evening she sent a rider for Henry and Eliza. Marcus had gone to them whenever they asked for him. Henry would understand this desperation that had finally made Marcus prisoner . . . .

But they could not leave Lapwai. The children were gravely ill; they dared not leave them—dared not bring them. But their letter was full of concern. They knew what could happen. Eliza had been alone in the house a few weeks before and some of the young indians had tried to force their way in. Henry had returned just in time. The indians were rising everywhere, Henry reported. Everywhere . . . .

Narcissa had a mental picture of the indians springing

like magic from the hills, from the plains, from the rivers, until the land trembled under their feet; their voices wailing their war chants while the missions cowered before the currents blowing east, blowing west, with every shifting wind. And she wept for their vulnerability.

1846

As if their latest outburst had eased the turbulence burning in them, the Cayuse were placid again by spring. But there was a rash of minor troubles. Marcus was thrown from a horse and injured his knee; they were unable to go to Tshimakain for Marcus to deliver the Walker's fifth child.

Narcissa had looked forward to seeing Mary Walker and Eliza. It was strange how the differences between herself and those others had faded to nothing. She had a need for friends now. The settler women couldn't begin to understand the needs that developed after years of living in this merciless place. They were blinded by the promise of a new life; they couldn't afford to admit the existence of dangers that might threaten their dreams. The loneliness and sacrifices had to be lived through before they forged common bonds.

Ten years—

It couldn't have been ten years, she thought sometimes, looking at the buildings still roofed with sod; at the grist mill still minus its roof from the burning in forty-two; at the acres of fields still unfenced. Where had ten years gone?

Those first months in the lean-to they'd made such lavish plans. There was to have been a boarding school for the indians by now, with a hundred—two hundred—students. They had been so sure, then, that friends and relatives would follow from the States. They had believed Waiilatpu would equal Fort Vancouver in importance by now, with the Cayuse settled on farms, their violence changed to meekness by their acceptance of Christianity.

—and what is the truth? We are thankful if we come through the night without being murdered. We are hollow people, empty, with foreboding of approaching failure. What have we accomplished for the price we've paid—

Not nearly enough.

Their pride had been trampled; their health ruined; they'd lost their child to this wild country.

—then why do we stay—

Because the thought of leaving was as painful as the uncertain future. After ten years their roots were deep in mission earth; they could not be pulled loose without them dying.

In February they traveled to Walla Walla to say their goodbyes to Archibald McKinley. The old factor was retiring to a farm in French Prairie.

"It'll be hard seeing him go, Marcus."

"Well, don't go crying at him. He'll growl at you like a lion if you embarrass him that way."

"I'll try not. I wonder what Mr. McBean will be like."

"He's a good enough man, I guess; but he's Catholic. He's bound to encourage Catholic missions here. The Cayuse are giving us enough trouble without us having to worry about the priests again."

"Pambrun didn't—" she began, and stopped. What she'd started to say was only partly true. When they started to come, Pambrun had favored the Catholic missionaries.

McKinley walked them to their wagon when they

240

started home. "We'll never forget you," Narcissa said. "There are no words to thank you for all your kindness." Tears brimmed her eyes.

"Now none o' thot! I'll not be puttin' up wi' a snivelin' woman in ma last week!" His eyebrows bristled; his scowl resembled a thunder cloud.

On impulse she kissed his cheek. "God bless you," she whispered, and climbed into the wagon before he could move to assist her. A fiery blush burned suddenly beneath the bush beard.

Marcus took a hand in his turn. "I wish you weren't leaving."

"If ye had an ounce o' sense ye'd be comin' wi' me."

"I know your speech by heart, McKinley. There's no use wasting your breath on it now."

"I tell ye, mon, it's dangerous to be stayin' here by yoursel'. I got few enou' friends I can call ma own. I've no mind to see a good one murdered for lack o' warnin'. I'm no just talkin' to hear ma brains make a noise, ye ken."

"I know that. But the Cayuse are quiet now. They're even coming to Sunday services again. There's been no trouble since Tamahas left."

"A rattlesnake coils up nice and cozy just before it strikes."

"I'll promise you this, McKinley. At the next sign of trouble I'm moving to the valley."

"Ye'd save time if ye'd just come along noo."

"I know the danger. But I've a duty somewhere. I told Tilhoukaikt I'd leave the mission to the Catholics, but the old scoundrel begged me to stay, crying like a baby."

"And likely went to his lodge then and held a council o' war over ye," McKinley finished darkly. "Ye can't put your faith i' thot old divil; not if ye value your hair."

Marcus grasped his hand again and climbed into the wagon.

"I'll be lookin' for y' i' th' fall," McKinley called after them as they drove away from the Fort.

McKinley's warnings echoed in Narcissa's mind for weeks. But during the fall all signs indicated tensions were easing. The indians had raised more crops than ever before. And Marcus heard the Catholics had given up their plans for a mission near Waiilatpu. The feeling of peace made talk of indian trouble sound hysterical. Yet Narcissa was afraid to trust the calm. More than ever she needed to talk with someone who could understand—

Henry and Eliza and the children came in August. She felt an unaccustomed tenderness as they rode into the yard. Somehow, in spite of past differences, Henry and Eliza had become dear friends.

Henry reported a quiet summer at Lapwai after a winter of harrassment. Marcus accepted it as further evidence of the new spirit of friendliness among the indians. She tried to put her doubts out of mind and enjoy their company while they were here. For the first time the four of them could talk together. Henry had left his belligerance behind in the passing years. His angles had disappeared; his face had lost the bony look that had frowned on the world for so long, and the added roundness seemed to soften his judgments as well. He could lean back in a chair and converse now, instead of pacing his way through a conversation.

She and Eliza laughed together over the children's mischief. They exchanged outgrown clothing, and compared heights. And when, without warning, Eliza would go still, eyes shadowed as she watched the little ones playing, Narcissa felt fear striking at her own heart.

—would the children be playing safely here, this time next year? Would the yard be here, and the house? Or would the sun shine on desolation—

Aloud, they talked of 'back home'. "I'm just plain homesick," Eliza confessed. "I try not to think about New York when I'm alone, because I end up crying every time."

Narcissa was too startled to answer.

"It's worse than when we first came. Time's rushing by; if they don't come soon it'll be too late." Eliza looked up then, laughing. "I keep thinking of how old they're getting, and forget about us being older until I notice Henry's gone bald."

They *will* get too old if they don't come soon," Narcissa said. "I don't think I could stand to make that trip again myself."

And they carefully did not look at each other for some moments, until the dark knowledge of their isolation was under control once more.

For the first time Narcissa felt real regret when the Spaldings returned to Lapwai. Leaving, Eliza said, "I wish we lived closer—" And Henry, after shaking hands, held hers for a moment.

For the second year the main stream of immigration drove down the Umatilla to the *dalles.* "Only the sick and starving come to us now," Marcus said with bitterness.

Narcissa didn't feel up to listening to his complaints again. "I'd better check to see if the two families that came this morning need anything."

He motioned her to stay where she was. "There's nothing needs doing at the moment. You better see if the women have diapers, though. They're both due any time now from the looks of them."

"There'll be others, Marcus."

He shook his head. "They don't bother with us since White spread word about the Umatilla Trail."

His mind was solidly against diversion. Men who'd

wintered at the mission gave good reasons for using the new trail. By way of Walla Walla they had to raft their wagons down the Columbia; on the Umatilla Trail they could drive all the way. But Marcus continued to blame White for the new route's popularity.

Wagons and riders dribbled into the mission meadows until there were six wagons and eight single men who asked to stay the winter. Marcus agreed to hire them on if they would take payment in supplies.

One slight young man came to their door alone; he looked at Narcissa with big dark eyes that were somehow familiar.

"Did you wish to speak to Doctor?"

A strange, eager smile captured his mouth. "I'd hoped you could give me directions for finding my sister's home—"

Her heart jumped as she recognized Eliza's brother. "Horace Hart!" She drew him inside; kissed him warmly; held him. To Mary Ann, watching wide-eyed, she cried "Run get father. Tell him it's Eliza's brother Horace, come all the way from New York!"

It was the Bliss family, last to come, who carried the measles. The father brought the ramshackle wagon at a run down from the foothills, the mission children watching from the fence. "That old schooner's gonna start flying in all directions any minute now," Francis said. "Must be indians after him."

Not indians this close to the mission, and in broad daylight. But they were in trouble. "Find Doctor, Francis. Hurry."

The boy's long legs scissored out across the field. She herded the girls to the porch. "You're not to come out to the wagon unless I tell you."

"What about Jonny and Francis?"

Jonny still hung on the fence, his eyes wide. "Over

244

here, Jonny," she called. "You stay with the girls."

Marcus was there when the wagon stopped, groaning like some ancient beast in its last agonies. A small man with a silver bristle on his face jumped down and ran to them. "My little ones are burning and tossing in that wagon. You the doctor?"

A white-faced woman looked out from the back. "You come on down, Mam, and let me in there." She did not move. "I'm Doctor Whitman. I want to help the babies, but there ain't room for us both up there. Come down now."

"It's measles," he said moments later, dropping back to the ground. "'Cissa, make beds on the floor of the end room in Mansion House. And cover the windows." He turned to question the woman. "When are you expecting the new one?"

"I reckon I'm three-four months along," she whispered.

"You had this?"

She shook her head.

"Good. I'll go get medicine now to help the little ones."

Narcissa hurried with him to the supply room. "Are you sure it's measles, Marcus?"

"They're sicker than most young ones with measles," he admitted. "What really worries me, Bliss said there's measles on the train that went on to the *dalles*. There's been indians following them from Fort Hall, begging and trading. If measles get started again among the Cayuse—" He didn't finish the thought; nor did he have to.

"They'll die like flies."

"I know. I know."

"Can't we do something?"

"Pray," he said. "It's gonna take a more powerful Doctor than me to handle it if measles spread among the indians this year."

The wagon families came down, one by one. Narcissa kept the children in the house. Marcus quarantined the settler children at the first signs. It was a particularly virulent form of the childhood disease. By week's end it was evident an epidemic could fan through the indian camps.

Marcus made his rounds and brooded. "It will be deadly for them. I've tried to get Umtippe to have his people burn anything they got from the settlers but he thinks I'm trying to get him to admit to thieving. It's probably too late anyway."

Nobody could have imagined the early blizzard that struck from the east. The snow started during the night and fell for two days, steadily, and when it did stop the sky still hung over them close enough to touch, gray and dark and evil. Narcissa crowded the wagon families into the houses. There was hardly room to walk between the beds.

"We've got to get the rest of them under roof somewhere, Marcus. Those children have to be kept warm."

"There's room for them at the mill when we can get the wagons up the slopes again. The minute the snow's gone we'll start moving them."

"The single men could ride up."

"I thought of that, but we're going to have to use the shed, too, and it ain't suitable for children. The men can bed out there and take their meals with us."

By the fourth evening the Youngs and Yarnells and Bittners were settled at the mill with provisions for the winter. Marcus and the young men came back through a second storm that had begun howling across the flats in late afternoon.

"It's going to be another good one," Marcus said, giving Catherine his snowy coat to take to the lean-to while Narcissa brought hot stew and bread and butter. She'd have to fix the extra men somewhere. They couldn't sleep in the shed in weather like this.

There was no getting outside this time. They had piled hay for the cow and turned the calf in with her; filled the feeders for the chickens; dumped corn in one corner of the pig pen; and hoped the horses could dig down to the dried grass.

"The field cattle will be hardest hit,"Marcus worried. "There's a hay stack in the northwest pasture; maybe some of them will get to it. Did anyone scatter hay for the sheep?"

"Mr. Bliss took care of it."

The second afternoon, late, they heard a scratching at the kitchen door. "Sounds like a dog—" But when Marcus opened the door the cold rushed in like an invader, blowing a figure straight past him. He wrestled the door shut while Narcissa stared at the scarecrow dripping water on her floor.

Never had she seen an indian so ugly. Coarse hair fitted his big head like a cap, the braids thick as a woman's arms. In the very center of his scalp a scab the size of a Mexican dollar seeped infection. His eyes were slits on each side of a nose sharp as a hatchet. His thin mouth showed the only defective teeth she had ever seen on an indian.

A powerful stench rose from the old buffalo robe he had wrapped himself in. She edged to the living room doorway to catch a gulp of breathable air. Marcus gasped, "Where the devil did you come from?" She felt no shock at his swearing; the man looked as if he'd come straight from Satan.

"I come with the wagon train, but the sons of bitches turned me out in the storm when we passed your road. They say you take me in."

Her eyes flew to Marcus' face. *We can't! We can't!*

But Marcus wasn't looking at her. "You can stay till the storm's over," he said. "Then we'll see."

"Good. Good." The guest slipped out of the buffalo robe to reveal filthy buckskins. "Now. Those damn farmers won't even give me no bread to get here."

"What's your name?"

"Ain't you heard of Jo Lewis? I can read and write good. I been to school three years. I know everything." He swaggered to a table and sat down.

"There's one thing you ain't learned, Jo," Marcus snapped. "That's to control your tongue in front of ladies. Any more out-of-the-way talk in this house and I'll put you back in the snow. Understand?"

The little pig eyes widened. "I ain't tell no lies. Those damn—"

Marcus slapped the table. "One more time and out you go!"

"All right! All right! A woman don't have to listen, she don't like what a man says." He spread his elbows on the table. "Now! Jo Lewis hungry!"

He was the crudest man Narcissa had ever seen. They could not stand to be in the same room without gagging, yet they could not throw him out while the storm blew. She put him in the farthest corner of the indian room, but the other occupants were so offended by his odor she moved him to the lean-to the second night. The next morning she found the breakfast bread had been devoured during the night, along with a bowl of butter.

"An ordinary man would be deathly sick after eating that much on a full stomach, Marcus."

"The trappers say an indian can eat five times as much as a white without stopping," he said. "This one looks like he could stoke up for a month if he had to."

"He goes out of my house the minute this storm lets up!"

248

By the next afternoon the snow lightened to a few sparse flakes drifting down from a steel gray sky. "We'd better see to the stock," Marcus said. "It could start up again any time."

"Not until you get Jo Lewis on his way to the Cayuse camp."

He took one look at her face and went after Jo.

—she wouldn't have that filthy thing in the house again if he froze stark naked—

That night the earth turned to ice. Snow, trees, ground, river: everything exposed to the bitter cold that snapped over the land was rigid by morning. They were still confined to the buildings, although the men could stumble and slide around the yard to care for the animals.

Marcus' worry over his field stock grew. The sheep could settle in the fence rows and keep themselves sheltered, but there was no haven in the flat country for the larger animals.

Three days after they sent him away Jo Lewis was back. Marcus found him snoring on the porch in his buffalo robe and nudged him with his boot.

"Who kicked Jo Lewis?" the derelict yelled. "Nobody can kick Jo Lewis! Nobody!"

"I didn't kick you. What are you doing back here? I told you to go to Umtippe's camp."

"They all sick at Umtippe's camp. I don't want get sick like that. They hot as fire; they laying dead all over the river bank, naked as new babies, covered with ice."

Marcus frowned. "How many?"

"How the hell I know? Lots and lots sick."

"Watch your language, Jo—"

The massive features assumed a wounded expression. "I not helling and damning around in your house in front of ladies," he whined.

"Wait here."

And the indian called after him, "Bring Jo something to eat."

"It has to be measles again," Marcus said, filling his bag from the supply cupboard. "I won't be long. And don't go worrying. Indians aren't going to be ornery in this weather."

"What about Jo Lewis?"

"I'll take him back over there. If Umtippe won't keep him I'll try to give him to Tilhoukaikt."

Tilhoukaikt accepted the guest, but reluctantly. Jo was back at the mission two mornings later. Marcus fed him outside and chased him off the porch. He crouched by the steps, shaking inside his mangy robe. "I shiver with cold," he whimpered. "Where I go now? Umtippe don't want me to stay; Tilhoukaikt don't want me; Doctor don't want me? Where in hell I go now?"

And Marcus, worried over missing cattle and horses, snapped, "Any corner would do, I reckon." He left then to round up the scattered stock. That evening Jo Lewis had disappeared.

The cold held to the land like a sprung trap. Measles attacked the indians at Walla Walla and into the Nez Perce country. Cattle and sheep continued to die. They had word from Lapwai that the Nez Perce had lost half their horses.

What indians were still on their feet rode out daily to hunt, but the mountains were caught in the crushing freeze; wild game died along with the cattle. Although the indians had planted corn and barley, they could look ahead to famine.

Marcus, moving through the longhouses, got the message from eyes glaring from dark corners as he passed: they believed the settlers had brought the cold along with the measles. And Jo Lewis returned.

250

"Umtippe say you scatter cold the way you scatter poison," he reported sociably, stumbling along behind Marcus on the icy ground. "But I tell him that not true. Doctor Whitman would not do that terrible thing."

Marcus opened his mouth for a grudging thanks, but Jo added first, "I tell them Doctor Whitman not powerful enough to call up this kind of cold."

Amused and stung, Marcus baited him. "How do you know I can't?"

"I know where cold comes from. I am educated indian. I know every damn thing, remember!"

"Where does the cold come from then?"

"You know Old Jimmy?"

"Never heard of him."

"Sure you hear of him. Old Jimmy that Christian indian lives up by Walla Walla Fort—"

"I'd know a Christian indian."

"Well—he this kind of Christian." Jo made the cross with a dirty forefinger. "*He* brought cold to punish indians because they not Christians. They wicked! They sinful rascals! They not do this when they pray every time." He crossed himself a second time. "Old Jimmy say the cold will go away tomorrow—next day—something like that."

"You know this too?"

"Sure I know! Sure! Indians pay Old Jimmy; he call away cold. He magic man, I tell you!"

Two days later the cold spell broke. Jo Lewis appeared again to remind Marcus of Old Jimmy's power.

Telling her about it, Marcus admitted his astonishment, not at Old Jimmy's power, but that the Catholics were this near.

For weeks the death cries keened over the countryside. Narcissa dreaded the long nights. Once those inside were quiet the wailing and chanting seemed to come right through the walls.

Near Christmas Dr. McLaughlin sent them a copy of the OREGON SPECTATOR dated November 4, announcing the ratification of the treaty between Great Britain and the United States settling their boundary at the Forty-ninth parallel. Marcus let out a whoop and ran to tell the settlers. Narcissa stayed to re-read the Governor's letter.

She was crying when he returned. "They forced him to resign from the Company because of the treaty—"

"That's the most idiotic nonsense I've ever heard! How in thunder do they think they'll get along without him at Vancouver? Douglas can't run that place."

"Vancouver's his life. They had no right to take it from him because he couldn't force the United States out of Oregon."

"He saved more of the territory for the British than anyone expected."

"Hudson Bay Company is no worse than the Americans," she said. "*They're* trying to force him out of his claim at Willamette Falls."

The news placed a heavy weight on her. If Dr. McLaughlin could be treated this way after a lifetime of service to HBC—to England—what hope was there for anyone else?

She brooded over the injustice, forgetting the coolness that had developed between them the past few years. He had been their friend from the day of their arrival, whatever had happened. As proof was his postscript to the letter:

I beg you to consider moving closer to the valley. Although I am no longer in command at Fort Vancouver I receive reports from many sources; and while I do not wish to alarm you, trouble is brewing among the indians. I fear for your safety.

252

1847

Marcus made his spring trip to the valley early and returned filled with new enthusiasm. Plans for Oregon's future were shaping fast; he could not help bragging that his trip to Washington five years before had at last borne fruit. The settlers had come as he predicted; their presence had carried the weight of claim to the land when the showdown came.

"If Congress doesn't get too bound up in this infernal Mexican War," he told her, "and forget us out here, we're on our way to Statehood."

"Forget us? How could they?"

"They haven't taken a step for setting up a Territorial Government."

"We have a government—"

"Provisional," he said. "Rule by whim of the public. We need a government established under the laws of the United States, so everyone knows where we stand."

Annual Meeting was set for the first week in June, at Tshimakain. Narcissa insisted on going against Marcus' wishes. "You've been sick all winter, 'Cissa. I don't think you should try it this time."

"I'm going," she insisted. "I'm tired from all these people."

Cushing Eells had brought the letter. "Mary and Myra would rejoice to see you," he told her. "It's lonely up there, year in and year out, with no one but the children."

There were important issues to be decided. The Mission Board had instructed them to look for a new site to replace Tshimakain. Marcus had brought back an offer from the Methodists at the *dalles* to sell their station there. Wascopum was a safer site than Tshimakain in view of the indian situation.

"Reverend Gary's leaving Wascopum this fall. They've offered to sell us the station with no charge for the improvements. I think we should take it. They're only asking seven hundred dollars all told."

Elkanah Walker unfolded himself and chewed silently for some seconds before asking, "What about the cost to us? This is our home, built by our own hands. Our children have been born here; some are buried here—"

Eells nodded while their wives looked on, their faces stretched tight. And recalling the little death she'd died when they voted her and Marcus out of Waiilatpu, Narcissa suffered for them.

But the Board had been definite in its instructions. In the end they voted to buy the Wascopum site for Mary and Elkanah; with the Eells coming to Waiilatpu. Neither of the women talked much after the vote was taken—.

They returned home through a countryside gone soft with summer. Coming down from the hills was like riding into a lake, the grass blue with flowers floating on long, fragile stems. The season had been busy at the mission, too. The apple trees were full green now. Petunias and roses painted a bright border around the house. Compared to the buildings at Lapwai and Tshimakain, Waiilatpu looked strong and prosperous.

The children came pounding to meet them through the

rye grass, as if their horses were swimming a river. Catherine carried Henrietta in front of her and Louise behind; Jon, Mathilda, and Mary Ann rode together; Francis brought Liz and Helen Mar. Narcissa took the baby and Marcus lifted Louise to his horse. The rest of them trouped around their 'cousin' Eliza who'd come to Waiilatpu for the school year. She was relieved to be safely home again, crowded or not.

The trip to Tshimakain had been harder on her than she admitted. She moved cautiously now to avoid the nausea that plagued her again; her arms and legs swelled; pains shot up her back like arrows. Narcissa spent most of her time with the children now. They picnicked, went swimming while she watched them from the bank, listened while she read to them or told them stories of her childhood in New York. Often Marcus would join them under the trees for an hour between chores, as if he felt the same need as herself to be with his family; as if the threatened trouble had sharpened their awareness of what their home contained.

A stranger found them one afternoon in the shade at the bottom of the hill. A small man, he gave an impression of strength; his sandy hair and brown skin blended with his buckskins, a quick smile lighted eyes and mouth.

"I'm Paul Kane, from Canada, traveling the northwest to paint the tribes. McBean at the Fort told me you could help me get to the Cayuse chiefs."

"Most are gone for the summer," Marcus told him, "except for Tilhoukaikt and Tamahas."

Paul Kane made friends with the children before they had returned to the house. The next morning they begged to go to the camp with the men but Narcissa refused absolutely, haunted by past attacks made on them at times when they felt most secure.

When Kane returned with sketches of Tamahas, the

children surrounded him like a pack of puppies. "Just let me get out my folio and we'll have a show." While he found the paintings he told them about his day. "When we got to the lodge we found old Tamahas sitting there naked as a jay, with the most savage expression I've ever seen on a human's face."

"And his face reflects his character," Marcus said.

"He sat there staring at me all the time I was working. When I finished he demanded if I intended to give the picture to you. Seems he thought if you had a picture of him he would be in your power."

"That right! That right!"

They all looked up together. Jo Lewis peered inside from the open doorway. She groaned as Marcus went to stop him there. "What is it now, Jo?"

"I got no place to sleep; no place to eat."

"I told you I'd feed you and give you a place to bed if you'd help me. You ran off somewhere, right when I needed you."

"Damn it, Jo had to see those traders put him off train."

"You've been to the valley?"

Jo nodded, heavy braids flapping. "But I work now, Doctor. I hungry now."

Marcus just looked at him.

"I stay and I work, Doctor. No place else I go now."

"Well—" Marcus conceded grudgingly. "Wait on the porch. I'll be out in a minute."

"I come inside?" But Marcus moved to close the door.

"I'll bring you something to eat out there."

Working, she could hear Jonny prodding Kane for more stories. "Tell us the rest about old Tamahas, Mr. Kane."

"Well I told old Tamahas I was keeping his picture for myself. And what do you think he did? He grabbed and tried to throw it in the fire."

"What happened then—?"

"I ran, sonny. I got out of there fast, and I rode all the way back here looking over my shoulder to see if there were arrows following me!"

In July they had a letter from the Walkers. After making the trip with Marcus to settle the deal for Wascopum, Elkanah had decided not to leave Tshimakain for at least another winter. Mary was pregnant again; the move would be hard on her. And they wanted more time to study the river tribes before moving among them.

"I should have figured on this. Walker wasn't too happy with Wascopum."

"What about the promise to buy the place?"

"I reckon we'll have to forfeit the hundred and fifty dollars we've paid down. What's bothering me is knowing the Catholics will grab up the site if we don't."

"Do you suppose Alan Hinson would move there temporarily? It's close to the Valley. He could put out his newspaper from Wascopum as easy as not."

Kane returned from a second trip to the Cayuse camp while they were talking. "Thought you were going to stay through the afternoon," Marcus said.

The artist's face was sober. "There's something going on over there, Doctor. They're rumbling around like a nest of hornets. Is there trouble?"

Marcus got up to look across the river. "I haven't heard of anything. How was Tilhoukaikt?"

"Like he had his mind on other things than having his portrait done."

"He didn't talk with you?"

"Just long enough to brush me off. Your guide said he had to council with one of his men who'd just returned from a trip."

"I'll go over with you tomorrow. We'll try to find out what's going on."

The Hinsons stopped on their way back from getting the printing press from Lapwai. They agreed to stay at Wascopum until other arrangements for manning the mission could be worked out. "Likely we can get someone from the States in the fall, Alan," Marcus told him. "The Board's been getting more offers from people willing to come here, now the trains come every year."

The Hinsons went on down river at the end of the week, Marcus riding with them. Narcissa felt a sense of desolation, waving them out of sight. Alan had married a girl from the valley before Annual Meeting; a girl warm-skinned and rounded, with green eyes and a heavy braid of brown hair she wore loose down her back; the kind of girl who looked better in a bonnet and gingham than dressed for church. When they said goodbye her own emotional farewells had been embarrassing.

Her senses betrayed her often this summer—enlarged, intensified—so that the children's shouts seemed to rebound from the sky; sadness cut sharp as death on soft evenings when they sat outdoors and talked of friends and family.

As Marcus rode into the yard that night they heard the faint pounding of hoofbeats from the north trail. They waited in the dark like wood blocks while the sounds increased—heightened—and carried Paul Kane to a stop beside them. Marcus led the way to the kitchen before Kane spoke.

"The indians are planning trouble, Doctor! Mr. McBean sent me. Your family is in grave danger, Sir. He wants you to come to the Fort at once!"

Narcissa struggled to breathe; fought nausea; sat down suddenly as the room whirled. The danger had been there

258

all summer, under the peaceful softness. Now it had broken through—

Marcus moved abruptly to face Kane squarely. "What makes McBean so sure the indians are up to something, Kane?"

"He said to tell you Yellow Serpent's son has returned from his trip to avenge Elijah's murder."

"That's been over two years—" she breathed.

"The indians near the Fort gathered when he came in. He said a few words and they began yowling like banshees, enough to shake the walls. Seems his whole band was wiped out by measles."

"Measles were everywhere the past two winters—"

"He called the roll of men that died. He'd call a name, and wait while the family wailed out for his death; then he'd go on to another. And it was weird, I tell you."

—they would claim revenge for all those young men, too, as well as for Elijah. And Dr. White wasn't here to deal with them this time—

"They always carry on when one dies," Marcus said, impatient of news of more trouble.

"McBean says this was different from anything he's ever seen, Doctor. They're calling a council. You must come, Sir! McBean heard your name mentioned more than once."

"We've been at their mercy before, and they've never done worse than make a nuisance of themselves. I think we're too important to them to be killed."

Narcissa shivered in the hot room. Marcus wasn't going to listen to this warning, either. But she had to try. "Maybe we'd better get the children up to the Fort, Marcus."

"Mrs. Whitman's right, Doctor. Once they hold council it may be too late."

"I can't leave," he insisted. "The settlers will be coming

within the month."

"Oh, Marcus! Most of them go the other way now."

"But what about the ones that don't—can't—go the other way? The ones that are sick, like Bliss; the ones that haven't money to get down to the Willamette? I can't leave them stranded because the indians are restless."

"We haven't got supplies this year even if they come," she said, knowing her arguments were useless.

"I've come through these scares too often to let this one send me running to the Fort. But you get the kids ready and go on with Kane if it will make you feel better. I'll come after the wagons pass."

—but it was him she was worried for—

"If you stay we'll all stay," she said; and he let the decision stand.

Kane tried one last time to change her mind. "Please bring the children and come with me, Mrs. Whitman."

"I can't leave the Doctor here by himself."

He looked at her, helpless. "I shouldn't have suggested it," he said, and rode away alone.

Through August the weather held hot and dry. The river sank; the ditches dried up. They carried water for the garden. The field crops turned dry as dust, maturing too soon. The men threshed grain with stalks a foot high, and were rewarded with half a yield.

It was as if the indians had put a curse on Waiilatpu. Old Jimmy, maybe? The one who'd brought the cold a year ago? She tried to pray, seeing the mission devoured by the heat and the tension, but God seemed far away, as if He had lost interest in them and the indians were taking advantage of His inattention. She knew it was wrong to think this way. She searched her soul for the habitual faith, but faith eluded her.

She dragged through the days. The children moped

after chores were finished, confined to the house by the threat of danger. She watched for signs of summer fever.

An advance party of immigrants came the last of the month, telling of a giant train dragging out across the continent, the last wagons suffering because the first ones exhausted grazing and supplies as they went. They reported harrassment by indians from one end of the train to the other.

She lived then with terror by day; woke in the night to hold her breath and listen, fearful her breathing might betray them. The Cayuse had stayed away from Waiilatpu during the hot summer. As fall came she felt their shadows long across the mission. She held herself tightly from day to day against hysteria.

Marcus expressed his tension in anger. The children stayed clear of him, barely talking when he was at the house. He was beside himself when scouts brought word the head of the train was at the Snake. "I've got to get supplies up here from the valley," he raged. And when she begged him not to leave her and the children alone, it was as if he hadn't heard.

"You said yourself only the sick and the needy will come—"

"There's five thousand on the way. The ones at the end of the line will be skeletons by the time they get here. I have to go for supplies, 'Cissa."

The fall rains started their dreary downpour before he was back with his two wagon loads, churning the dust to mud. He was like a miser with his precious stores when the wagons began to come, weighing out barely enough to get each family on down to the Willamette. He paid no attention to angry talk from those who had money to buy more. He tried to steer travelers to a new trail he'd followed coming cross-country with the supplies, but they were afraid. These stragglers were the ones who'd lost their assurance along the way with their cattle.

The soggy meadows began to clog with wagons of those who couldn't decide between the known dangers of the river cliffs and the imagined dangers of an unmarked trail. They lingered, reluctant to leave this refuge where there was some food, at least, and care for the ill.

The ones who chose the old trail sent back word that indians were waiting along the cliffs. Their thieving became banditry; wagons were stopped and looted. And stories were whispered of women being forced to submit to indignities that were not put into words.

Marcus, furious, rode to intercept the main party, trying to convince them to take the shorter, less-known trail and avoid the indians. Some brave ones followed his advice, but the timid and the sick continued to camp near the mission buildings.

One morning the Cayuse were back, and with them Jo Lewis. He had come and gone during the summer; now, with settlers camped conveniently close, he settled in. Narcissa nagged Marcus to send him on his way, but the derelict refused to leave. He wandered among the wagons, a grinning demon, frightening the children and laughing loudly when the women, nerves raw from attacks along the trail, gave way to hysterical tears.

In desperation Marcus gave in to the requests to lead the ragged settlers to the *dalles*. And again Narcissa fought his going. "I can't take care of things here by myself—"

"We have to get these people out of here," he insisted. "We'll all be starving by Christmas if I don't get them down to the Valley."

"Wait a few more days. They'll go when they see it's no use staying."

"They won't leave until they're forced to. They're sick

of the trail; they'd as soon stay here all winter. There isn't room. There's not enough food. You know that."

While he was gone more wagons filled the vacant spaces. Time after time Narcissa was called out into the rain to measure supplies for some new arrival. She was afraid to trust anyone else; it was too easy to be tempted by the cries of hungry children and give some more than their share.

Narcissa was in bed with a hacking cough when Marcus returned. She dragged out to the kitchen, calling Catherine to come help her. Wrath burned in every word that Marcus spoke. At Walla Walla he'd found Jesuits conferring with Young Chief for permission to start a Catholic mission near the Fort.

"I tried to tell them there'd be trouble if we got the indians arguing over religion. Blanchet informed me they were there at Young Chief's invitation; that McBean felt need of a Catholic mission in the area; that they intended to convert indians, and Americans too, if they showed interest."

She sat down suddenly, too sick, too tired, to stay on her feet. "We can't have them here—"

His face swam; his voice had the hollow sound of distance behind it. "I warned them if there was trouble the blame would be on them. I told them not to come to Waiilatpu begging help if their food ran out this winter."

"You shouldn't have said that—" The Catholics had helped them many times; McLaughlin and McBean and the others . . .

"Why should I help them? They're deliberately stirring up the indians. They know the Americans are mainly Protestant. They'd like nothing better than to see the indians destroy us all!"

The rains continued into October. Late arrivals were

quartered everywhere; two families shared the cabin at the mill; the Mansion House was jammed full with twenty-nine; the blacksmith shop housed nine; their own rooms overflowed—twenty-one people in space designed for a dozen.

Marcus turned the main room into an infirmary as the settlers came down with fever and measles. Narcissa threaded her way between the pallets to answer their nagging questions, trying to keep the household going. Marcus was at her to let others do the work, but she was afraid to trust anyone with the cooking. The settlers magnified the mission's stock of supplies by comparing them with their own empty wagons. They couldn't know what this place would demand of them before the winter ended. They hadn't seen people die of starvation.

She drove herself to stay on her feet. If she could only eat something— She tried. She tried. But swallowing was an effort, and oftener than not nausea rocked her stomach at the smell of food. She managed to take some milk now and then; or a bite of bread. Getting into winter dresses, she was startled to find her skirt overlapped four inches at the waist. She hadn't imagined that much— But her arms and hands were thin as sticks.

She picked up a mirror, fearfully, and saw her eyes like dark holes; her face white as paper; her hair— What had happened to her hair this past year? It was faded and limp and straggling—

What had happened to her? What in the name of God had happened to her, here in this terrible place? She wasn't a woman now; she wasn't Narcissa Prentice, of Steuben County, New York; she was some ghastly, ravaged stranger, dead or near to death . . . .

—and there was not time for even this small, harrowing moment of truth. Someone was calling. Always and forever, someone was calling—

264

Marcus caught a lingering cold which he refused to pamper. His energy grew as short as his temper. She thought sometimes she would go out of her mind listening to his endless arguments. Yet there was something so frightening about his brooding despair when he fell silent that she prayed for something to rouse him to anger again.

Francis came in from chores one morning with a story of a big meeting of indians at the Fort. Marcus, staring into the fire, roused himself and reached for the boy's arm. "What are you chattering about?"

"Jo Lewis says there's a big council at Walla Walla to choose a site for the Catholic mission. He says Young Chief has promised to give them Waiilatpu."

Marcus' face went white, then red; he jumped up and ran into the downpour in his shirt sleeves, shouting for Jo Lewis. Narcissa ran with his jacket but it was too late; he was shaking Jo Lewis by the fronts of his ragged buffalo robe, his head streaming from the beating rain. "What's this lie you've been telling?" he yelled.

"That ain't damn lie, damn it all, Doctor. I was there right beside Young Chief, and I hear him tell black robes they can have Waiilatpu if they want."

"You lie!" Marcus shouted. "How can Young Chief give Waiilatpu away? It belongs to me!"

Jo Lewis shook his head with furious movement, up and down and left and right. "He not give house away; he say make mission for black robes at Tilhoukaikt's camp; plenty land there."

"Not at Tilhoukaikt's camp either!"

Jo tried to pull away from the avenging hands. "Why the hell you so excitable, Doctor?" he cried. "I don't give your place away; Tilhoukaikt say give it away."

"I don't care who tried to give it away; there'll be a hassle if any Jesuits set foot on my land!"

"—and it don't make no difference," Jo broke in,

"because Bishop Blanchet say he won't take your land, your house. He say there's plenty damned land for everyone. Father Bruillet will stay at Young Chief's camp; far away to Young Chief's house." Jo jerked on the robe again and it slipped from Marcus' fingers. The indian splashed through the rain toward the indian camp while Narcissa ran to Marcus, throwing the jacket over his soaked shirt.

"What the devil are you doing out here, 'Cissa? Get back inside."

But she held him there. "What are we going to do?"

"Do—?" He was like a man without eyes. He reached for her shoulders for support.

"Is this the time to leave, Marcus?"

"The houses are full of people depending on us. What would they do if we left?"

"The indians have never been like this before—"

"We can't leave."

Marcus worked then with desperate urgency, as if he could prove his claim to Waiilatpu that way. She watched, silent, as he strained against odds that would have dwarfed three men's efforts. Couldn't he see the fate of Waiilatpu didn't rest in his hands? The Cayuse would decide the outcome of this struggle, whatever he did.

She didn't try to talk to him. He wouldn't be swayed by the arguments she could offer; weariness, danger, despair. He was running from these omens of defeat, refusing to admit their existence.

Narcissa moved in a vacuum of exhaustion as the settlers' children came down with dysentary and measles; as her own children fell ill. She heard the death chants from the indian camps. She experienced these conditions with detachment, as if they were happening far off, and she a spectator. She cared for the ill impartially; she cried for the immigrant youngsters as easily as for her own when she could do nothing to ease their misery. She

266

cleaned them and fed them and prayed over them. What more could be done?

Jo Lewis crawled to the kitchen door one evening, shivering and groaning. They made a bed for him on the floor, and Marcus, with grim humor, took advantage of his weakness to give him a scrubbing. The Cayuse came for him still. She had given up protesting his going. He had assumed a fatalistic attitude. "If they want to kill me they don't have to call me over to the camp to do it."

But the *te-wats* focused powerful opposition to his visits, and as the epidemic spread it was obvious they were reaching the Cayuse. "That new drug Dr. Richardson sent me this fall works against dysentary, at least, but they won't take it." He rubbed at his face, his eyes closed. "Someone's spreading the word that I'm poisoning them."

"Don't they see our people are sick, too? Do they think we're poisoning ourselves?"

"Their people die while ours get well. They never had these plagues before the whites came. No wonder they listen to the *te-wats*."

Someone knocked. Mary Ann whimpered and Narcissa hurried to her. When she looked up again Marcus was gone.

His steps dragged back along the porch an hour later. He stopped just inside the door, his shoulders hunched, his hands dragging at his arms.

She was rocked by foreknowledge of another death. "Who is it, Marcus?"

"Salvie Jane Osburn."

She took a deep breath. "I'd better go. It's only been a week since the baby died—"

But he put an arm across the doorway. "Mrs. Saunders is with her; Mrs. Kimball is taking care of the little ones."

"I ought to help—"

His eyes were deep shadows, as if he'd taken all the suffering he hadn't been able to relieve into himself. They threatened to devour him whole. Guilt and remorse were there. And fear.

She reached out to him. He buried his face against her; she felt his tears like spots of fire; she was consumed by a vehement rage that the world could do this to him.

Next morning her rage had settled to a cold hatred that ate in her like acid. When Tamsuky and two of his men came to the door she tried to turn them away. "I won't call the Doctor for you. You don't want his help; you only want to hurt him more. Get out of here!"

"Cayuse die in the night," Tamsuky growled, holding up both hands with fingers outspread. "More than this."

"If you'd called Doctor in time he could have helped. Go back and whine over your dead children. You deserve what's happening to you."

He took a quick step forward. She jerked her eyes up to meet his and gave a little cry. They held the same dark anguish she had seen in Marcus' eyes last night— *Did* Tamsuky feel what Marcus had felt? Could she make him understand this terrible sickness did not play favorites?

"Docta poison Cayuse," he grated. "All over Cayuse lands he throw poison; whites take land."

"It's measles and dysentary that are killing your peo-ple," she cried. "They're killing us, too!"

"Only Cayuse die; Walla Walla die; Nez Perce die. Whites do not die."

"Come with me," she said, her voice shaking. "I'll show you."

She ran to the Mansion House and burst into the Saunder's room. They stared as she ran through to the Osborn's corner, followed by the indians.

"Mrs. Osborn, they say we're deliberately spreading the sickness to kill them and not us. Let them see Salvie Jane.

Let them see they're believing lies."

Silently Mrs. Osborn lifted the curtain around a bed. The savages stared at the dead child. Suddenly Tamsuky threw back his head, laughing. "Too bad! Docta make mistake; give poison to white child."

Helen Mar and the baby were both vomiting when she got back to the house. As she held them through the spasms of retching the echo of Tamsuky's cruel laughter came to her and her fury raged anew.

"I could kill them all." The words grated under her breath. "Tamsuky, Umtippe, Tilhoukaikt; I could kill them all."

There was a movement from the couch behind her. She turned to see Jo Lewis lurching through the door. He'd better leave! She'd told the filthy tramp to stay in the indian room—

By next afternoon Mrs. Osborn and two more of her children were ill; Crocket Bewly came down with dysentary. When Marcus came at dusk she was reeling. He sent her to bed with orders to stay there.

It was deep night when she was dragged from sleep by his hand on her shoulder. She sat up with a start, certain of another death.

"I'm going to the camp," he told her and left quickly. She checked on the children, then waited in the main room for him to return. She must have dozed; she was jerked awake a second time by voices outside, and the sound of horses. Her senses leaped to the fact of Marcus' death—

She stumbled to the open door, almost falling into Henry's arms. He steadied her while Andrew Rogers shut the door, looking in at the sick in the next room, his expression unbelieving.

"Where's Marcus?"

"The indians came for him," she said, still trembling.

"Come sit down." Rogers' voice was gentle.

"When did he go, Narcissa?"

Something in Henry's manner warned her; Marcus was in grave danger—

"I've been asleep. I can't be sure—"

"We'll go after him." He placed his hands on her shoulders. "You'll be all right?"

She nodded.

She had no idea how long it was before she heard them returning. Her heart choked her with its frantic beating while she listened—listened—for Marcus' footsteps. . . .

She sat back all at once as he and Henry came in the door.

"Now," Henry said, "we're going to settle this. It's time you got out of here, Marcus. Past time."

"We'll talk about it in the morning. I'm tired now. I'm going to look in on the sick here and get to bed—"

"We will not wait until morning! Those indians are planning your murder right now!"

Narcissa's breath made a ragged sound in her throat. She'd heard it—thought it—so many times; but this time—*This time*—

"That's a game they're fond of, Henry. Actually, killing me is something else."

"Marcus! Listen to me now! Not four hours ago Rogers and I sat in Yellow Serpent's lodge and heard an indian come in and ask him if the Whitmans had been killed yet. Peu-Peu sent me down here to beg you to leave Waiilatpu."

Her eyes never left Marcus' face. Now, finally, a look of uncertainty showed there.

"Jo Lewis is telling everyone you're poisoning the Cayuse to keep them from giving Waiilatpu to the Catholics. Don't you know two hundred Cayuse have died

270

already this winter?"

"Of course I know it! I don't want to hear it again!" He appealed to Narcissa with his eyes; looked back to Henry. "Where would we go? *How* would we go? We have seventy-five people here; at least half of them are ill. It would take days to move them all. If things are as bad as you say, it will just arouse the indians worse if they see us trying to escape."

Henry shook his head, slowly, steadily.

"Where would we go if we do leave? McBean doesn't want us there. He's in strong with Tamahas and Young Chief. He wouldn't want to risk his position by defending us."

"Marcus, all I know is that you and Narcissa must leave here. I doubt the Cayuse will bother anyone else; it's you Jo Lewis is blaming their troubles on."

"Running away would be admitting that everything I've done here in the past twelve years is a failure—"

Henry sighed. "Maybe we're all failures. Is there any point in compounding the failure by sacrificing your lives?"

Slowly, slowly, the room began to spin around her; the shadows deepened and swirled and came closer; the fetid sick-room odors thickened in her throat.

"—Marcus—"

"What is it, 'Cissa?"

"I have to get outside—"

One of the children whimpered; she half-turned, and Rogers said quietly, "I'll see to it." She went out into the night and breathed the damp air and felt life coming back to her.

"Can we go for a walk, Marcus?" If she could get away for awhile, free herself from the problems that plagued them like the visitations of Job— She wrapped her shawl tighter.

271

He put an arm around her shoulders and walked her toward the fence. The night was blotted with dark clouds, but there was a moon behind them; she could see well enough by its light. The lank, leftover grass beat at her skirts as they walked out into the meadow; the ground was spongy underfoot. She led the way to the hill.

From the summit the outlines of the buildings were blurred. Dim lights burned in all of them, but the whole of Waiilatpu seemed nebulous—a dream conjured out of the hopes of individuals not strong enough to bring it to reality.

—is that all it is, after all? Is that all *it is—*

"Do you suppose Henry's right, 'Cissa?" Marcus said. "It's not much to show for twelve years." There was a lightness in his voice now, as if he were discussing some village in China which didn't touch him at all. "The indians can wipe it all away in a night if they want to."

"I don't see how." Marcus, denying all they'd done here, was more frightening than the Cayuse.

"Oh, they can, easy. They'll burn what will burn, and carry off what won't; they'll knock in the walls and smash the windows. In one winter the rains will beat the bricks to mud and the rye grass will grow up around the place, and there'll be hardly a trace, come spring, to show we were ever here."

"The people won't forget us if we go—"

"The Cayuse, you mean? We haven't even touched them."

She was chilled to the bone by his words, spoken without anger. He should have been angry and bitter, discussing the destruction of all they'd worked for.

"Stikus and Lawyer aren't against us," she said.

"There may be a dozen on our side, out of hundreds."

"What would have happened to the children if we hadn't taken them?"

272

"They'd have grown up somehow."

His indifference reduced their labor and conviction to a ridiculous effort. She wouldn't allow him to do this!

"That's right," she said. They would have grown up *somehow*. This way they're growing up proud, and I won't have you belittling what we've done here. Not any of it. In twelve years we've never turned anyone away."

"You hear a different story in the valley. The settlers complain because we wouldn't sell more of our supplies; because we charged instead of giving them; because—"

"What about the sick? No telling how many people would have died if you hadn't been here."

"And now they're trying to kill us for it. Is it worth dying for, 'Cissa? Henry has the right to ask. Is it worth dying for?"

She kept her eyes on the candlelights that was all she could see of Waiilatpu. She was afraid—afraid—Marcus without faith was a stranger; and how could she plead with a stranger to remember the things that held their life here together.

His hands gripped her arms. "I promised you great and glorious things when I asked you to come out here with me," he said, his voice halfway between tears and shouting; "and what have I given you? Twelve years of— *nothing*." His words blurred. "Twelve years of pain and loneliness; twelve years of struggle. Twelve miserable years—"

—*now God*, she prayed. *If You mean to help us, help me now*-

"You've left out part of it, Marcus," she managed to say. "Twelve years of pride and hope and love mixed in with the other—they were real, too. Making your dreams come true isn't all that counts. It's having dreams in the first place that make the difference. The important thing is that we tried."

"We're left with nothing in the end."

"Oh, Marcus, twelve years of trying isn't failure."

"I don't know what else you'd call it."

"I don't know, either. But I know it's not failure, and I won't listen any longer while you try to convince us that it is."

His arms went around her shoulders; he leaned on her, his face against hers. "—I can't leave. No matter what happens. Not even for you—"

Her eyes burned. "I know."

And for that moment she was sheltered and comforted, there on the open hill top, in spite of the cold wind.

On the way down the hill they paused at the picket fence around Alice's grave. "I guess I couldn't have gone either—"

They found a messenger from Stikus waiting. His people were dying. Could the Docta come? Five Crows, too, was watching his people fall and die; he prayed for help. And Young Chief—Towatoe—asked for the Docta—

Bitterness was heavy in Marcus' voice. "Why doesn't Stikus call on Blanchet? He's promised to find him a mission. Why does he send for me?"

"Stikus is the one who's talking for us, Marcus. He's been our friend from the day we came here."

Marcus had told her on the way to the house that not all the indians were in favor of killing them. The ones who had come for him earlier had taken him to a secret meeting of Cayuse who did not agree with Tilhoukaikt and Tomahas. He must help Stikus now.

He reached for his bag.

"You're not going?" Henry's tone was unbelieving.

"I've always gone when they called, Henry." His voice sounded very tired. "I guess it's too late to change now."

274

"What can I say to convince you your very life is in danger—"

Marcus, packing his supplies, ignored the question. "Come ride with me, why don't you?"

"Are you serious?"

"Yes." He snapped the bag shut. "The indians aren't after your hide—not the Cayuse, anyway. Maybe if you come along it will keep me from their wrath for one more trip. Besides, we haven't had a chance to talk. I'd enjoy your company."

Henry's face softened. "I'll come," he said. "Of course I'll come."

They left in a downpour. Their horses, hitched to the porch rail, were running water. They would be soaked long before they'd covered the twenty miles to Stikus' camp.

Marcus took her hands and held them hard in his. "I've left medicines on the table in case any more come down while I'm gone."

"I know what to do."

"And don't worry. Try to get some rest."

"I will," she said, knowing she would not sleep until he was home again.

"Work to keep Helen Mar's fever down."

Someone came leading a pack horse loaded with supplies. Marcus went to check the lashings.

Henry came to her. "Thank you for going with him," she said. "He needs someone."

"You both need someone!" Henry's voice held anger. "Will you come to Lapwai with me when I stop back for Eliza?"

She shook her head.

"There isn't anything I can say to change your mind? We can take the children, if that's what's bothering you—"

"Don't worry about us, Henry. Please don't worry. We've come through these things before; we'll come through this."

Unexpectedly he put his arms around her. "I shall worry—" he began, and could not continue, but stood looking down at her, pleading silently with her to change her mind.

The tears that were always near the surface now filled her eyes; she touched his face, and there was nothing of the antagonism that had haunted them all these years between them now. The danger reaching out for her and Marcus—for all of them—had washed away the distrust; shared disappointment brought them together in a love that was free from passion and jealousy.

"Thank you, Henry," she whispered, and felt his lips touch her forehead before he went to his waiting horse.

Rogers insisted she must get some rest. She checked the sick room and knelt to touch Helen Mar's flushed face. Eliza and Mary Ann were asleep in her bed. She lay down on the extra cot in her clothes, and did not wake until morning.

Helen Mar was struggling to sit up when Narcissa hurried to her; her eyes like dried leaves; her face all skin and bones; her nightdress soaked. As Narcissa knelt beside the pallet the little girl began to cry in soft whimpers.

She had not known this kind of fear since she had watched the indian bring Alice up out of the river. She reached for salt water and poured it over the shivering child nightgown and all. She wet the child mouth with water and changed the bed and sat beside it talking softly. Some were waking around her. Narcissa left their care to others; all her will focused toward keeping Helen Mar alive. She would not allow her to be taken! She refused to leave Joe's child; as if she were holding death at bay by will power alone. Time after time she murmured frantic prayers under her breath. Again and again she challenged God: *"You can't take Helen Mar. You can't take her! You can't—*

She tried to pray *Thy will be done* as Mrs. Hall had told her to do in times of crisis, and could not. If God took Helen Mar Meek it would have to be without her consent. Brushing the black hair aside off the burning forehead, she would think of Joe. How could she tell him if Helen died? And she would picture him holding her that last moment before he left her with them; see his face baring that hopeless, helpless love—Trusting her with his treasured child to guaranty her place in a world he could not give her—

In the evening Rogers brought her some potato soup and stood over her until she tasted it to make him go away. But he did not go away; he insisted she must rest again.

"Twice you've fallen over, Mrs. Whitman, just sitting there. If it would help the little girl for you to be sick, I'd see some call for you to stay like this. But it won't help her—"

He kept at her until she lay down on the couch near Helen's bed. She drowsed there, refusing to give in all the way to sleep. Once she roused and saw Francis and Jonny sitting at the table, a lamp turned low between them, reading. Jonny turned and smiled at her and she lay back. Finally, in spite of her will, she was carried down and down into a dreamless sleep.

The next time Narcissa woke Marcus was bending over Helen's bed. She could not see his face, but as he pulled the cover around the child he shook his head slightly.

Narcissa sat up quickly. "How is she, Marcus?"

After what seemed hours he said, "She'll be all right soon."

He settled slowly into his chair by the fire. She sat across from him in the rocker he'd made her to match his.

—he looked so tired—

"Why did you come back tonight, Marcus? You could have slept, and come back tomorrow."

He rocked without looking at her. "Stikus was afraid for me to stay. He cried, begging me to go. He warned us to leave Waiilatpu as soon as I got back. He says he can't hold the Cayuse off much longer." He looked at her then. "Do you want to change your mind?"

"Has anything changed since we decided?"

"One thing. Stikus guaranteed the ones left behind won't be harmed if we leave."

"He can't be sure."

"I trust him. 'Cissa, he says the death vote will come very soon."

Helen Mar cried, and Narcissa sat on the pallet again and held the little girl and sang to her until she quieted. She went back to Marcus then, standing behind him with her hands on his face, her own face against his hair. "I won't leave the children—"

He took her hand. "All right, 'Cissa. I was just trying to scare you into going with Henry when he gets back."

"Where is Henry?"

"His horse slipped and he injured his leg going down. He's coming in a couple of days, after the swelling eases."

"Have you had anything to eat?"

"I'm not hungry." He lifted her hand; kissed it. "Why don't you go to bed now?" he said without opening his eyes.

"I'm all right—"

"You've been on your feet for the last two weeks. Go on now. I'm here."

She came around in front of him. The lines in his face

were deep; his hair white at the temples.

"Marcus, have you slept at all since you left here?"

He opened his eyes; for a moment they blazed blue and clear and bright as they had when she first met him. He smiled. "Go on to bed, 'Cissa. I'll rest here and listen for the children."

She slipped off her shoes and lay down in the bedroom, pulling a blanket over herself. Sleep lifted her then, whirling her round and round and down—

She roused, hearing an imperious pounding; hearing a harsh voice crying, "Docta! Where are you, Docta?" She struggled to come awake. Marcus mustn't go with them this time—

But sitting up, heavy with sleep, she heard no further cries. She must have been dreaming, she thought and lay back into the receptive blankets; letting herself drift on the currents of sleep without trying to break free. Marcus was always scolding her for imagining the indians were coming for him—

—and the noises and rumbling and shoutings began again, far away but there; and dogs barked outside; and horses were running; and the pounding began again—

She frowned in her sleep. It was only a dream. Only a dream. . . .

And the dream would end soon.

THE END

POSTSCRIPT

Narcissa and Marcus Whitman
were massacred
November 29, 1847

John and Francis Sager
were also among the victims
at Waiilatpu Mission
on that date and in the days following,
as was Helen Mar Meek,
who died from measles.

ALSO FROM IMAGE IMPRINTS

A SONG HEARD IN A STRANGE LAND
Narcissa: Her Story-Book I
1985

EXPLORING THE OREGON COAST BY CAR
Second Edition - Fourth printing
1986